SPOON LICKER

Cassidy Barker

SPOONLICKER

Cactus Moon Publications, LLC
1305 W. 7th Street, Tempe, AZ 85281
www.cactusmoonpublishing.com

First Edition

ISBN: 978-0-9996965-7-6

This book is for my mother, Kathleen

Acknowledgments

Thank you to the Walton County Crime Scene Unit for having me as an intern and being patient with my plethora of seemingly random questions. Anything I got wrong is only the fault of my own or was altered to better fit the flow of the story.

Note from the Author

None of the faulty investigative practices by characters in the book reflect anything I witnessed during my time at Walton County. The entire crime unit of Walton is comprised of honorable and wonderful people.

Table of Contents

CHAPTER 1

He wanted to lick the spoon. He combed through his notebook, running his hand over newspaper clippings and his own series of scratchy notes written off to the side. There were so many mysteries, so many spoons, and nobody claiming any of it. He cracked his neck as he read through the most recent additions, hoping for connections while also wondering if he should expand his search to states that immediately surrounded Georgia.

April 23, 2013
Atlanta, Georgia

He walked home alone every night after striking out at the bars. Once, a flasher mistook Martin Brixx for a girl and hopped in front of him, wagging his diseased penis before darting away. That didn't bother Martin so much; he even lifted his phone to take a picture but couldn't capture one in the time it took for the flasher to realize Martin was male and lacking the shocked face that gave him his jollies. When a young, white boy in a ski mask showed Martin his knife and gave him enough of a poke to dispel a drop of ruby blood from the side of his throat, demanding his phone and wallet, Martin swallowed, Adam's Apple visibly bobbing, and handed everything over. If the rest of his friends were present, he might have put on a front and refused, acting like a small guy with a knife couldn't frighten him. He didn't want to go to the police when that happened, but his mother refused to fund him a new phone unless he made a report. The relentless woman also insisted he report the flasher, something he told her only because he found it funny but regretted when she began squawking with concern. Considering he was living on his own for the first time and having trouble making rent, he wasn't in the position to turn down this offer. So, Martin made his way to the police department and filed both reports, cheeks red as he explained the flasher. The officer who filled out the reports said, "It's good that you told us, though it would have been better sooner. Those kinds of guys normally prey on young females and we want to avoid further incident."

Now Martin made his usual trek to his haggard apartment, drunk and too busy on his new iPhone to pay attention to his surroundings. He knew the way home by heart and let his feet take him there. He could feel the dampness beneath his armpits and was grateful he chose to wear a black shirt out tonight. His long, brown hair was glued to his neck from a coat of sweat. He grunted in frustration as he tapped at his iPhone to no avail, fingers sliding all over the surface. The phone was sticky and his fingers sweaty, a combination that may have worked with an older version of any phone. He repeatedly wiped his hand on his shorts. Martin felt a car whiz by in front of him, nearly taking his shirt with it. He stopped just in time and laughed nervously for the only indication that he needed to look up came from the change in terrain from sidewalk to street. He turned into the parking deck he often cut through. He stepped over the miniature wall that existed only to keep other cars from pulling into the deck from anywhere other than its one entrance. He pulled up on the crotch of his khaki shorts as he did to avoid any unnecessary knocking.

While Martin walked, dark blue eyes followed his movement. The man was stationed at the bottom floor of a poorly lit parking deck that mercifully, for him anyway, lacked surveillance cameras. He merged into the shadow behind a mini-van waiting to see what Martin would do next, if he would take a cautious look around or, at the very least, put down his cell phone for even a moment.

Martin continued to tap away at his phone, watching Facebook videos he would forget about as soon as he clicked on another. He made one upward glance to be sure he wasn't headed into one of the deck's pillars but relied on the limited peripheral vision in front of each step he took, though it was only fuzzed vision in the background of his device.

The man rolled his eyes as he rolled his sleeves, taking in quickened but silent breaths. He read all police alerts in the Atlanta area and knew of Brixx's previous run in with a knife. His pulse raced with excitement. He wrapped a bar towel around his hand after polishing off the jagged glass left behind from what may have been a car-jacking in the same deck. It was beautiful and ready to have a new purpose. Tonight, that glass would do something more than just lay there amongst its other shattered cohorts. Because of its iceberg shape, it was chosen, chosen to be in control of a human's life.

He held the glass in his towel-wrapped hand at the ready. He slowly walked into his path, waiting for his shoes to be in the same field of vision as Martin's. When at last they were, Martin cussed and dropped his phone. The frail thing shattered there between the four feet, two covered by black, nonslip shoes and two in a pair of loafers covered with bar tar. Martin's mouth was agape and questioning, but his expression quickly became one of anger. He let some guy get the better of him before, but he wasn't going to let that happen again. He puffed out his chest and clenched his fists. "Empty your wallet and give me your credit card. You're going to replace that, jackass."

The man only smiled. It was usually a handsome one but now was that of a rabid animal, peeled back from his teeth. Martin searched the man's dark blue eyes, wondering if he should go ahead and punch this guy in the face. He was imagining doing it, saw himself rearing back a fist and connecting, then saw his mother's face when he would inevitably tell her this story and how disappointed she would be. The last thing he saw was this projection in his mind, his mother's disappointment, as the glass was plunged into his stomach. Martin's eyebrows drew together in questioning and he felt himself stagger and grab the man's shoulder for support. The images began to fade as the man pulled the shard upward, fighting through tough skin in what seemed like an effort to split Martin in two.

When Martin's chest ceased to move, the man wiped the glass on the dead boy's shirt and tossed it back with the rest of its friends found by the car. It cracked in a few places and fell apart, so it was just as obsolete as the others. It surely could not have been used to take a life.

He picked up the lifeless body, muscles twitching with the effort of dead weight, and took it over to his own car, a sleek

BMW. He threw the body inside the trunk where a cradle of sheets lay waiting.

May 10, 2013
Athens, Georgia

Her hands shook as her eyes scanned through the dim light for a familiar face or a friend. She sipped nervously at her Amaretto Sour, ignoring the discomfort in her jaw. She tried to stop thinking about the way the bartender had looked at her when she ordered her drink, like she was some dumb college freshmen sorority girl. Which, she was, aside from dumb, but that didn't make it okay for her to be stereotyped! She'd be a sophomore soon enough, one with a 3.7 GPA. Rebecca Caster drew another sip of her drink through the doubled skinny straws and self-consciously ran a hand through her not-blonde-enough-for-Tri-Delt-so-Phi-Mu-has-to-do hair.

"Can I buy you a drink?" A boy wearing a backwards base-ball cap approached her, grinning through his sweat.

She made a face and lifted her cup. "I've got one already." She turned away and felt a tug at her stomach. Her new sisters had forgotten to tell her they were leaving this underage-student filled bar and heading to a new one. Rebecca turned back around and grabbed the boy by his shoulder. "Actually, let's take some shots," she smiled. It was returned with an even bigger one. He pushed his way through the throngs of people to get to the bar. Rebecca downed her drink while she waited. He came back with two little cups with limes hanging on the rims.

"Tequila," he said. "But don't you try and take advantage of me tonight! I'm not that kind of boy," he winked and handed her a cup and clinked his plastic against hers before downing the shot. He stuck the lime in his mouth. As Rebecca laughed then followed suit, he studied her body, taking careful notice of her perky breasts in a low cut shirt. He dragged his eyes back up in time to see her shudder with distaste from the alcohol. Feeling caught he said, "Sorry. My eyes got tired for a moment and fell so I had to pick them back up. Actually, that's not true, I was checking you out. Want another?"

Rebecca laughed at his honesty and gazed at the boy. He was probably her age, maybe a year up. Not many legal drinkers came to a bar like this. She thought again about her fellow freshman sorority sisters, and then nodded. "I would love another," she said with a grin. "What's your name by the way? I'm Rebecca."

"Mack. Let's go downstairs, there are less people so I can get to the bar easier." Mack guided her to the darkness that led to the stairs with his hand just above the curve of her ass. While they walked, *he* watched.

Three more shots of tequila later, Rebecca found herself at a loss for balance, or inhibitions. She slung her arms around Mack's neck and laughed. "Hold me up! I can't do it myself anymore!" She tried to find Mack's eyes, but his face wouldn't stop swimming around in front of her. She grabbed at his face to hold it still, then pressed her mouth against his. His lips parted and his Pepe Lopez flavored tongue poked his way into her mouth. She greeted his tongue with her own and explored.

CHAPTER 1

Rebecca pulled back, letting spittle from a sloppy kiss rest around her lips without wiping it away. "I want... you... Maaaaacky. to take me home. Home to your place," she sputtered.

Mack drew back in surprise. "No, no. We just met. That's not a good—" he stopped as his mouth filled with a warm warning liquid. He darted away to avoid puking in front of her. Rebecca didn't see Mack again. Others would, though. He would be the boy plastered all over social media, passed out, head first, in a trashcan amongst the bile of many others. She tried to hide her disappointment, he was a jerk anyway, and scanned the room. There was nobody she recognized, nobody to talk to. There weren't many people in general in the dank basement. Most probably avoided it due to the smell of stale urine that seemed to seep from the walls. Rebecca decided it was probably time to go, lest she found someone to hang out with for at least another hour.

He watched from a corner as she looked around the room. She looked like she was making her way toward the stairs. He climbed them two at a time and waited half inside the door of a single empty bathroom, appreciating the darkness and lack of people. He didn't have to wait long. There she was, stumbling up the steps and blindly grabbing at the walls for support.

"Woah, woah, woah. You look like you need some help!" Rebecca looked up at the older, albeit extremely handsome, stranger in front of her. He was holding out a large hand.

"Who issss, are you?"

"I work here."

She accepted his helping hand and let him lead her to the landing. "Shhthanks."

"You look like you could use a pick-me-up. Am I right?"

Rebecca nodded as a tear dripped down her flushed cheek. "I do!"

She followed him into the bathroom. It was a tight squeeze. Her stomach churned at the sight of the broken, clogged toilet. She caught a glimpse of herself in the mirror and was thankful for the poor lighting. She turned back to the handsome stranger. He was pulling a small bag from his pocket. Inside it was some kind of white powder. Cocaine, she guessed. He noticed her look of apprehension.

"Have you ever done this before?" He asked. She shook her head no in response. "It'll give you a lot of energy. All you have to do it close up one nostril, like this. . ." he demonstrated by pressing his index finger against the outside of his left nostril, ". . .and suck up through the other one with this." He rolled up a dollar bill in a tight little cylinder.

"And this'll, this'll make me feel happy? And have more energy?" He could see by her face that she had already given in. Always the gentleman, he cleaned off the edge of the bathroom sink with his shirt. He poured a little of the powder onto the surface and separated it into two neat lines. He handed her the rolled up dollar.

"More energy than any vodka with Red Bull could give you. Just make sure you don't breathe out onto the lines, it'll send the stuff everywhere," he let out a hearty laugh to give her the last bit of reassurance she would need. It was fine. She should relax.

CHAPTER 1

Rebecca bent down and stuck the dollar inside her nose. She held it over one end of a line and began sucking up as she moved the bill over the powder, watching as it disappeared into her vacuum of a nose. She smiled and glanced at the handsome man.

"Did I do it right?"

He smiled and said, "You sure did. Oh, no, that one is for you too. I'm all set already." He waved away the rolled up bill that she held out to him.

"Oh-Okay." She returned his easy grin and bent down again, feeling like a badass chick. She stood up and wiped the last remnants off of her nose.

"Rub it on your gums," he instructed. She did as she was told. He gave her a more serious look. "Make sure you don't tell anyone where you got this. I could lose my job. Not to mention it would piss off all of the people who have been hounding me for this stuff. You just looked like you needed it. You understand?"

Rebecca nodded. "I won't tell a soul!"

"Now, onto the more important matter. How do ya feel?" His eyes lit up as the smile reached them.

"I feel amazing!" she told the charming stranger. "I just wanna run! And dance! Thank you so much! This stuff is amazing I have so much energy I don't even feel drunk anymore I feel so good and so happy!"

"Alright, off you go, have fun." He opened the door and watched her run off, praising the placebo effect. It worked especially well when coupled with stupidity.

Rebecca Caster died with quite the cocktail in her system. Cocaine was there, but also crushed up Xanax, bleach powder, rat poisoning, and just a smidge of ricin. Better to be safe than sorry. One might say it was just a tad overdone.

June 13, 2013
Savannah, Georgia

Sean Smith steered the speedboat filled with his drunken friends through the Savannah River. The man was just as bland as his name, but still felt the constant urge to impress his friends. So, he proposed to them that they get a weekend away from Atlanta and their lives (some of which were duller than others) and go to Savannah. The guys agreed, excited by the trip, especially when Sean told them he had already rented a boat.

In the back, Roy was doing an Irish jig with a can of Bud Light opened in his hand. Sean could hear Kevin asking what the fuck he was doing, and Roy's response that he was pretending it was St. Patrick's Day. All of the men in the back rolled their eyes. Sean did not. He might have if he had been turned around to see everyone else do it, but that was the only way. Everything his friends did or said was cool, and he felt a particular envy toward Roy for being the group's clown.

Mikey roared from the back of the boat, "Sean, slow down! Stop this thing!" Sean complied, easing the boat into a smooth stop. He joined the others that were all on one side of the padded cushions, peering over the edge of the boat.

"What's goin' on guys?" He so often struggled to find the perfect "casual" speech.

"There's a fuckin' gator right there," Kevin said, a smile on his face. Sean looked into the water and there was indeed an alligator. Its eyes were floating alone above the surface of the water, occasionally joined by the flick of a long tail.

"I'm gonna swim with it," Roy stood up and pretended like he was going to jump in. It was all for show of course: to scare his buddies and make them laugh. That was Roy's role, one that Sean wanted.

"What's going on over there, fellas?" A man had slowed beside them in a boat with one of those outboard motors.

"We've got a gator over here, man!" Mikey yelled.

The man threw them a thumbs-up and looked on with interest even though any view he could have of the alligator was blocked by Sean's rental.

"Well, Roy, maybe you won't go to it, but I'll bring the gator to us!" Sean decided this was his moment to freak the group of guys out himself and make them laugh. He was more daring than Roy. At least, he was going to pretend to be. And now he had the newest audience member. Sean wanted that man to think that *he* was the group clown. He wanted the stranger to wonder what it would be like to be friends with such a goof. Sean grabbed the life float and stood on the very edge of the boat, praying that a strong gust of wind wouldn't come along. He glanced over his shoulder and saw that the stranger was still there watching. *Good.* His friends waited.

Sean threw the life float out to the gator, hoping to have it land over those muddy eyes. His friends roared with laughter. Roy shouted above it, "Bring it to me, buddy!"

But the float didn't circle over the alligator's head. Instead, the beast pushed upward and showed off its brilliant lines of teeth in a mouth that could have easily swallowed a full watermelon whole. It caught the donut and bit down, pulling.

"Alright now, reel it in," Kevin encouraged jokingly. But the alligator must have thought Kevin was talking to him, because he pulled back the same way a shark would abruptly jerk its prey and Sean began to lose his balance. Despite being a couple of brews deep, the men still had a good enough reaction time to leap up and grab Sean by his feet. Sean tilted forward and his hair grazed the water. As the alligator swam to separate Sean's skull from his neck, the men pulled him inside the boat.

Sean's face had gone pale. At first, the boys didn't say anything. They were looking over their friend to make sure he was all right. When they saw that he was fine, they broke into laughter.

"What the fuck were ya thinking, Seany? You could a made a nice dinner for that gator!" Roy chortled.

Sean looked over and saw the stranger was still watching him. He hadn't laughed. He just stared. Then, he pulled the engine of his boat and went on his own way. Sean didn't give the man another thought because he was now in his circle of friends who were laughing like children at a monster-smelly fart. He had succeeded in making them laugh, and that was all that mattered. But he ran a hand over his wet hair and shuddered.

That night, the men told and retold the story of Sean's almost-alligator feeding, each with a different version as if the others had not been there. Each time, they laughed. Their laughter was a drug to Sean, and he couldn't seem to get enough of it. So, when the boys started passing out one by one, he was disappointed to say the least. He took his own Miller Lite into his bedroom on the bottom floor of the rental house. Sean flicked on the TV and left it on the Home Shopping Network. He never bought anything, but he always watched.

Around four in the morning, Sean felt a tickle on his foot. He opened his eyes and shielded them to the unwelcoming bedroom light. Standing at the foot of his bed was the stranger from the motorboat. But the man Sean barely registered. All he could focus on was the fangs and whiteness from inside the Water Moccasin's mouth that the stranger held with a simple hook. Before he could let out a noise of any kind, the man flung the four-foot creature onto Sean's face. Sean felt those great fangs penetrate his neck as the beast's body coiled next to his head. The snake sunk into Sean's carotid artery. He widened his boring brown eyes at the stranger, begging for mercy. But that was no longer up to the stranger. Sean was at the hands, or fangs, of the snake now.

Since the Water Moccasin had found an artery, death didn't take long to arrive. Within a minute, Sean was gone.

CHAPTER 2

Lanny Pape scratched his cheek while he sat at Matrix, an expensive bar among many other expensive bars in Atlanta. It was his first time entering the place. For a few days he had walked past Matrix, transfixed by the blue lights that illuminated the choice liquors and the smooth marble bar counter; he desperately wished to run his long fingers over its surface. But Lanny Pape had never been inside a bar before. He had been a bit nervous going in with only the rudimentary knowledge of bar etiquette he had learned from movies.

Lanny surveyed the other customers, trying to figure out who it was that he was looking for. There was a couple to his right, talking only in whispers and giggles. A few frat types were hanging at the end of the bar with a pitcher of Bud Light. To his left sat an old man who coughed phlegm into his hanky. Lanny wrinkled his nose and turned away from the sight. A thin girl burst through the door and found herself a seat one away from the old man. Lanny watched as the guys at the end of the bar gave her a once over, then returned to whatever inane conversation they'd been having.

"What'll it be?" The voice came through Lanny's fog of thought. His eyes focused on the short man in front of him.

"Uh, a ginger ale and lemon juice?"

"Sure, just one second. By the way, I'm Johnny and the other bartender is Warren. Let either of us know if you need anything." Johnny turned away from the customer. He was used to those guys coming in to the bar and ordering something that should have alcohol in it. They were the AA guys who were riding along on a wobbly-wheeled wagon. Johnny placed the drink in front of Lanny. The guys at the end of the bar flagged him down.

Lanny overheard tidbits of the conversation, that the other bartender, Warren, was grabbing the keg and to just wait a minute. On cue, another man came through the back of the bar, carrying the quarter-keg over his shoulder. He replaced the nozzle on the new one and tossed the empty one at his peer, almost knocking him over. "You can take it back," Warren said.

Warren took a look up and down his bar. His eyes first fell on the old man next to Lanny. "Sal, how ya doing on that drink? Ready for a new one?" He asked.

"Nah, this'll prolly be the last today, Warren," he replied in a quiet, croaky voice.

Warren noticed the small girl. When he looked at her, she squeaked and blushed.

"And what will you be having?" He asked with a wide smile.

"Well, I'm not actually sure," she admitted. "I've had two glasses of Cab Sav tonight, but I'm no longer in the mood for wine. Still have another bottle at the house. You know what, I think I'll just have a vodka martini," she decided, sliding her ID across the bar. He gave it a cursory glance.

"Do you have a vodka preference?"

"Tito's."

"Straight up or on the rocks?"

"Straight up, and with olives please."

While the bartender set to work on the girl's drink, the old man turned toward the girl.

"What's your name, sweetheart?"

The girl returned a polite smile while she leaned forward to understand him through his almost-closed mouth, "Amanda."

"Amanda, huh? Lovely, lovely name," he coughed again. "What are you doin' out here by yourself?" He mumbled.

"I had to drive myself out here," she gave a slight laugh, "I'm meeting my boyfriend at Ringo's in a little bit."

Warren set the drink in front of Amanda, with a slight smirk on his face. Lanny could see her hand visibly shaking as she reached for her glass, her eyes on the handsome bartender's face. Sal continued to stare at the small girl beside him. He then turned to Lanny.

"The girls just get prettier and prettier, am I right?" He offered Lanny a wink with a tight-lipped smile.

Lanny didn't actually hear whatever Sal had murmured. But he gave a nod as if he had and hoped that was an appropriate response. He studied Sal, wondering if this was his guy. He looked into the quiet, old man's saggy eyes and saw mountains of slain girls piled in his basement. But... it wasn't him. He couldn't have been who Lanny was looking for. His killer didn't prefer young women. His killer didn't have any preference at all, if he was right.

"Ready for another one, fella?" Lanny looked down and realized his drink was almost empty. It wasn't Johnny asking, it was

Warren. Lanny met the man's deep blue eyes. His gut began to communicate with him with quite some rigor and persistence.

"Uh, please. Yes, lemon juice and ginger ale." Lanny said.

"Ya know, if you threw some gin in there, it'd be a great drink," he flashed his white teeth.

"No, thank you, just the lemon juice and ginger ale," he repeated.

Warren quickly put the drink together. Lanny sipped. He remembered the way Warren had smirked at the girl, Amanda, and wondered if she was his newest target. *Where did she say she was going? Was it Ringo's? Yes, I think it was. I bet Warren will show up there later.*

Lanny spent the next hour or so finishing drink after drink, defying the limits of his bladder by refusing to get up from his stool. He watched how Warren interacted with customers, how he mixed drinks, and wondered what it'd be like to watch how he killed. Lanny just wanted to lick the spoon again.

Warren finished his side work, always there for the rush but never the close. He consulted his watch and set off at a brisk pace toward Ringo's, pure adrenaline rushing through his body. He took great pride in his work and wished he could boast of it. But no, this was a private job, however necessary. Warren worked to make the world a better place. He walked past the entrance to Ringo's and parked himself in the little alley next door, then waited. On the inside, Lanny was keeping tabs on the girl from Matrix. Her bleached blonde hair made it easy.

She tossed back a shot of vodka without flinching. Lanny thought it looked just like water, and that something that clear couldn't possibly have any taste. He sat at a round high-top table with two chairs. Ringo's was packed with rowdy heathens that reeked of cheap beer. Nobody noticed him. He watched the girl, Amanda, as she leaned in to say something in a short guy's ear. A shrug followed the whisper. A fat man with more than just a beer belly bellowed into Lanny's ear something indecipherable. Lanny shrugged off the fleshy arm and grimaced. The man was now in front of him shouting and laughing. His eyes were as red as the blood Lanny so wished would appear from a nice knife wound in his great gut. In between bursts of laughter, the man dribbled puke down his front. Lanny finally hopped off of his chair just in time to see Amanda slap the short guy and flee.

Warren was pleased when he saw Amanda walk out of the bar, alone, with mascara running down her face. He took a step forward, but paused when he noticed a short, muscular guy run out after her.

"Babe chill out. Wanna talk about it, tomorrow?"

"Yeah," she gave a defeated smile, "yeah, I'll probably be over it by then."

He smiled and returned to the bar. *Probably back to find some floozy to keep him company for the night.*

Warren jogged over to his car that was just one block down. He circled around the block to see the girl wobble into her own Jetta. He slowed down and pulled to the other side of the road, waiting for another car to pass and provide him with a safe distance. Lanny was on it. He pulled right up behind Amanda in his beat up Ford truck. Warren still gave a cushioned distance between his car and the truck. The girl started her engine after three tries, and all three of them were off.

Lanny glanced at Warren in his rear view mirror: jaw set, eyes alert, one hand on the wheel. Lanny felt a flutter in his own stomach and retrieved a safety pin from his shirt pocket. He expertly undid the pin with one hand still on the wheel and pricked his thumb. He jammed his thumb in his mouth and savored the metallic taste. Lanny's thumb stayed planted until it began to wrinkle. Ahead of him, Amanda's car swerved in a snakelike way at fifteen above the speed limit.

Warren let out a small groan as the crappy truck in front of him turned into the same apartment complex as the Jetta, Peachtree Station. He drove a bit past the drive and one road over. He parked his black BMW next to a flickering streetlamp. He stepped out of the car and gave his legs a good stretch, his neck a good crack. Warren slid along the shadows and spied Amanda, still fumbling with her keys outside of Apartment 23. He saw no sign of the Ford truck. He waited. She dropped the keys that gave an echoing clang into the air. He sighed. "Stupid, stupid, stupid," the words echoed inside his head. She slowly bent over, and he could see every vertebra along her spine. She gave one go at the keys and missed as if they were under water. On the second try she got them and then succeeded in unlocking her door. Warren set off toward the apartment.

Lanny kept his head low in his truck. He'd parked between two even bigger trucks, feeling quite secure in his location. He could just see the dark green door that led to his destiny. All he had to do was wait. He felt a bit like a cop on a stake out, only with a different goal in mind. He drummed his fingers on the steering wheel, anxious for the performance. A small yelp of excitement escaped his lips as he saw Warren jog up the steps to Apartment 23. He clasped his hands over his mouth, and then giggled, realizing nobody could actually hear him. He focused again on the green door, wondering how Warren was going to make his entrance. Jimmy the lock? Find an open window? Or maybe kick the door down! Yes, that seemed like a badass entry for the seasoned killer. But, to Lanny's surprise, Warren didn't even try the knob to see if it was unlocked. Instead, he gave three curt knocks.

Amanda wiped at her mascara-stained eyes and walked to the door. She expected it would be Colby, ready to make up and fuck. She swung the door open with what she hoped was a pouty look on her face. It was replaced by a look of confusion, then, as she took in the handsome bartender's chiseled face and sparkling white teeth, sultry excitement.

"I remember you. What could you be doing here?" She batted her eyelashes like little girls are taught to do.

Warren's smile widened. "Just bored. Lookin' for something to do…" He trailed off and met her eyes with his own blue ones.

"Well, would you like to come in?" The girl stepped aside, ready to let the stranger in.

"I'd like that." He was mildly surprised that she didn't wonder how he found her apartment, but this was also a girl who just drove drunk. He followed her in to the tiny kitchen and watched as she busied herself pouring glasses of wine.

"We switched places! Your drink sir," her hands shook as she gave him the long stemmed glass.

"Cab Sav?" he asked.

"How did you know?" she asked.

"Just a guess."

The two clinked and sipped at their wine. "Would you like to sit on the couch?" She smiled coyly. Warren agreed and sat on the edge of the suede loveseat. He let the girl settle in right next to him.

"So, what do you do when you aren't bartending?" Amanda asked. His foreboding gaze having already hypnotized her. Warren told her he just tried to make the world a better place. She took another sip of wine.

"You have lovely hair," Warren complimented, and it was not untrue, "I love the way it curls."

The girl thanked him and patted at her silky hair. Then her eyes widened. "Oh! I think I left my curling iron on! Thank goodness the place is still here. Still, I better go turn it off. You stay here," she commanded, then added, "I will be back for more." She flitted up the narrow staircase and stumbled over the last step. But she didn't spill her wine. Warren gave his neck another good crack before grabbing a nice little steak knife from the kitchen, pocketing it, and taking to the stairs.

Lanny thought six minutes was enough time to wait. He practically jumped out of his car with excitement and trotted up the steps to that green door. He put his ear against it and listened, nothing. A rise of panic began when Lanny thought he might have missed everything. He patted his Smith and Wesson snub-nosed revolver in his pocket, hoping Warren wouldn't make fun of him for the small gun. Lanny tried the knob and it gave. He turned it slowly and pushed through the green door, ready for his life to begin again.

Warren crept up the stairs and heard the girl humming from one of two bedrooms. There was no worry of being seen by a roommate. Warren was always prepared to take care of any unexpected problem. He pushed open the door and the humming got louder. It was some Beyoncé song, thought he couldn't quite recall the name. He stepped into the room. The walls were bare save one photograph of the little guy that had chased her out of Ringo's. The bathroom door was cracked. Warren could see the girl's reflection in the mirror. She was running the curling wand through her hair, readying herself to provide her boyfriend with some payback. She never cheated before, but Colby had cheated her on at least three times she knew of. Beyoncé gave her courage, but she still felt so wrong for what she was going to do.

He stepped on a loose board and it let out a good squeak. The humming stopped. She poked her long neck through the door-frame.

"Oh, hullo there. I was just freshening up... but it seems you don't need that from me, do you? Tell me, what is it that you need from me?" Her voice dropped to a low, husky growl and she only felt mild embarrassment for the way she was acting. Amanda reminded herself she would never have to see this guy again, so it didn't matter what he thought.

She was only slurring the slightest bit. Warren flashed a guilty smile. He walked toward her. She opened the bathroom door fully to reveal some lacy black underwear covering her bony body. Warren had remembered seeing a strap of blue fall down her arm at his bar, and almost found it endearing that she had sexed herself up for him. One hand was still holding the curling wand in her hair. With the other, she fingered the front clasp of her bra and let it snap open. Her skinny fingers traveled down her pale torso, and into the front of her thong. "Come help me?" She asked.

Warren didn't answer. He strode forward and held her soft face in his big hand. He let his lips meet hers for one brief kiss, close-mouthed. Her eyes stayed shut and he smiled. Then she stopped. "Wait, no, I don't want to do this. I'm not a cheater. I'm sorry. You have to go." He wrapped one hand over hers on the curling wand and gently slid it from her grip. He could feel her body shudder inwardly. He put his other hand over her mouth.

"Shhh. You may not be a cheater. But you are stupid, stupid, stupid. You just drove drunk, or at least mildly intoxicated. What if you hit someone? What if you crashed your car into a family of four?"

"What? Uh- yeah, I guess you're right. How would you know that? Yeah, but I'm not drunk. I'm *not* drunk. Just a little tipsy." She saw the look in his eye. "No, not even tipsy. I'm fine, but you really need to leave. I'm not going to do this."

The wand had already singed parts of her hair. Warren pulled it free, gently. But the gentleness didn't last long. "I don't want to have sex with you," he said. He didn't think twice about his tool or what all he could do with it, just plunged the hot iron into the girl's left eye, letting it burn the flesh of her eyelids. He pushed it in further. The sound was almost the same as frying bacon. His heavy hand muffled her screams. Her good eye widened a comical degree; he thought it was going to pop right out of her head. That would be a nice memento.

Lanny pushed through the bedroom door to the muted screams of the girl. He arrived just in time to see the end of some sort of stick or barrel protruding from her eye. The eye contact she gave him, perhaps in a plea for help, lasted less than a second as Warren sent a knife through the side of her neck, in and out, nice and quick. Her body went limp and he caught it gallantly in his arms before setting it on the ground. Lanny looked on with admiration as Warren stood up. He couldn't help himself; he started a slow clap.

Warren whirled around at the sound of a single person's applause. He didn't miss a beat. He began marching toward Lanny, the knife raised, ready to plummet again into tough but soft human flesh. When Lanny saw this, he reached his sweaty hand into his pocket and pulled out the S & W.

"Please, just hear me out." Lanny pointed the gun at Warren's head.

Warren stared at the tiny gun shaking in this man's hand. He lifted his gaze to the man's face. He saw that queer sort of fellow that ordered ginger ale and lemon juice.

"Ok. Let's talk." Warren stopped advancing. He stood slightly rocking back and forth on his feet and with his arms crossed. Lanny kept the gun raised, just to be safe. He talked from behind its force field.

"I've been looking for you Warren. Only, I didn't know it was you I was looking for. That is, until I looked into your eyes. Then, I felt it. I *knew* you were my guy. The one I'd been looking for!" Sheen of sweat had broken out across Lanny's forehead. He began talking faster and faster, as if all of the words were trying to break out of his mouth at once. Warren kept his lips shut tight, more so out of curiosity than any kind of fear. Lanny continued.

"I keep myself up to date with the newspapers. When stories broke, some murders only a week apart, I got very excited. You see, most people, the police included, believed these murders to be the work of different killers, as I am sure you know. I started expanding my search, collecting news from all over Georgia.

"It's genius. You, you are genius. I just knew it had to be the same guy behind it all. I can't explain why or how I knew, I just did. Well, I hoped I did. It was a hunch and I went with it. But, when I saw you behind the bar at Matrix, my stomach turned in excited flips. Like, there you were! Making some drinks, cool as can be." Lanny stopped and took a big breath. He realized he hadn't taken one that whole time. He glanced down at the skinny girl's unmoving body and failed to suppress a great grin.

"I'm not admitting to anything. But what is it that you want from me, fella?"

"Warren, I want to lick your spoon."

"What the fuck?"

"That doesn't sound quite right, I know, may I?" Lanny lifted his free hand, palm facing up, and advanced slowly toward Warren. He kept his finger on the trigger of the raised gun to be safe. Warren was, for what felt like the first time (aside from contemplating the ignorance of people around him) dumbfounded. He gave the knife a toss in the air, causing Lanny to flinch. But Warren merely caught the blade by the tip after it went a half rotation. He offered the handle to Lanny.

Lanny could feel himself salivating. He felt like Pavlov's dog hearing the bell and receiving food after such a long wait. He shoved the gun back in his pocket and held the knife close to his face. He wanted to savor the moment. Warren didn't exist right then. Lanny ran his tongue slowly up the blade, starting at the bottom, twitching with pleasure. After one long, slow lick, he lost control of his tongue and let it dance over the blade, uncovering its true shiny surface. He finally plopped the blade in his mouth and stood motionless, sucking it as a baby would his binky. A young girl of about eleven stood in front of him, encouraging him.

"Lick it all off, Lanny! Now think, how often do I let you have the whole spoon to yourself, huh? It's good right?"

Lanny nodded, his lips carving a smile into his face.

"Man, what the fuck?" Warren repeated.

The haze cleared from Lanny's eyes. The girl was gone, replaced by a man who was looking at him as if he had poured ketchup all over his French fries instead of in one neat pile to dip at a noncommittal leisure. Warren wondered if there would be cuts inside the fella's mouth, surely on his tongue at least. Lanny pulled the knife from his mouth; it was sparkling clean like it had just been through the wash.

"What was that?" Warren was getting a bit annoyed whilst waiting for an explanation.

"Ever lick the spoon of brownie batter, or cookie dough?" Lanny asked, feeling more comfortable by the second as he digested the new blood. He still wasn't fully there. It was as if he were trying to hang on to the wisps of the fantasy the knife had brought him.

"No," Warren answered honestly, "I never ate that crap... But what does that have to do with anything? I mean, you just up and licked that knife that was covered in blood. Don't you think? What if the chick had AIDS or somethin', huh?"

"She didn't."

"And how would you know that? I oughta kill you right now for being so openly stupid. How could you—"

"She didn't. My gut always tells me what I need to know. Look, Mr...."

"Worth. You are?"

"Mr. Worth, Lanny Pape, licking the spoon is always better when you enjoy it with the company of someone else, like a sibling, or a friend. It's nice sitting back and watching someone do what they love, whether that be baking... or killing, and then licking the spoon of their handiwork, sharing the moment with them."

Warren busted out laughing. It was deep and hearty, one that almost forced others to join him. Here he was, fresh off of a murder, with a witness who wanted to, what, lick his spoon? *What the flying fuck in hell?* It was all too much. Here, his own customer, a guy he hadn't seen coming! He would scold and punish himself later for not paying enough attention, but for now, only laughter came.

Lanny wasn't quite sure why Warren was laughing, but he joined in anyway. It was hard not to. Warren had a great laugh. Lanny's was a bit twitchy alongside it, but it felt good to laugh. Warren wiped an actual tear from his eye and tried to control himself. But every time he looked up to see ole Lanny standing there with that knife in his hand, he got lost in another fit of giggles.

"Oh, my God. I," Warren laughed, "Okay, I need to start cleaning up. We need to get the fuck out of here, fella. Jesus Christ, alright, make yourself useful." He ripped the pillowcase from the pillow and tossed it to Lanny. Start wiping shit down. Starting with that iron." He gestured to the girl's body. "But, wait, you aren't into some freaky necrophilia stuff, right? Because if you cum on that body, this is all on you."

At first, Lanny felt tears jump to his eyes. Warren was just another jock, making fun of him. Only he had skipped the homo jokes and jumped straight into "so-pathetic-he-only-fucks-the-dead." But, he realized, Warren was being serious. They weren't that well acquainted, and the guy was just taking necessary precautions. He dabbed at his eyes with the pillowcase while Warren had his back turned.

Warren had picked up the girl's now cracked iPhone and was trying to break the code. *1-1-1-1, nope. 2-5-8-0, miss. 0-0-0-0, bing!* He scrolled through her most recent pictures to make sure she hadn't taken one of him when he was bartending or wasn't looking. Once, a group of girls just breaking the seal of twenty-one came in one night, trying so hard to flirt with him. Of course, he couldn't blame them. He tended to smile as he made drinks and faced the bar so customers could see everything that was going into it. Always taking necessary precautions, never to be blamed for something like roofies. That was when a flash went off in his direction. Of course all of the girls were too drunk to be embarrassed. But still, it was something he knew to look out for. Always learning, always evolving.

Thankfully, there were no pictures of him. Next, he took to her text messages to see if she had alerted any of her gal pals of the handsome stranger she'd be spending the night with. Only one text to a Becks alluded to such a thing—*Gonna be a good night. Fuck Colby, Colby who?*" This was followed by one of those winking emojis.

Warren wasn't worried about that. After all, it just set up the perfect scenario for the police to capture their "guy." Random guy brought back from the bars to the house for a night of passion. The boyfriend stops by to apologize. The boyfriend arrives to moans and grunts coming from upstairs. He yells. She pleads. The other guy gathers up his clothes in one arm and runs out in his underwear. Colby notices the curling iron. The rest, well, that is for the imagination of whatever the officers want to decide. Yes, thank you for playing such a nice role.

Warren surveyed the room, making sure he covered all of his bases. "Looks good."

Lanny threw the crumpled pillowcase back onto the bed. Warren grabbed him by the arm, hard.

"What the fuck are you doing?"

Lanny had no answer, he only stood gape-mouthed struggling to come up with something, but still not understanding what he had done wrong.

Warren rolled his eyes. "Take it with you. I saw you wipe your eyes on that thing, and who knows what else it could have picked up. Take the pillowcase, take the knife. Although I assume you were going to do that anyway." He was right. Lanny had slid the knife into his pocket to put on his nightstand later. Warren went on to tell Lanny to burn the pillowcase when he got home, and if he had to keep the knife, keep it to himself. "Don't show it to any weirdo friends." Lanny nodded, taking in every word, not allowing himself to take any offense. The two trotted down the steps. Lanny started to open the door again.

"Christ, did you open it when you first got here too? Wipe both knobs with the case. Avoid the wet spots from your tears. Who knows when the technology is going to improve again, could be tonight?" Warren quickly strode over to the couch and picked up his wine glass. He could have wiped it clean but opted to take it with him. He was that way with most things. If it had the potential to break down as evidence, it would be burned or otherwise destroyed.

The two went down the steps. Warren followed Lanny to his truck, rolling his eyes yet again at its spot in the lot of the now-dead girl. He hopped in anyway and told Lanny where his car was. As he was stepping out, he turned and reluctantly flicked Lanny his card. It was his bartending card that he gave out mostly to the rich folks at private parties he worked. His cell phone number was printed at the bottom in a bold black. Lanny flushed and thanked him and was on his way.

CHAPTER 3

Detective Morgan Purdy gulped at his coffee, hoping taking it in bigger swells would force it to kick in faster. It was four-thirty in the morning, and he and his partner had gotten the call about fifteen minutes prior. Purdy had gone to bed early as usual when he was on-call, but it never made the abrupt wake-up any easier. His partner Brian Jenson looked just as bleary-eyed, if not more, in the passenger seat of the 2010 Crown Victoria. When they pulled into the apartment complex, a few squad cars were there already. Some officers were busy taping off the scene and barely took a moment to acknowledge the newcomers. One opened his mouth just to say, "D.O.A.," dead on arrival. Purdy and Jenson both pulled on a pair of black, latex gloves. The two then stepped into shoe covers before going through the door.

The green door to apartment 23 was ajar. Purdy stepped around it and nodded to the blue-suit inside. A boy with shaggy, greasy hair falling into his eyes was further into the entryway. He had snot running down his wet face. He was wearing a wife-beater tank and cargo shorts. "Hi," he said simply through a sniffle.

Purdy looked the guy up and down before sliding past him, hand on his gun's butt, ready to pull it out at any second. He took a quick survey of the room and relaxed. Empty save this guy who smelled of stale beer.

"Are you Colby? He make the call?" Jenson asked, both to the officer and the boy. Both nodded. More blue lights lit up the windows, but they had all turned off their sirens. Black cars began to pull up as well. Outside, Purdy caught sight of a flash of red hair as well as flashes of light from a camera. The blinding light started off from afar and came closer as its handler moved in from the perimeter. She took a few shots of the doorway, waiting impatiently for everyone inside the apartment to get out of her shot, then finally stepped inside.

"Miranda," Purdy gave his ex-lover a nod.

"Morgan," she returned, "and hello Brian."

Jenson flicked his hand in greeting, keeping all of the attention on Colby.

"Man, I don't know what to do! That was my girl up there!" He buried his face in his fists. Alejandro Rivera had begun placing numbered markers around the place while Miranda took the photos. He set one down beside the half-empty bottle of Cabernet Sauvignon.

Jenson placed his hand on Colby's shoulder. "I'm going to need to ask you some questions." Colby nodded. Miranda took establishing and close-up shots all around the kitchen and living room before taking to the stairs. Purdy followed.

They went through the only open door and didn't have to look hard to find the body. There she was, dressed in some lingerie. Lividity had set in; the body was covered in bluish-purple patches that resembled enormous bruises.

"What's that, there in her eye?" Purdy asked.

34

Miranda bent over the body with the camera still in hand. "That would be a curling iron. You know, a tool used to curl a women's hair." Purdy grunted at her condescending tone.

She went on, "And right there, the side of her neck, that is a clean strike. This guy knew exactly where to hit." She took a cluster of pictures of the side of the neck where the knife was, as well as of the eye penetrated by a curling iron. Miranda scanned the area behind her lens, taking more shots of the splatter next to the body.

At that point more investigators filed into the room, one was busily sketching, another taking inventory of everything the deceased was wearing: black bra with a front clasp, Victoria's Secret, lacy black underwear by the same name, no shoes or socks, one red beaded bracelet. Purdy slipped out and joined his partner downstairs. Jenson was standing up, and flipped his notebook shut.

"Get anything good?" he asked Jenson.

"Maybe, we'll have to wait and see. No arrests to be made, right now anyway. We should start to bag some of this stuff."

"Okay. Is Paul on his way yet?" Morgan asked, referring to the coroner.

"Yeah, he should be here any second now."

On cue, Paul walked in with his own clipboard, a pair of orange latex gloves on his hands, and his glasses pushed up on top of his balding head. He had an orange stretcher that he was dragging along behind him. "Upstairs?"

"Yessir," Morgan nodded. He and his partner followed the man upstairs, ready to assist in moving the body.

As Morgan Purdy made his way back to his one-story house and his wife Ellen, Lanny Pape was walking through the door of his small apartment in Brookhaven. He fumbled his way through the door and locked it without looking. He sat down on the couch he found at someone's dumpster sale. It was pea green and sagged in the middle. He took to the sag and pulled out Amanda's knife. His reflection glared from the surface: green eyes that rarely sparkled, straw-like strawberry blonde hair, and smatterings of almost-there freckles. He wasn't ugly, nor was he attractive, more so just forgettable. Lanny wondered if he had ever made an impression on anyone. He doubted that even his many foster parents would remember his name.

But Lanny didn't care if he was memorable. He just needed one person, just one, to make him feel special. It didn't have to be a lover, but even a friend, a sister…

Lanny scarcely saw his sister, about once a year since he was about eleven. She was eighteen at the time and off to college. Jodee wasn't exactly book-smart. She was street-smart though, as well as a talented athlete. Unlike Lanny, Jodee was able to stick with one foster family. They loved her and signed her up for all of the sports she wanted. She spent her youth playing soccer, basketball, and tennis, but soccer was always her one true love. When she turned eighteen, Jodee made her way to the brother she saw maybe once a year for five years.

At that time, Lanny was living with the Jeffersons, or maybe it was the Johnsons. They were an okay family, aside from Brian the teenager who picked on Lanny relentlessly. Jodee picked Lanny up and took him out for dinner, it was Olive Garden as he recalled. As he sat shoving breadsticks down his throat, Jodee informed him she would be going to Furman on a full soccer scholarship. Lanny knew all about scholarships, even at eleven. Earning one would be the only way he could get into a college. Except, he didn't know anything about sports' scholarships. He was hoping for a nice academic one.

Jodee droned on and on about the coach and the team and how beautiful the school was. Lanny just nodded dutifully but was really struggling to hold back the tears. This hadn't been part of the plan. Jodee had made him a promise the first time they'd had to go separate ways. But, nowhere in Jodee's collegiate plans did Lanny see a spot for himself. Jodee mentioned the dorms, how she'd picked a roommate from the rest of the upcoming freshman soccer player litter, but nothing about a place for Lanny in her new life.

He sat in silence throughout the dinner. He only scraped the cheese off the top of his chicken Parmesan and munched on that, ignoring the faces Jodee was giving him. None of it was right. Jodee had *pinky* promised, kissed the fist and everything, that she would find a way to legally adopt him. But that no longer fit into Jodee's plan. It seemed to Lanny that she might have completely forgotten about it. So, they finished eating, Jodee took the bill, and she drove him back to the Johnson's or Jefferson's. She unlocked the door for him to get out, but Lanny was stuck. He sat there with tears welling in his eyes.

"What's going on, Lan?" Jodee had asked. But the concern on her face looked phony. He didn't say anything. He just pulled a shiny object from his pocket. It was short and jagged but gleamed like it had just been polished. He remembered feeling a sort of satisfaction when Jodee seemed to stop breathing. He held it out for her to see, not by its handle but by the tip. It was to force her to remember her promise, as well as the entirety of that night. Jodee finally let out a breath. She looked over at her lost little brother and placed her hand on his muss of haystack hair. Lanny ripped out from underneath what felt like dead weight and jumped out of the Honda Civic. He threw the knife into the passenger seat and ran back into the white-bread world house that he would only live in for another three months.

And now Lanny had a new toy. One that he hoped would be the first of many to make for a fabulous collection. He pushed all thoughts of Jodee and what she might be doing from his mind. These were replaced with giddy ones of Warren Worth and his magnificent blow to the girl's neck. It was so calculated and precise, really amazing to watch. Warren had agreed to come to Lanny's Thursday evening for tea. Lanny enjoyed the idea of "having a cup of tea" with someone other than the ghosts of his past. They never were much for conversation; even they always ended up leaving.

Lanny found it difficult to focus on his job over the days leading up to his next meeting with Warren. On the morning of, he walked into work as usual and offered a small wave to the woman at the desk in the front of the building. He did not know her name or her exact job title; she was merely part of his every day scenery. On this particular morning, he was extra careless. He was part of the crew that was to prepare the bodies for display at Bodies: The Exhibition in Atlanta. Lanny was working with a particularly nasty set of lungs from a Chinese man who died at the early age of forty-two. The blackened lungs would be great next to the case full of cigarette cartons. Guests would see the lungs, and swear off cigarettes, until they got cravings that night, and deposit their cartons inside.

Lanny almost missed a crucial step that day. He had spent the entire previous day separating and dissecting out the man's lungs. Lanny always worked with the lungs. Occasionally he would do the heart, but he tried to avoid such meticulous work. Today he brought the lungs over to the silicone polymer bath and was milliseconds from placing them inside, when he noticed the weight was just a bit off. He tested it in his hands for a moment; at first believing the lungs were heavier because this man had taken in that much more tobacco than the others. Lanny dismissed this absurd thought and his eyes widened in shock as he realized what he had forgotten. He turned and guarded the lungs, treating them now like he was a mother with a newborn baby. Lanny couldn't afford to let the others see what he had been so close to doing. He would need to take extra care of this set. He placed the lungs in a bath of acetone and put it in the freezer. The lungs were heavy because of all of the water still inside that had not yet been drawn out by the acetone.

As he waited, Lanny pricked his calloused thumb and put it in his mouth, his back turned to the guys still dissecting their parts of the specimen. Foolish mistakes were not something he was accustomed to.

Warren pulled up to Lanny's Brookhaven apartment at exactly five in the evening, as discussed. He was a punctual, no nonsense man. Too many distractions would lead him down the road away from his evolving state. He stepped out of his matte black Bimmer and straightened his collar. He let out a sigh and trotted up the steps. He knocked briskly three times.

Lanny opened the door with a smile. "Please, have a seat anywhere you'd like." Warren surveyed his options. There was a snot green couch juxtaposed against a La-Z-Boy leather recliner, a few barstools at a counter, and two seats at a small wooden table. He opted for a seat at the table, intending to get straight down to business. Lanny busied himself in the kitchen and Warren could hear the clinking of china. Lanny carried over a tray with two cups of tea, a bowl of sugar, stirring spoons, and a plate of lemons.

"It's green tea, I hope that's alright." Warren could see the nerves behind Lanny's smile.

"That'll be just fine." Warren took a cup for himself and squeezed a lemon over it. He looked on with amusement as he watched Lanny take spoon after spoon of sugar. "So Lanny," he began, and the other man looked up with his spoon hovering above the sugar bowl, "tell me a little bit about yourself." Warren wanted it clear that he came on his own terms, and that the discussion was going to go in whichever direction he chose.

"Well, I am from Georgia. Initially North Georgia, but now I obviously live here. I work for Bodies: The Exhibition in Atlanta. Both of my parents are dead. My sister, she may pretend I am also dead. I love reading Raymond Carver. I went to UNC

Chapel Hill on a merit scholarship, and quite a big one I might add. I worked my way through college, though my parents did leave a bit set aside for me. I was employed ..."

Warren's ears perked up when Lanny mentioned his job at Bodies: The Exhibition. He didn't hear much after that and was ready to move to the core of the conversation.

"Lanny, sorry for interrupting, all of this is very interesting, but not what I'm after. I guess I'd like to know why you seek to, oh there is no real word for this I suppose, but partner with me?"

"I told you. I want to lick the spoon."

"Yes, I remember all that, but I guess I need more of a background. Or at least what your ultimate goal is."

"There is not much to my background, really. But I guess my ultimate goal is to be happy. To admire and appreciate someone who has such passion for his work that he makes it an art form. And I mean that both for the bartending and the killing. It's all beautiful. Everything you do is beautiful."

Warren didn't care much for the flattery. "Why aren't you frightened of me? I am a bit concerned that you still haven't asked why I do what I do."

"Okay. Why do you do what you do?"

Cheeky bastard. I guess I asked for it. "Lanny, I seek to make the world a better place. Before I go into full disclosure, I would like to point out that you are already an accessory to one of my 'crimes'. Therefore turning me in to any authority, while a dumb move on your part, would also be a waste of energy. There is not one man on this earth that I would not be able to elude. I'd also like to know if you have any living relatives, or next of kin."

Lanny's face went white. He swallowed and the saliva took a particularly rough journey down his dry throat. He didn't want to tell about Jodee. But Warren's deep blue eyes were boring into Lanny's soul. It was like the man was reading his thoughts. *Jodee left me. She wasn't there to protect me, so I shouldn't worry about protecting her. I have a new person now, someone else to take care of me. I need to show my loyalty to him now.* Lanny looked down as he gave his answer and solidified his loyalty with Warren overall. "I do have a sister. But she left my life long ago."

"And her name?"

"Jodee. Jodee Pape."

Warren produced a small notebook from his pants pocket and wrote something down. He was the opposite of a cop but performing the same practices. When Warren looked up, his face had taken on a broad smile showcasing perfect teeth.

"Good, Lanny. Okay, let's get on with it, fella. I seek to make the world a better place by eliminating those who are not properly evolved: those who make dumb and life-threatening decisions on a daily basis without even realizing it. For some reason, Earth has stopped with the tests and no plague lasts long enough anymore. So I have taken over on a small scale.

"You see, someone or something needs to start implementing natural selection again. Everyone has gotten into this comfortable routine. The Internet has taken over and people fight from behind those cyber walls. And it is a shame because we are not alike. Nobody is. Alfred Russel Wallace wrote a book called *Darwinism; An Exposition of the Theory of Natural Selection with Some of its Applications.* He said, 'Why do some live rather than others? If all the same individuals of each species were exactly alike in each respect, we could only say it is a matter of chance. But they are not alike.'"

Lanny wondered if that was the exact quote, and how long it had taken Warren to memorize it. Then again, this man memorized drink orders, drink recipes, names, and everything else almost every day.

"I have an eidetic memory, yes." Lanny shuddered as if Warren really were reading his thoughts. In reality, Warren spent weeks memorizing that quote. There was no such special skill nestled in his brain. Warren continued, "It is only proof that I am further evolved than the majority of humans inhabiting this earth. So I have taken over in implementing natural selection because 'Survival of the fittest' almost seems to be a thing of the past in this day and age, and that is not the way things should be."

Lanny hung on every word. His tea was long forgotten. Actually, neither of them had taken so much as a sip so far.

"So Lanny, what do you think," Warren was growing impatient with the silence.

"I-I think it is absolutely incredible. I guess I also want to know when our first case together is."

Warren chuckled as if amused by a small child. "How about tomorrow? Sometimes I like to find a target and find out everything about them. But most of the time I act on impulse, a low stalk for a few hours and then I pounce."

"Don't you work tomorrow?" Lanny asked.

"Yes, but at night."

"And you want to do this during the day?" Lanny was incredulous.

Warren again laughed. "It doesn't matter when. Day, night, I can always find a blanket to cover myself with. Sound good?"

Lanny nodded and the two planned to meet early in the morning and go on a little road trip to South Georgia.

Dressed carefully in all black, despite the August heat, Lanny skipped to his truck while picking at the collected lint on his fleece shirt. He didn't feel the sweat falling down the spine of his back. He opened the door to his truck and jumped in, humming the tune of "Pop Goes the Weasel." Lanny had perfect attendance throughout all of his years in school, and that carried over to his work life. That Friday morning he was finally using one of his many built up vacation days. He felt like a rebel *with* a cause.

Warren had given Lanny instructions to park at the Georgia Aquarium, on the Penguin Deck, and then meet him at the deck's exit. Lanny gave no qualms about having to pay to park even though he really didn't understand why Warren couldn't have picked him up at his apartment. But he wanted to show Warren he would be easy to work with. So, he parked on the Penguin and took the elevator to the first deck. He stepped into the sunshine, annoyed at himself for forgetting sunglasses. Every guy under cover had sunglasses. He put his hand in his pocket and gave himself a little prick on the already-opened safety pin. Lanny saw no sign of Warren's car. He jammed his thumb in his mouth and sucked vigorously. With his other hand he consulted his iPhone. It was 8:27 in the morning. The men had decided, well Warren had decided, that the meeting time would be 8:30.

Lanny figured Warren would appreciate his being early. A lot of people walked past Lanny on the sidewalk and barely stopped to notice his outfit that was so unsuited for Georgia heat. There were a lot of weirdoes walking those streets, but most didn't come out until the evening at the earliest.

By the time Warren pulled up, Lanny had a coat of sweat over his face and neck. The rest of his skin was covered by all of the black. Warren took one look at the man and rolled his eyes. It was moments like this that he wished he split his personality into two different bodies to place bets.

"Get in," Warren commanded. He popped the locks. Lanny slid easily into the buttered seat. Warren sat there looking at him, the car still in park, not caring that he was technically in the middle of the road.

Lanny chuckled nervously, "Shouldn't we get going?"

Warren said nothing. He reached behind his seat and retrieved a large white paper bag. He tossed it to Lanny. Warren put the car in drive and pulled into the Shell gas station. "I'll wait here."

Lanny peered into the bag, worried he would find a ski mask and a gun. Instead he saw a few t-shirts and khaki shorts. He turned and surveyed Warren. The man was dressed simply in a blue Salt Life tee and faded cargo shorts. Lanny stepped out of the car with his head down, a bit ashamed of himself. He started toward the gas station when Warren called out for him to wait a second. Lanny watched as Warren also stepped out of the car and popped the trunk. He rummaged for a moment and Lanny heard a lot of metal clanging. He finally came up with a beach towel. Warren tossed it to his sweaty counterpart.

"Wipe yourself down a bit. I don't need any sweaty glute imprints on my seats."

Lanny caught the towel and ignored the sting he felt when the corner of it whipped into his eye. He took the punishment, as well as the bag and towel, and walked into the gas station. The Middle Eastern man barely looked up from his magazine behind the dirty plexiglass window that separated him from the customers.

Lanny shuffled into the bathroom and locked the door behind him. He looked for a clean place to set the bag and settled for the sink. There were three shirts, a green one, a blue Salty Dog, and a faded yellow shirt with a fish on it. Lanny thought of Warren's blue shirt, though a different shade, and chose that one. He pulled the fleece over his head and finally realized how hot he had been. He looked like black sheep gone through slaughter, with only bits of wool attached in random spots. Lanny slid out of his black pants and wrapped himself in the towel while he pulled out the khaki shorts. He rubbed the towel vigorously up and down his legs until they were red with irritation. He stepped through one leg, then the other, and pulled them up. The shorts were a little big for him, but Lanny didn't think it would be entirely noticeable. He then began wiping his torso down with the towel, trying to ignore the pasty reflection mimicking his actions.

When he was totally dressed, he looked in the mirror. His hair was sticking up in sweaty chunks. Lanny parted it to the side and smoothed it down, using the excess sweat as a nice paste. He looked even younger than normal and like a total frat star. For some reason, he thought Warren would appreciate the look. Lanny allowed a small smile at the mirror and tried to puff up some confidence to go with his new persona. He stepped out of the bathroom.

This time the man behind the counter stared. Lanny channeled his inner douche and decided to flip him the bird. "What are you lookin' at?" He demanded shakily. Lanny noticed the rack of cheap sunglasses and pulled a pair of simple black ones, then set them in the concave slope of the counter that went beneath the plexiglass. The Middle Eastern man rang him up and Lanny slid him seven dollars, then left without waiting for whatever coins would be returned. To go with the "douche" persona, Lanny hooked the sunglasses around his ears from behind his head.

Warren was standing outside the car, leaning against it. He looked cool as can be, but even Lanny noticed the look of irritation on the man's handsome face as he got closer. The persona was gone, he was back to his nervous and unconfident self.

Warren didn't say a word about Lanny's appearance, so naturally he immediately began second-guessing himself. He followed Warren's suit and got into the car. Warren put the car into reverse and pulled out of the spot, then into drive and pulled onto the main road. He turned on the stereo and punched the AUX button with his thumb. His phone was already plugged into the port. Warren glanced at his phone and clicked "Shuffle all."

"Ain't no rest for the wicked..." by Cage the Elephant cut into the silence. Lanny saw Warren mouthing along to the words in his peripheral vision. He then began thinking how little he actually knew about Warren. But he didn't want to ask right now. Instead he settled back into the leather seat and turned his air vent so the air conditioning would hit him directly. The angry glare from the sun hit his eyes, so he removed the sunglasses from the douche position and put them on in the intended way. He leaned back and stared out the window, watching land and people and trees whiz past.

At about ten o' clock, Warren slammed on the brakes as some redneck cut him off. He cussed and held down the horn. Lanny sat up from his slumber. "Revolution" by the Beatles was now playing. He realized that he didn't actually know where they were going. He realized he was on the road with a seasoned killer, whom he had blackmailed. He realized he could be well on the way to his death.

"Wh... where are we going anyway?" Lanny attempted nonchalance.

Warren's brow was still furrowed from the dumbass that had cut in front of them. Right now he was weaving to the right lane and speeding up in order to gain some comeuppance.

The question took a moment to gain his attention. It sat in the air for a good thirty seconds. It wasn't until the black Bimmer was in front of the obnoxiously huge truck with camouflage trim and confederate flag bumper stickers that Warren bothered to answer.

"Clarenceville. A bit less than three hours to go."

"Oh. Gotcha. Sounds great." Lanny didn't settle back into his seat. He was rigid. Beside him, Warren chuckled.

"I'm not going to kill you."

Again, Lanny wondered about Warren reading his mind. He didn't answer. Another heavy silence filled the car as the song switched again.

Warren glanced over at Lanny. "Look. You outsmarted me. I don't think you understand how rare that is, for me to overlook something, or in this case someone. I never saw you coming. Now, I am not looking to eliminate those that are above the large gap, the gap that separates the favored individuals, us, from the average men out there.

"Fella, mankind has populated and reproduced and taken over with the common goal of being the strongest force in the natural world. We surpassed that point long ago. Now there are idiots running wild with no force to stop them. There are too many people, and unfortunately people with gifts and higher faculties are a rarity when compared to the number of semi-savages. I see your gifts. And I intend to use them. I guess you could say I'm sort of like God."

Lanny flushed, pleased with the assessment. He settled back into his seat and almost hummed out loud with 38 Special's "Hold on Loosely." He *was* special. And Warren saw that in him.

The sun beat down through the windows into the car. It was almost one in the afternoon. They were close to Clarenceville. Lanny pressed his face against the window to take in the scenery. Buildings were sparse. A gated area filled with horses whizzed by on his right. Lanny found horses to be utterly terrifying. Cows, on the other hand, he adored. He let a smile creep onto his face as they passed a few grazing here and there on tufts of green grass. At some point the road had turned to dirt. There were a few more buildings now, though some looked extremely decrepit. The only people they could see were sitting in lawn chairs that must have been stronger than they looked considering the weight they had to bear. Confederate flags flew proudly above more than a few front doors.

Lanny was confused. He didn't see how they were going to pick just one target. He entertained the thought that Warren might be intending on a mission similar to Sherman's March to the Sea, taking down this whole town of primitive beings. "So, what is the plan of action anyway?"

Warren kept his eyes straight ahead on the dirt road. "We are going to the grocery store. Then, we are going to the local watering hole, I'm sure happy hour is all day for these fools."

"How do you know where everything is? Have you been here before?"

Warren didn't answer. He did, however, slow as they passed a faded blue house. A broken wire fence surrounded the place. The windows had lost a lot of face due to the constant flying rocks. Lanny swore he saw a face peering out from behind one jagged piece of glass in the upstairs window. The face looked just short of haunted. It disappeared.

Just as he was about to mention the house, Warren sped up a bit. They pulled into a large gravel lot. To Lanny, it resembled fairground parking. He squinted through the sun and noticed they were in front of an old grocery store, "Marty's Mart." There was a beat up truck and station wagon in the parking lot. Other than that, a few bikes left about haphazardly. Lanny enjoyed the audible crunching of the car's tires over the gravel. Warren pulled in next to the single streetlamp. Lanny didn't think that was the best idea, for the lamp looked as if it was ready to give up the good fight and totter over. But he didn't say anything. He just stepped out of the car and stretched his limbs.

"Aren't you glad you changed clothes?" Warren asked not unkindly whilst performing a few back twists.

"Yes, I actually am." Lanny gave a chuckle. "Thanks for that, by the way."

"Yeah, fella, you got it." They set off toward the store.

Warren made a jagged path so that he could peek into the cars in the lot. He didn't seem to find anything of importance and continued into the store. A bell gave a weak ring as they walked in, alerting the fat, pimply adolescent behind the counter to put down her phone and greet the customers.

"Welcome to Marty's," she said unenthusiastically. Her blonde hair clung to her head under coats of grease. Lanny saw her though. He knew that she was working this dull job to save up for school. She wanted to get out of this town and her parents weren't going to do anything to help. He knew that she was a ghost in her high school, if not severely picked on. He knew that she got nervous every time the bell over the door sounded for it could be one of the popular girls walking in to give her an emotional beating.

The sound of a laughing group of pre-pubescent boys rose from one of the aisles. Lanny was grateful that Warren didn't start off in that direction. Instead he walked lazily to the far side of the store. Lanny followed his lead. There wasn't a soul in the frozen foods aisle. Warren picked out a small box of frozen chicken nuggets. He inspected it, then turned to Lanny. "Would you mind grabbing us a shopping basket?"

Lanny hitched his breath, nervous about the boys. Kids that age were the worst. He remembered his own days of being tortured, not only by Brian Jefferson or Johnson, but by every kid he suffered through middle school with. Boys at that age would force you to the ground and make you pull out your penis, and then call you a "gay fag." Lanny left Warren's side. He straightened up a bit and went back to the front of the store. The blonde cashier was back on her phone.

Lanny made it to the stack of baskets and struggled to pull one from the top. He finally ripped it apart. He heard some giggling and turned around. Four boys were standing at the front of the candy aisle. They were watching him. He slid his hand into his pocket and realized he had left the pin in the black pants. He panicked. Then, Lanny stood up straight and puffed out his concaved chest. These kids, he was sure they could smell the insecurity on him. He decided he would walk straight toward them and try to act as if he were the formidable Warren Worth. He was about fifteen feet from the boy in the front of the group when he made eye contact with their leader. He froze. The kid smiled at him, revealing a row of scuzzy teeth that were in desperate need of a mother reminding him to brush before bed and in the morning. Lanny abruptly turned to the right and speed-walked his way back to Warren. He could hear more laughter behind him and only walked faster. The footsteps behind him made no effort to be quiet. The squeaking of sneakers echoed around him.

Lanny began to panic. He just needed to find Warren. He turned right at the end of the cereal aisle and began walking straight to where they had started, whipping his head around to look down every aisle along the way. Warren was now looking at the wide array of soups. Lanny let out his breath. He marched toward Warren.

Warren looked up from his can of tomato soup when he heard someone coming. Then, he realized it was more than one. Four boys trailed behind Lanny. Some were throwing crushed receipts they must have found deep in their pockets from the local McDonald's. There was a pained look on Lanny's face. Lanny stopped right in front of him and tried to appear calm. "Here's the basket." Warren dropped in a can of soup and a bag of crackers along with the chicken nuggets. He then turned square on with the boys, silently boring his eyes into them one at a time. Warren took a few steps toward them until he was about nose to nose with the scuzzy-toothed leader. He said nothing, only let his breaths come out like an angry, awakened dragon. The smallest kid of the group nudged the boy in front.

"Hey, Alec. M-maybe we should just go man." The other boys nodded in agreement. They wanted to peel their eyes away from Warren's dark blue ones. Alec swallowed, determined not to show his gang any weakness.

"Whatever. These guys are fags anyway. No use messin' with gay-fers." He turned on his heel and walked away. The others followed.

Lanny tried to figure out what had just transpired between Warren and the boys. It was like he held them under a spell, like he had cut them with just his eyes. Whatever the trick was, Lanny was appreciative.

"Look. You cannot tell me you still let kids like that intimidate you." Warren turned to face Lanny. "They're less than half your age, Lanny!" He looked frustrated. Lanny didn't respond, which was a smart idea on his behalf. He didn't say a word as Warren walked up and down rows of messily stocked food items. They came across a screaming toddler and large, exhausted woman. She was trying in vain to secure a binky in the toddler's mouth. Warren squeezed past her and acted like he didn't hear the screaming baby. Lanny followed.

Warren picked out a pack of cinnamon-flavored gum and a bottle of wine before heading back to the front of the store. He set the gum, the wine, the box of nuggets, soup, and crackers on the counter. He then grabbed a bottle of water from the cooler next to the register. It was warm. He set that on the counter too. "Grab yourself a soda or something," he told Lanny. Lanny set a Sprite along with the other items.

The girl behind the counter noticed Warren's face without her phone as a distraction. Her face turned bright red and looked a bit sweaty. She began scanning his items. "I *love* this flavor of gum," she said just to say something.

"You can have a piece, if you'd like," Warren flashed a smile, charming as ever. The girl couldn't actually respond, only giggled and revealed shining silver braces.

She finished scanning. "Will that be cash or card?"

"Cash," Warren handed her damp hand a twenty and a ten. She counted out the change and gave it to him along with a wet receipt. Warren gave her another smile that would make her quiver down below for days.

"Have a great day!" she called out with much more enthusiasm then she had when they came in. The bell gave another pathetic ding as they left the store. The bikes were gone from the lot, but the same cars were left. Again, Warren peeked into each of them on their way back to his car. Lanny walked in a straight shuffling path.

They reached the Bimmer and Warren clicked his automatic remote twice to unlock the doors. Lanny stood outside for a second while Warren leaned in and turned on the car, putting the air conditioning on full blast. They had been in the store less than half an hour, but the heat in South Georgia was tremendous and only an idiot would climb into the leather seats of a black car without the AC running full blast. He made that mistake shortly after purchasing the car two years ago and jumped out with a yelp, deeply ashamed of himself.

"Look, I am sorry I let those kids get to me," Lanny apologized.

Warren waved his hand as if he were swatting a fly. Then Lanny saw he was swatting at a large buzzing bug around his head. They were frequent here, and usually swarmed in packs. Warren ducked into the car; Lanny followed suit.

"Don't worry about it. You've just got to toughen up a bit. I get that that isn't your personality. But any time someone makes you inferior, remember your intellect. That is the true test of a man's real worth these days. Well, it always has been, but for a while Neanderthals ruled. We are taking back the kingdom of earth. You can't worry about shit like middle-school bullies anymore." And Lanny, he was a true intellectual.

Warren put the car in drive. Lanny asked, "So did you find a target? Perhaps one of those kids?"

"No, Lanny. Those kids aren't even developed. You never know what one of them could turn out to be. They still have a chance to be molded or influenced by something positive."

Disappointed, Lanny pressed on, "Okay, well did you pick anyone out from the grocery store."

"Between the screaming baby, stressed mother, and counter girl? No, no candidates from the store."

"So off to the bar?"

"So off to the bar."

The trip to The Bar was a quick one. The wisecracker who built the place must have known it would be the only one to spring up in Clarenceville and took some comedic liberties on the name. The shutters were falling off the windows and the broken wooden steps to the bar's entrance were just waiting to prick the right prick and start a lawsuit. A Dodge truck, an old '95 Buick, and a Nissan waited patiently in the parking lot on their owners. Warren again walked alongside each car in the lot and again found nothing. He took a quick trot up the steps, avoiding the splintering, and Lanny followed.

The only people in The Bar were two old men, one in a Braves cap and one with a straw hat sitting next to him, and the bartender. The bartender looked to be in his sixties and friendly enough but still ready to bash a guy over the head with a bat. He nodded to Warren and looked Lanny over with eyes that crinkled into crow's feet. Warren pulled out a wooden bar stool. Lanny did the same. The chairs creaked under their weight.

This bartender didn't worry about time limits and greeting them within thirty seconds. He took his time ambling over to them. Lanny noticed he had a slight limp.

"What'll it be, fellas?" He asked in a smoker's voice.

"A Budweiser for me," Warren responded. The barkeep turned his attention to Lanny.

"Um, a lemon juice and ginger ale please."

The man gave him a look. "Add some gin to that and you've got a great drink. How 'bout it?"

Lanny shook his head. "No thank you."

"Alright, then." The man drew a beer from one of three pour spouts. He set the Budweiser in front of Warren, foam dripping down the side of the glass. Warren picked it up without wiping it off and took a long gulp.

"Can we change the damn channel, Scotty? I can't watch this game. We're getting killed. And by the damn Mets no less." The man in the Braves cap groaned.

Scotty set Lanny's drink on a coaster. He let out a raspy chuckle. "And what else is new?" He flipped it over to the Golf channel. The signal was shitty, but these men were used to a wavering television screen.

Lanny and Warren sat sipping their drinks, eyes intent on the screen.

"Say, Scotty. Any word on ole Creary?" The man with the straw hat asked. All of their southern accents were thick, except for Scotty's.

Scotty looked somber and sat on his own stool behind the bar. "Yeah, he's outta the hoosegow again. Damn retard. I'll bet we'll see his face in here before too long." He glanced at Warren.

"They let him out? What about Linda, and that kid?"

"She took him back. 'Spineless as usual. I'm tellin' ya the cops 'round here are hardly such. Lettin' him out again. That man needs to go somewhere federal."

"Scotty don't slip your tongue too much now," Braves cap said.

"Speak of the Devil," straw cap muttered.

On cue, in walked Pat Creary. He had on denim pants that were ripped at both knees and coming apart at the bottom. He was wearing a wife-beater tank top, stained, that didn't quite reach the bottom of his beer belly. He sat at the bar, right next to Warren Worth. Warren could smell the man's beer sweat and sour breath.

"Out so soon?" Scotty asked with disdain.

"Whaa? Ain't ya happy to see me?" Pat Creary had a deep voice, already sloshing his words. Warren cast a side-eyed glance at Lanny, then again faced forward.

"Oh, you bet." Scotty said.

"How 'bout a beer, Scotty?"

"How about a water? You already seem a bit unsteady."

"I'm unsteady? Man, you're a gimp. Ya just refuse to use the damn cane!" Creary roared with laughter and clapped Braves cap on the back until he joined in. He only gave a nervous laugh. Nobody disrespected Scotty, aside from Pat of course. Scotty was well liked, a good guy.

Scotty ignored the jab and hopped off the stool. He hobbled over to where Lanny and Warren were sitting. Warren had about four sips left of his beer. "Ready for another?" Scotty asked. Warren shook his head no.

Scotty turned to Lanny, "You sure you don't wanna turn that drink into a Ginbuck?"

"Yessir, thank you for asking though."

Scotty nodded.

"I'll take a Ginbuck or whatever the fuck," Pat Creary said loudly.

"We both know you've got your own flask next to the dip in your pocket, Pat. I am not going to be a part of you getting drunk and possibly killing another dog or giving your wife another black eye."

The man with the Braves cap and the man with the straw hat lowered their heads, uneasy. They both knew a double-barreled shotgun lay in the bed of Creary's truck, ready to be used on someone who said the wrong thing. Scotty knew this as well.

But Pat just gave a laugh. "You know somethin'? You're right, I do have a flask here. But no tip for you."

"Why should today be any different?" Scotty replied.

"And by the way, maybe I will fry me up some doggy tonight. Say, how is that ole pit of yours doin' anyhow?" Pat mixed a smirk in with a grimace.

Scotty stiffened at the mention of his beloved dog, Rocky. Rocky was at home with the wife, probably lying in the spot of sun that shone through the window at this time of day. He lowered his voice to just above a growl, "Now, Pat, don't you go threatening me, or my dog, or my wife for that matter. I know you've got that shotgun; I've got some of my own protection too." He turned away and ended the conversation. Pat lifted his flask and took a long swig. Then, he turned toward Lanny and Warren.

"Is that one of your guys' Bimmer out there? Sure is a pretty thang."

"Thank you. It's a rental. Thought I'd treat myself." Warren answered simply.

"Yes suh. I'd like to take a spin in that," Pat put a meaty arm around Warren's shoulder. Now it was Warren that stiffened. Lanny chewed on an ice cube, terrified. But Warren simply shrugged off the arm and continued drinking his beer.

"You must not be from around here we got this thang called southern hospitality. Bet you fags never heard of that, huh?"

"I suppose you're right," Warren would not let the man goad him. Lanny could see the wheels turning in Warren's head, wondering if this Pat Creary would be their target.

"How much do we owe you?" Warren asked Scotty.

"Let's call it two dollars," Scotty replied.

Warren stuck a ten under his coaster and stood from his stool. A piece of his shorts had latched onto a piece of splintered wood. He ripped it free and went for the door with Lanny in tow. He gave a little salute to Scotty as he walked toward the door.

"Is you fag boys leavin' already?" Creary called, slurring his words.

"Yessir, you have a nice day." Warren tipped a bit of an accent into his words. They let the door swing shut behind them and Warren made his way toward the newest addition to the parking lot. It was a faded red Ford pick-up truck, lifted an obnoxious amount off the ground. Warren wondered how a drunkard like Pat Creary even made it into this car without spilling onto his ass. He had to stand on his tiptoes to look inside this time. And when he did, he froze. On the inside, Warren's blood boiled, from both excitement and rage. The combination of the two extremes swirled together through his body. On the outside, Warren was calm. If he hadn't been on his toes longer than a seasoned ballerina, Lanny wouldn't have taken notice. But he was, and he did.

"What is it? A dog? What's in there?" Lanny noticed the window to the backseat cracked only about a millimeter. Then, he listened. He could hear the faint panting. "A dog?" he repeated, repulsed.

Warren came down slowly to his heels without saying a word. He made a swift turn in the dirt and walked back into The Bar. "Uh, Pat, is it?"

Creary turned slowly, his head almost lolling on his shoulder. "Whassup?"

61

"That your Ford out there? The truck?"

"Beautiful lifts on her, am-I-right?"

"Yessir. But, did you forget something in the car?"

"Nah, man! My flask issss right here!" Creary pet his silver friend with adoration.

Scotty was appalled, he seemed to know what Warren was talking about right away even though Pat couldn't put it together. "Holy shit! You left Nelly out there? Pat it's over one hundred degrees outside what the fuck is wrong with you?"

Creary was unfazed. "Okay, I'll take the kid home. Her ma is prolly back from that damn church anyhow." He stood to leave and tripped over one of the legs to the stool. He giggled. "Might wanna fix that leg there, Scotty." He stumbled outside, pulling his key from his pocket. Pat fell through the door.

Lanny saw Pat coming and panicked. He didn't want a confrontation, so he ran to the other side of the truck and hid in line with one of the wheels. Seconds later, Scotty, Warren, and the two men with hats were rushing out the door.

Warren strolled to his Bimmer to watch from there. Lanny scooted to join him. "Are you going to let him drive that truck?" He whispered in panic. "There's a child in there!"

"Lanny, it is not my job to interfere with the decisions of others. I'm just the one who takes care of the mess after the fact. You see, if I interfere now, nothing changes. This man is just going to get drunk another day and probably do the same thing when I am not here. So let this run its course, and we will see if I have any work to do." Warren spoke in a low voice, but without attempting at a whisper.

"There is no way in hell you are driving that truck!" Scotty yelled.

"Well, hows else do ya 'spect me to get the kid home, then, huh?" Pat asked.

Lanny couldn't understand how someone could get that drunk that quick before realizing the man must have started drinking long before he got to the bar.

Pat fumbled and tried at putting the key to the lock. He dropped it and bent slowly to retrieve it before giving it another go. He barely got it on the second try. The man with the straw hat and the man with the baseball cap looked on in disbelief.

"Pat, you can't drive that car, son," The man in the straw hat warned.

"Shut the fuck up you ole shit," Pat giggled and pulled himself into the truck. Everyone watched, hoping he would lose his grip and fall the ridiculous height onto his back. But he made it in and began to start the car. The wails from the child had risen. Seeing as nobody else was going to interfere, Scotty ran forward and reached across Pat's lap. He tried to pull the key from the ignition. Creary gave him a poke with a knife he had pulled from the console and warned him to back off.

"Stew, call Coley!" Scotty called over his shoulder. The man in the straw hat pulled out an old Nokia cell phone.

"Sherriff Coley ain't gonna do shit," Pat laughed.

Scotty was fuming. "He will if you kill that child. Let me at least get her out of the car."

"Fine, take the kid. Fine," Scotty eyed the knife sitting calmly in Creary's lap. He opened the back door and stepped up to the inside of the truck.

"Hey, Nelly, it's okay," he cooed to the four year old. He undid her car seat and gently lifted her. He was just bringing Nelly to his chest when Pat took off, with both the driver side door and back door open. Scotty jumped backward off the truck and landed on one leg, the bad one slightly bent just above the ground, but with Nelly safe in his arms. "I hope he crashes into a tree or something," Scotty muttered.

Lanny and Warren had left just before Pat Creary had taken off. Now they sat in a driveway to a McDonald's, waiting. The Ford truck whizzed by, swerving on the road. Warren pulled out to follow.

"I just thought of something," Lanny said. He'd figured out that Pat Creary was going to be their first job as partners. Warren's eyes were straight ahead. He was only half-listening. Lanny continued anyway, "This car stands out around here, you know. The BMW. Won't people take notice? And assume things?"

"That's not going to be a problem. Do you know how many people probably want a man like that dead? And, we don't even know him. We remained calm the entire time. We are just two bystanders passing through town. And, it's not like we are going to leave any evidence behind."

Lanny said, "But what about Scotty? Won't they suspect him? He got awfully mad…"

"Scotty will be fine. Like I said, the town wants a man like that dead." Warren sped up on the road to keep up with the out of control truck. Lanny shut his mouth and just looked ahead, trying to get excited.

Linda Creary was in the church on her knees, ignoring the fractured wood. Her hands were clasped tight and she sat up straight, just as she had for the past two hours in prayer. Her rosary beads hung loosely between her hands. She prayed as she did every day. She prayed for courage. She prayed for change, for a better life for her and her Nelly. She prayed for a way out of her terrible marriage without committing any sins. She heard the loud rumble of the engine that was her husband's truck and jumped up from her knees. She went to the end of the pew and bowed to the altar before hurrying out the door.

The truck had kicked up a cloud of dirt in its wake. Linda barely noticed the black BMW. She began to jog back to her house, grateful that it was only a ten-minute walk away. Then again, almost everything in the town was a ten-minute walk or less. She passed under the single stoplight in Clarenceville and slowed to gaze at the baby doll on the corner, and the flowers that wilted long ago. Nobody ever touched them. She picked up the pace and by the time she made it to the one story house, her white blouse was see-through from all the sweat.

Warren watched as Creary pulled in front of a house and fell out the car door. A woman appeared, almost out of nowhere, and caught him before he hit the ground. She didn't look terribly concerned, just frustrated. He heard her scream into the man's face *Where is my child?* Warren saw all he needed to see. He grabbed the pack of gum from the pile of groceries in the back seat and began to chomp. "Hungry?"

Lanny turned to Warren, bewildered. "Not particularly," he said. Warren smiled and turned the car around. He drove to the McDonald's and pulled into a spot. He was never allowed Mickey D's growing up, so he ate it weekly now while still maintaining his figure.

"We've got to give it a little time. Let the sheriff show up, if he even will, let things calm down," Warren said when he noticed Lanny hadn't unbuckled his seat belt. Warren sighed and made his way toward the front door. He got in line behind a slim woman and her fat kid. He whined when she told him that no, he couldn't get both cookies and an apple pie. He had to choose. But the kid ended up winning out. Warren was just ordering a McDouble and fries when Lanny appeared by his side. Lanny mumbled to the girl behind the register that he just wanted a small fry. Warren paid the girl and jogged outside to lock his car. He returned and spotted Lanny with the food in the corner of the restaurant by the bathrooms. Warren sat down and unwrapped his burger. The cheese looked plastic, but he ate it anyway. And, as always, it was oddly delicious. "Lanny, you should have known what you were getting yourself into. I understand this is your first job, but Jesus you don't need to be this dramatic about it."

"I'm sorry. It's just, I don't know. You're right. I'll be fine. What's the plan?" He asked, though lacking the enthusiasm Warren expected. *Ah, he'll get used to it. Once he feels the rush of removing an idiot from the planet, he'll be fine.*

"So, we finish eating here. Then we can take another drive by the house, see what's up. We will park somewhere nearby, probably in those woods or at another house, and walk over there. I imagine the road will be deserted when the initial commotion is over."

"Are we going to shoot him?" Lanny asked.

"Oh, no, of course not. It's still the afternoon and that would be much too loud and noticeable in a place like this. We wouldn't have a chance to get out. No. Actually, Lanny, I want you to decide our MO this time around. Be creative. That is most important. My kills are all so different and target different people that it keeps me from reaching serial killer status in the eyes of the law.

"The police just assume these murders are unrelated and done by many different people. This is just one other way I stay a step ahead of the game. To be with me, you need to keep up with my game. Do you understand?"

Lanny understood. He was the one who pointed that out to Warren after all when they first met. He put it together no problem. Of course, he couldn't say this to the man. "So this is like a test?"

"Yes, and no. I want to see your ingenuity and what exactly I am working with. There is no failure, however. If I decide your idea is good, I'll use it. If it doesn't work, I will not blame you, but myself."

Lanny thought to himself for a moment. He figured the punishment should fit the crime, or at the very least, the person. It could be something he loves turned against him. Lanny remembered the drunken way Pat lurched about. It had sickened him. He visualized the flask and Creary putting it against his wet mouth. Any man who had a flask had to fill it with something of his own supply. "Can we kill him with a bottle?"

Warren grinned, already knowing where Lanny's train was headed. "What kind of bottle, fella?"

"I dunno. Not a beer bottle, I think that would just shatter. But a liquor bottle. One that is mostly full, I think, would do best." Lanny's face was lighting up. He had forgotten to be nervous about his pitch. "Let the alcohol kill him! It'd be better if we could make him choke on his own vomit, but hell, this is good enough... right?"

"I like it, Lanny. I really do. Blunt force trauma to the head. That sounds just fine to me. It really does." Warren wiped the fry salt from his lips and stood to use the restroom. Lanny realized he had to go too but decided to wait until Warren was finished.

The two emerged from McDonald's like a new team. "Actually, maybe we could just make him choke on his own vomit," Lanny said. "Then nobody would be looking for a killer after all."

"I told you nobody's going to be mad that that man got killed."

"Well, wouldn't the vomit thing be more *creative* anyway? Plenty of people have been killed by being hit over the head with something."

"Yeah, and plenty have died from choking on vomit." Warren liked the bottle idea because it was something he would've come up with. They said it and now Lanny was being a nuisance and wanting to deviate from the plan.

"Right, but it's always ruled as accidental. Not murder."

"It'll be ruled as accidental in this case too," Warren said, exasperated.

"But we'll know it wasn't." Lanny kept his eyes low as they stood outside the car while Warren started the AC on the inside.

"Fucking fine. But if it doesn't work... it's the bottle. This better not be a *stupid* idea," he sneered.

Lanny didn't say anything, couldn't celebrate the small victory without pissing off Warren, and they drove to the blue house Lanny had noticed earlier. It was a few blocks (of woods) down from Creary's house. Lanny looked back to the window and again could have sworn he saw a boy's face for a mere second. The place gave him the creeps. But Warren seemed to feel right at home, knowing exactly where to go and what to do. He drove to the far side of the house and under the shelter of trees. He parked and went to the trunk. All he retrieved was a pair of binoculars. He strutted through the door that was loose on its hinges, pushing it with his boot. Lanny followed. Despite the brightness of the day, the inside of the house was dark. Lanny felt goose bumps prickle his arms. Warren said, "Let's go upstairs. We can get a good view from the window." Warren took off and immediately found the staircase. Lanny wondered if that was because he was already familiar with its location.

Linda cowered from Pat when he raised his hand. Her swelling from the last round of black eyes may have long been gone, but the memory was fresh. She closed her eyes in anticipation of the hit. She heard a crash of glass but didn't feel a thing. Linda opened her eyes to find her husband on the ground, face in the dirt, and Scotty the bartender standing over him with a broken Coors light bottle, or piss water as he called it. Standing next to Scotty was Sherriff Coley, who was now holding Nelly.

"Oh my baby! Thank you, Sherriff, thank you!" He shifted the sleeping child onto Linda's shoulder. He tried to avert his eyes from her see-through blouse but failed and caught a smack on the head from Scotty when Linda wasn't looking. "Are you gonna take him back to jail, Coley?"

Sherriff Coley glanced at Scotty, who shrugged. "I think we oughta let him sober up. The most I could say right now is drunk drivin' and—"

"—and child abuse!" Linda interrupted.

Scotty took Linda to the side and spoke to her softly. "Linda, you left your child with him. And he was drunk long before he even got to my bar. There isn't much to say or do right now…"

"Are you sayin' I was neglectin' my child?" She was shrill.

"No, course not. But others might see it that way. Me and Coley here, we're just gonna drag Pat inside and get you away for a while. Keep surveillance on the house, keep him *in* the house. Might even do the whole house arrest deal. Look, can you stay with Caroline down the street for a while?"

"I don't want to be an imposition. Maybe I'll just get out of town. Go visit my sister Alexandria in Statesboro or something." Linda no longer cared about Pat. Now she only saw the opportunity to get away. "But, Scotty, do make sure he stays in this house. I do want to leave him. For good though, not temporarily. Do you understand?"

Scotty nodded somberly, "I do."

"If he comes lookin' for me, well, I believe he'd kill us all!"

"We'll take care of it, Linda. But I agree this is best for you and Nelly. Getting completely out of town is an even better idea. Why don't you go pack some things while me and the Sheriff here drag this sack into the house? You'll want to get out of here before he comes to."

Linda turned toward the house when Scotty called to her. "And Linda? Take the damn car with you. This bastard does not need to be driving." Linda nodded and went to fill a couple of suitcases. She didn't feel sentimental at all as she entered the bedroom she and Pat shared. She only stuffed her hand between the moldy mattress and box spring and came out with a rubber band of twenties she'd saved and hid from Pat over time. She wasn't committing any sins. She was only going to leave Pat for a little while, without divorcing him. There was nothing wrong with that.

She thought for a second and pulled her blouse from her head and replaced it with a new one. Linda caught her reflection in the mirror: clad in only a bra, covered with scars from broken bottles and jagged nails, a few burn marks. She shuddered at her appearance and pulled on a nice green tee. She balled up her damp blouse and threw it on the bed. *Let him sleep with that.*

Linda took her Nelly and left the room. Scotty and Coley had just pulled Pat onto the couch and were sweating from the effort. He began to stir, and her heart began to pound. Her feet took her outside to the truck. The keys were still in the ignition. She put Nelly into the car seat and waited for Scotty and Coley to come back outside.

"We'll miss you around here, Ms. Linda," Coley said. She nodded in agreement and let him hug her.

"Thank you, Scotty. Both of you. Please, just keep him here. I'll come back one day." She leaned into Scotty and he gave her a fatherly kiss on the head.

"Get on, before he wakes," Scotty said.

Linda hopped into the car and let the weight of her entire leg fall onto the gas pedal.

Warren lowered the binoculars as the Ford truck hummed past. "The wife is gone. I guess that's good," he said, mostly to himself.

"What are we waiting on now?" Lanny asked.

"For Scotty and the Sherriff to leave. And ah, there they go, right on cue." Warren flashed his teeth at Lanny. "I swear, things so often go to my plan, I feel like I'm God, controlling everything from my subconscious." He turned back toward his car and retrieved a knife.

"I thought we were gonna make him throw up?" Lanny was hurt that Warren was dismissing his plan.

"We are or bash him in with a bottle. But we need a backup just in case, right?"

Lanny shrugged. The two made their way from the back of the house. As they passed in front of it, Warren ran his knife along the broken wire fence, enjoying the music it made. Lanny swallowed a lump in his throat. It was nerves. He scanned the dirt road and felt comfort in the fact that it was completely vacant. Warren stuck the knife into his back pocket and walked with confidence, slightly dragging his feet in the dirt as he went. He was humming a tune Lanny couldn't make out. While Lanny couldn't match the man's confidence, he could take the same precautions in dragging his feet.

Warren and Lanny walked to the back door. It was slightly cracked, so Warren nudged it open with his knee. He started in before pausing and going back outside. He stomped his shoes free of the dirt and indicated that Lanny do the same. Then, it was okay to proceed. They could hear moans from inside. Warren decided to use Pat's groggy state to their advantage. They could creep along without being noticed until they were ready. Then, there would be less of a fight, less noise, less chance of getting caught. Though Pat had just gotten out of jail, there were bottles strewn about everywhere. It was mostly vodka, but a few whiskeys were thrown in the mix. More than half of them were already empty, the rest had about a third of the way to go. Warren walked slowly, heel to toe, over to the fridge. He picked up a dishtowel from the counter and pulled open the freezer. He gave himself an internal pat on the back. He pulled out the cold bottle of Grey Goose, which was probably the nicest thing the Creary's owned.

Pat opened his eyes half-way. "Whaaa the fuck?" He said hoarsely. "Linda!" he yelled. "Linda bring me a damned drink!"

McDonald's wrappers covered most of the carpeting in the living room. Creary was on the couch in front of a TV with antennae. His finger was in his belly button, picking at something dried and crusted. Lanny stayed in the entryway between the kitchen and the living room, hovering light on his feet, ready to flee at a moment's notice.

Now Warren strutted right behind Pat. "Linda, my drink," he said, irritated. Warren smirked and held the bottle in front of Pat's line of half-sight so he could see the Grey Goose. "The good stuff? Guess you wanna get fucked tonight. Glad you got a new one after finishing the other off, whore." Pat laughed and choked on saliva that had pooled in his throat. He hocked a loogey. *Real sexy.* Warren noticed a bit of blood trickling down his neck from his scalp. There were a few glass shards tangled in his hair as well. Warren correctly surmised that Scotty had been the one to crack a bottle on their pal's head.

Warren handed the bottle to Lanny after unscrewing the lid, bartender's habit, and then grabbed Pat Creary's head between his lean but meaty arms.

"What in the fuck of shittin' hell?"

Warren held a little tighter with his left arm so that he could use his right to grab the dishtowel from his pocket. He placed it over the top of Pat's head so he could put his palm down in added pressure to tip the head back. Once he had the man in place, now using his left hand to hold his mouth open by squeezing in and forward on his cheeks, Warren glared at Lanny to get moving.

Lanny walked in front of Pat with the bottle in hand. "Ooo pussshy ash bish!" Lanny turned the bottle completely upside down into Pat's mouth. He guzzled it at first, not hating it, and then began to choke it up. Once they got over half the bottle down, the men put Pat flat on his back. As a seasoned drunk, it would take a lot to get the man upchucking.

"Induce vomiting," Warren instructed.

Lanny didn't want to stick his fingers anywhere near this guy's mouth, but he said, "Yessir."

Pat's eyes bulged like a bullfrog as Lanny came at him with his pointer and middle finger pressed flush together. He stuck them into his mouth and Pat tried to bite down. Warren squeezed harder on his cheeks. Now Lanny jabbed his fingers in and out as deep as he could. First, Pat gagged with no vomit. Lanny continued. The gags continued until one came with substance. It was a little at first but then came in gales. The men held the man down so that he couldn't flip himself over.

Vomit pooled in his mouth and then spurted like underwater volcanic eruptions. Lanny wanted to join in when a splatter of throw up hit the side of his cheek. Pat's eyes were looking ready to pop out of his head. The cords on his thick neck stuck out as he struggled. After a few minutes the struggling ceased, the vomit continued but now at a leisurely pace, and the pooled bile in his mouth began spilling out the sides from overflow. A few more minutes and Warren pronounced Pat Creary dead.

"Ready to go," he asked, as if he was merely tired from a long day at the theme park.

"No!" Lanny shouted.

Warren arched his brows at Lanny. "Well, what is it?"

"I need a spoon..." Lanny looked at Warren who sighed before walking back over to the fresh corpse. In a moment of staggering brilliance, in his own opinion, Warren grabbed the cap of the Grey Goose bottle and scraped it up against Creary's neck skin. It was almost dry, but it would have to do. He handed it to Lanny and looked away in disgust as Lanny shoved the cap straight into his mouth. His face visibly relaxed. While Lanny went back in his memory to whatever fucked up place he loved, Warren began his search for the empty Grey Goose bottle that Pat had mentioned, the one Linda apparently finished off on her own. It was nowhere to be found in the kitchen, just a bunch of cheap brands like Svekda.

He took his time walking around the small house. He peered into the trashcan only to find it overflowing. Warren decided that would be the last place he would look. He went to the bedroom and again came up short. He even checked the kid's closet of a room for good measure. Again, he found nothing. Warren kicked open the bathroom door and gagged at what he saw. The toilet was un-flushed, the curtain liner was covered in mildew, and an unidentified lump was sitting in the corner next to the tub. But, in the tub there was a bottle of Grey Goose. It was empty. Either the wife had tried to drown her sorrows (and maybe herself) or she was getting rid of the alcohol in vain to make her husband sober. He laid the dishrag in his hand and picked up the bottle, triumphant. The cap was already off, but that wasn't a concern. He carried it over to his trophy, the wife-beater choked to death. He finished pouring the first bottle into the man's already-full mouth, then uncapped the second and left it by his draping hand. He wiped everything down with the towel. He turned to collect his protégée and halted. Lanny was in the same position, rolling the cap around on his tongue now. It was like his mind had entered a different plane of the universe and left his body behind.

"Lanny, Lanny!" Warren yelled into his ear. Lanny didn't snap to automatically, but slowly came around. "Time to go. And you and I are going to have to have a long talk about this blood-spoon-licking thing. Lanny followed Warren out the back door. They left it open so that the flies could have easier access to the body, and maybe a wild animal of some sort. That would be cool. The road was just as barren as they left it and the two made an easy walk back to the car.

CHAPTER 4

Jodee Pape glanced up at the young Kaitlyn Rice as she blew her whistle and started the clock. The girl pushed off of the line, cleats digging into the freshly cut grass. Her brow was furrowed, and her eyes were set on the line of cones that were one hundred yards away. This was the eighth time Kaitlyn had to run the Manchester United fitness test. She had to run to that line of cones twenty times. For the first ten, she had to make it in twenty-five seconds with a recovery time back to the end line of thirty-five seconds. The eleventh minute she would have twenty-four seconds with a recovery time of thirty-six seconds, then twenty-three seconds with thirty-seven recovery and so on.

For the sake of the Furman Women's Soccer team fitness test, the girls only had to make the times in fifteen of the twenty runs, while still running for the entire test. Kaitlyn was a freshman on the soccer team. She had shown tremendous athleticism and talent on all of Jodee's recruiting trips (resulting in the full scholarship), but she could not make it past twelve levels of the test. So making her run until she passed, even though they were already past preseason, was Jodee's way of making an example of the girl.

"Kaitlyn, slow down. You've got a long way to go!" Jodee yelled as Kaitlyn ran past. That really was her problem, aside from nerves and the apparent inability to catch her breath. The girl would fire out of the gate, making the first few in twenty seconds then she'd run out of gas.

Jodee had such an urge to punch the kid in the face. She had talked Kaitlyn up to the older girls on the team after she committed, and this was how she showed up to preseason. Not a good impression on her teammates, who had come to dislike her.

"Let's go, you're doin' great!" Jodee called out as Rice went by on the seventh run. And she was doing well. According to Jodee's stopwatch, Kaitlyn was right on pace. This excited Jodee. No matter how pissed she was at Kaitlyn, she needed to get that girl on the field before they would travel to play Georgia State. It was already mid-September; every game was important.

The sun began to rise above Jodee and Kaitlyn, the fabulous mist hovering above the field dissipating. The rest of the team would be arriving for practice soon.

Jodee squinted her eyes at the sunrise and turned her attention back to the athlete. She couldn't understand why Kaitlyn refused to have teammates watch her, cheer for her, while she ran. Well, maybe she could. At this point the breakfast club consisted of only Kaitlyn running every Monday and Thursday. It was embarrassing and she probably felt like the support was fake and forced. And maybe it was. But still, wouldn't that just light the fire under your ass?

Cars began to fill the lot as Kaitlyn began the twelfth run. Jodee wanted this for her, to at least surpass her previous record. As the short girl darted past, Jodee could hear the frantic breaths from fifteen yards away. *Oh, no. Come on, Rice, come the fuck on.* Kaitlyn hit the line of cones at thirty-eight seconds.

"Make it back! You missed by a second, so you'll have to make up for it later!" She could see the girl giving up. Her face was taking on that corpse-y pallor they had all come to know and love. She was pure white, even her lips.

"Come on, Rice! Make it there." Kaitlyn made it back to the line just as the girls filed onto the space of green behind her. Jodee thought, *This is it. She's giving up again.* But then a yell from Jenna, a junior, lifted Jodee's spirits.

"You've got this girl! Get your gear today, let's go!" Jenna's cheers brought more out from the rest of the team.

"Come on, Kaitlyn!"

"You can do this!"

"Don't give up!"

Kaitlyn had five seconds of rest left on the line before the next run. She was bent over at the waist, and Jodee could see the rise and fall of her breaths taking over her whole body. But she was slowly standing up. Then something happened that brought tears to Jodee's always-dry green eyes.

Janey and Mo, two girls who were *not* fans of fitness tests (both having had Breakfast Club appearances in past years) stepped to the line on either side of Kaitlyn. Mo clapped her on the back. Jodee blew the whistle and the three girls were off. Kaitlyn was running with a newfound energy.

"Thirty-eight seconds on this one, seventeen to go. PACE!" Kaitlyn hit the line side-on with her right foot and began her jog back on the left. She was smiling. Jodee had called out "thirty-eight" as Kaitlyn was already turning back. There was an eruption of cheers from the end line.

81

"Make it back, Kait. You've got it girl."

"Let's go, Mo!"

"Yes, Janey."

Some of the team ran to the other side of the cones to cheer from there. Kaitlyn sailed through levels fourteen and fifteen. She wasn't completely controlling her breathing, but it was better than before.

As Kaitlyn was jogging past, Jodee reminded her that she just needed to make the next one, the sixteenth, then she could jog the rest of the test. Rice threw up a thumb as she passed, nodding her head. Mo and Janey gave her another pat.

"You're making it even if I have to drag you!" Mo promised. Or threatened. The girls made it back just in time to turn and sprint. Kaitlyn no longer gave a fuck about any pace. She sprinted far ahead of the other two, making it down in fifteen seconds.

"Damn, Kait," Janey called from somewhere behind her.

The whole team was going crazy. Then, when Jodee thought her girls couldn't make her any prouder, the entire team took to the field and jogged with Kaitlyn through the last four minutes.

As soon as Jodee blew the whistle signaling the end of the test, Kaitlyn dropped to the ground in partial relief and partial exhaustion. It was probably more of the latter. The girls all laughed and clapped for their fallen teammate.

Jodee made her way over to the girl in the grass. "Good work, now get up." She pulled a wobbly Kaitlyn up by her arms.

"Jesus, Jodee," one of the seniors laughed.

Jodee knew she was being rough, but it served a purpose. It was a reminder of how long it had taken to get to this point. It was also a reminder that there was still a grueling two-hour practice to get through and she planned to have the entire team do fitness at the end.

Jodee returned to her neighborhood that was nestled beneath a canopy of oak trees. She turned into her gravel driveway and turned off the car. She sat there for a few minutes, still buckled beneath the seatbelt. It was never something that Jodee thought about or planned, but that happened almost every day without fail. In that time, she failed to think of anything. Or, she succeeded in blocking out everything. It was such a private reflection time that even she would not be able to recall ten minutes later what ran through her mind during the quiet minutes on the driveway. Perhaps the subconscious was taking over. She stepped out of her car and stretched her legs. Scar was already at the window, scratching to get through it to her master. Jodee smiled.

She unlocked the front door and pushed it open, leaving the key in the lock, and took a step back. Scar leaped out at her as if shot from a cannon. Jodee ended up on the ground, as she always did. It wasn't from the sheer force that came with Scar's leap, she was only a border collie, but from the all over relaxation of her own muscles that came whenever reunited with her dog. Scar buried her black and white face into Jodee's lap. It didn't matter that it had only been three hours since their morning walk; it may as well of been three years.

Scar panted and stood up. She glanced at Jodee with pure love before trotting off to find the perfect spot to squat. There was no need for a fence or leash. Scar remained by Jodee's side and no tempting squirrel could change that. Jodee left the dog to it and retrieved her key from the lock, entering her house. She shut the door to keep out any bugs, knowing that Scar would give a soft bark when she was ready to come back inside.

The darkness of her home calmed Jodee. Eclipse curtains may have been one of her best ideas. She walked through the darkness into the kitchen, only then did she turn on a light. Jodee pulled out her Belgian waffle maker and the mix. She scooped her share and cracked an egg in the bowl. She attempted to do it one handed and ended with the ball of yolk cradled in her palm while the cracked shells scattered into the bowl. Jodee laughed at herself and began scooping out the shells when she felt her phone buzz in her back pocket. She slid it out with the hand she should have also used to crack the egg.

There were four new messages from Matt. Jodee sighed. He was getting too into the relationship too fast. They were supposed to go out to dinner tonight, but Jodee changed her plans. Matt's last text was a series of question marks. Jodee heard the faint bark at the door and walked with the phone illuminating her path to let in Scar. She typed back to Matt that she had to cancel. Even Jodee realized how cold that sounded by itself, so she threw in a frowny face with the unfelt apologetic "sorry." She padded back to the kitchen with Scar at her heels and finished making her waffles.

CHAPTER 4

She and Scar shared the loveseat as they ate and watched old episodes of *Dexter*. Jodee wanted that kind of man. Not a serial killer, but one that wasn't wound up with emotion. Ever since she was little, the only kind of guys she went after were the ones who showed her no interest. Matt had been that way at first, distant, but her spell had been cast and it ended with a backfiring curse on her as always. Instead of watching the show, a new one played in her mind. In this one, she was on a date with Dexter. She leaned to try and plant a kiss on his cheek and he quickly found an excuse to move out of the way. She placed her hand on his leg and he had to stand up to go to the bathroom. Jodee felt herself getting aroused and damned Matt for being so needy.

She consulted the clock and stood up from the couch, stretching her limbs. It was time to head to the office. She had to get through an entire list of recruits to call for the day, as well as prepare to host a few. There were some strong potentials from Florida and Connecticut coming in to see their program, as well as one family who would be touring the campus at noon. She threw Scar a treat, turned the TV on to daytime television so that the pup wouldn't feel alone, and locked the door behind her.

Jodee had written up a few practice plans when she got a knock at her office door. Ms. Nancy, one of the college advisors, was dropping off the family for a meeting. Jodee forced a smile onto her face as she graciously accepted them and asked them to take a seat. She watched the way the girl, Anna Walker, nervously looked at her parents for reassurance before taking a seat. Jodee always felt a little bit awkward around parents, seeing as she didn't have any.

"So," she began by clapping her hands together once then leaving them clasped and taking a seat across from the family, "what'd you think of the campus?"

Once the Walkers left her office, Jodee returned to her seat behind the desk. She hadn't been to one of Anna's games yet, or knew anything about how she played, but she was familiar with the club team and coach. She'd promised to attend one of the games in the near future.

Jodee spent the majority of the rest of her workday on the phone, calling her contacts in club coaches as well as the house phones of the recruits on her list. During the calls, she did a lot of gazing at the photo of Scar sitting on her desk. It was the only photo of family she had in the office; the rest were pictures of the past teams she had coached through the years at Furman. The team photos were like pictures of her family. She played a part in the molding of each and every one of those girls' lives. When their parents handed them off to her during their freshman year, she became their interim mother/guardian while they were on campus. She knew everything about each of them, always kept a close eye on their social media accounts and listened with a keen ear whenever one of their names popped up to see what they'd been doing. That was one of the reasons she could never see herself having a kid, she already had about thirty at a time.

She got through her list of calls and turned off the light in her office, ready to call it a day. Jodee dodged anyone that might ask her to get some dinner; she was planning for it to be an early night. Jodee made the drive home and went through the routine of being mauled by Scar, letting her out to the bathroom, and preparing a small dinner for them both. She then settled back onto the couch to flick on a movie with Scar curled up next to her. Jodee lived for films. They took her mind off of everything else in life, the bad and the good. She could just disappear into the story showing in front of her and forget the world for a while.

Jodee yawned and decided to move the party to the bedroom, so she could wash her face and do the whole nightly ritual before falling asleep to the TV. But first she walked with Scar outside so she could pee once more before she would wake Jodee in the morning to pee again.

The night had turned cold and dark and Jodee felt her nipples harden through her small t-shirt. Goose bumps covered her skin. She sat down on the front step and gazed at the sky. Every now and then she would do this, stare at the stars for a while, listening to the serenity of an empty night around her with the rest of the world already tucked into bed. These were some of the moments she treasured, but also cursed. It was during these times that her mind would wander and work overtime for the time lost during movies.

There were so many stars in the sky that were so far away, and she wondered about death. What would happen? Where would she go? The unbroken sky above her gave no answers, only more questions. Jodee stood and bounced on her feet while Scar started another stream, watching Jodee watch her. "Ok, let's go then," Jodee turned knowing Scar would follow.

She locked the door and went to the back one too, though it hadn't been opened all day. She checked the front door again before going upstairs, pulling on it to test the lock just as she did every night. Once satisfied, she went to her bedroom.

Jodee covered her face in water before massaging Neutrogena face wash all over. She bent over and rinsed it clean, then blotted with a towel. She squeezed toothpaste onto her toothbrush, peeking at herself in the mirror for only a second. She was curious. She was always curious. Some nights she gave in, and others she didn't. She had a feeling tonight she was going to give in. Jodee stuck her toothbrush in her mouth and tried to distract herself by scrubbing at her molars. But she kept peeking at the mirror. She would just make eye contact with herself before pulling away. It was too easy to make the connection. But her eyes kept flitting up.

She spit into the sink and put her toothbrush down. Both of her hands gripped the ring of the sink. She leaned in so that her face was just up to the mirror with her eyes closed. She opened them and instantly connected with what she called her Otherland Self. Her reflection seemed to separate and become its own. The face that stared back at her was equally terrifying and amazing. It was Jodee, but an angry Jodee, one that seemed mad at her. It was evil. *That* she could feel. After a few seconds that felt like minutes, Jodee pulled away. She would not offer the mirror another glance tonight, not until it was day again and she wouldn't feel the temptation of the Other-land.

The Other-land Self was something Jodee had come up with a year or so after she graduated from college. She had found herself at a party filled with hippie-types. She'd only seen blurred faces as they flitted about around her. The theme had been rainbow, or something of that nature. She remembered seeing rainbow suspenders and rainbow shirts. But the lines of the rainbow curved in too many different ways for her eyes. She had had way too much tequila.

Her friends found someone they knew, so Jodee was left to fend for herself. She walked around the house, not talking to anyone, just observing. She made her way into the kitchen where she stole a red cup and filled it with water from the sink faucet. She continued her tour and found the bathroom. Amazingly no line was formed outside of it. She realized she should empty her bladder, so she staggered in and shut the door, too drunk to bother with figuring out the lock. She peed hard. Jodee felt like her whole body could relax into the bowl.

She fell into a light sleep sitting up on the toilet, in a state of complete relaxation. Two guys burst through the door giggling. Jodee woke with a start and peed a little more. She instinctively covered her vagina. The guys giggled and assured her they weren't going to look. They then asked if she wanted to stay and watch.

"Watch, watch what to watch? What?" Jodee asked.

"Easy, is that some kind of Seuss riddle? Oh, we're just kidding! Take your time!" The taller one laughed. She didn't feel like they were laughing *at* her, just laughing out of pure joy. She smiled too, because why not? There was no toilet paper on the roll. Jodee asked the guys to check under the sink. The shorter one complied and came up empty. He grabbed the rug off of the floor and tossed it to her.

"Just use it! I'm sure you're not the first one to do that tonight. It feels a little damp," he erupted into another fit of
giggles. Jodee wasn't one to do the shake, and she really didn't
care enough to worry about how gross and unsanitary it was, so
she wiped with the probably previously used rug. She left the
bathroom to the two guys and searched for her friends through
the smoke-filled haze of the room. Still unable to see anyone she
recognized, Jodee continued her tour through the house to the
basement. She wanted to get away from the loudness and re-
group.

The stairs down were like an optical illusion that converged
together until they met at some point far away. They were
unforgivingly steep as well. She found the handrail on the wall
and took careful steps down into the darkness. The steps creaked
and she thought about whether this trek into the basement was a
good idea. At last she made it to the bottom, where there was one
door to her immediate left. She put her ear to it and couldn't
make out any noise. She thought she was either going to walk
into an orgy or find the infamous quiet white kid at the school in
a corner with a gun, bracing himself to take the lives of frantic
partiers. She took a breath and turned the knob, wishing she'd
had the foresight to knock. Jodee pushed the door open and
heard a soft chuckle coming from a girl.

The girl was sitting at a barstool with her elbows resting on a
tall table. An attractive guy with shaggy dark hair was across
from her, separating something out from tin foil. Jodee's first
thought was that he had some kind of bread or other baked good
in there, and her second was that if that were the case, it was an

edible of some sort. She was worried walking in on what could be a drug deal. She didn't want them to freak out and stab the witness. But instead they both turned and offered her friendly smiles.

"What's up?" The girl asked.

"Just trying to get away from the loudness upstairs," Jodee replied.

"Same. Well originally, I came to buy, but then realized I wasn't in a hurry to get back to the crazy. Not 'til this has kicked in anyway," she laughed and Jodee offered a chuckle as well.

"Are those edibles?"

The guy answered and Jodee's cheeks grew pink at his mere acknowledgement, "Nah, I'm sellin' LSD."

All Jodee knew of LSD was what she had learned from an episode of *CSI*. Some guy had put LSD in motel air fresheners, and it made guests freak out and kill whomever they were staying with. She told this to the boy and girl. They both laughed, not meanly though.

"Trips can be different. I've never had a bad one, though," the boy finally said, and the girl nodded in agreement. "That kind of stuff is pure Hollywood. This isn't that kind of shit."

"Interesting…" Jodee said. And she was interested. She had tried weed before and didn't care much for the stuff. She was a virgin to these hardcore drugs. But, in the presence of these two people who seemed so chill and friendly, the drunkenness in her took a turn for the wild and curious side. "So… how much for like, a hit?"

The guy laughed, again not in a mean way. "I'll give you a square for ten bucks."

That sounded cheap to Jodee for a drug that would have such a strong effect. She agreed and he gave her what looked like a small piece of paper.

"How do I do it?" she asked, no longer afraid to sound inexperienced. They wanted to be her guides and introduce her to a whole new world.

"You just place it on your tongue and let it dissolve," the girl told her.

"And how long does it take to kick in?"

"Eh, usually about thirty minutes to an hour. It varies."

"Will I know when it's hitting me?"

"Oh, you will *definitely* know."

Jodee had dozens of other questions, and the guy and girl answered them all with patience over the next fifteen minutes. At the end of the interview, Jodee popped the square on her tongue.

"And now, wait for the fun to begin," the guy winked and Jodee blushed again.

Just after, more people burst through the door. The guy sat up, expecting more buyers. Instead it was Melissa and Kristen who were looking for Jodee.

"*There* you are. Jesus Christ we've been looking for you everywhere, JoJo!" Kristen nearly shouted.

"What are you doing?" Melissa asked with a furrowed brow, taking in the two at the table with tin foil.

"I just bought some LSD," Jodee said nonchalantly.

"Are you fucking serious?" Melissa scolded, then slid her eyes to the others, "No offense, but this is a former athlete. She shouldn't be doing stuff like this." She said this with offense intended. Melissa never seemed to actually get drunk, so she was always the one making decisions and with the head on her shoulders. The guy shrugged in response.

"Well, let's gooooo gigolo!" Kristen grabbed Jodee by the arm, "We're going to the bar!"

Jodee allowed herself to be dragged by her drunk*er* friend and offered a wave to the two. She wished she had gotten their names. Melissa threw a judgmental glance over her shoulder on the way out.

Jodee was silent on the taxi ride over to the bar. She wanted to catch exactly when the drug hit. Melissa sat beside her and Jodee could feel her softening the further they got from that hippie house. Kristen leapt out of the car with Jodee's arm while Melissa paid the driver. As soon as they got inside, Jodee found herself a nice leather couch and waited. She watched Kristen and Melissa share a round of shots; Jodee declined any more alcohol. It seemed only a moment had passed before the colored lights around the bar blended together in a dreamlike way. Jodee felt a serene smile on her face as she enjoyed the view. She wanted to share it. She tugged on Melissa's blouse and pointed up, "Isn't it beautiful?" she said.

"Yeah, Jodee, yeah it's real pretty." Melissa may have disapproved of Jodee's choice, but she knew better than to bring down someone who was on a drug like that. It could lead to a really bad trip. She'd seen a *CSI* episode about it.

When the girls set off for the short walk to their apartment, Jodee felt the alcohol from earlier in the night creeping up on her. She didn't try to fend it off. Instead, she stopped and tossed her liquor into a nearby bush.

"Ok, let's get you home," Melissa said.

"Hey, how come you never seem to get drunk?" Jodee asked, smiling.

"Good breeding. Now let's *go*." The three girls made it back to their place.

Melissa and Kristen were yawning, ready for bed, but Jodee felt more awake than ever. "Come on guys, let's do something else. Let's watch a movie, or a TV show."

Melissa sighed, "Jodee, we're really tired," she saw in her peripheral that Kristen had just passed out on the couch, "Kris is already out." She pointed.

"Just one show, come on Lissy," Jodee was pleading now.

Melissa sighed, "Ok, but let's watch it in my bedroom."

Jodee was overjoyed. She bounded up the stairs with Melissa trudging behind her. She flung herself onto Melissa's fluffy duvet and clicked through the channels, landing on *That 70's Show*. Jodee could hear Melissa's sink water running and the electric buzz of her toothbrush. She bounced up and galloped into the restroom. From the perimeter of the small room, she caught a glimpse of herself in the mirror over Melissa's shoulder and smirked. She thought she looked *good*, near flawless even. Jodee couldn't keep the cocky grin from her face.

Melissa spat rabies foam into the sink. "What are you looking at?"

"Myself." Jodee said with a wink.

"God stop, just go back to the bed."

Jodee tried, but she turned back over her shoulder to get another good look at herself. A shove from Melissa sent her on her way back to the bed. But she spied herself in Melissa's closet mirror and sent hidden sultry glances in that direction. She heard a soft yawn from beside her and pulled her gaze from the mirror. Melissa's breathing was getting slower, and her eyes were starting to flicker with the strain of staying awake. Jodee gave her a light slap on the cheek.

"Come on! Stay awake. I haven't had a dick in so long. Let's talk about that. Or anything. Let's enjoy the show!" Jodee laughed.

"God, Jodee, don't be so crass," Melissa yawned again, "And yeah I'm staying up." This was just a lie with good intention to become the truth. As soon as Jodee's attention was back on the television, Melissa's eyelids fell hard. A movement from Jo opened them again, and then they fell even harder. Each time, Melissa's eyelids seemed to accumulate glue that made it harder and harder to them... or maybe it was that famous sandman sand. That mixed with the booze.

Jodee felt alone when her friend lost the ability to stay up with her. She got out of bed, making a lot of noise in hopes of accidentally waking Melissa, and made her way back to the bathroom. She stared and giggled. Then, she felt the need to move. Jodee left Melissa's room and started making trips up and down their one set of stairs. She would pause at the bottom and top each time, allowing herself a glimpse in another reflective surface. Jodee found Kristen's small Nikon camera and began to take pictures of herself. In some she would smile, and in others she would give that same smirk. She felt like a flawless-skinned vampire. Jodee wanted to get closer to her reflection, and closer to her face.

She made her way to her own well-lit bathroom and hopped on top of the sink. With her nose pressed against the glass, Jodee stared into her own eyes. Her bright green eyes stared back. They stared until they were no longer her own bright green eyes. No, these eyes belonged to someone much angrier. This someone seemed to have a personal vendetta against Jodee and Jodee alone. Jodee tried to tear her eyes away from the mirror but couldn't. There was a mixture of curiosity as well as a pull from the other side that overrode the fear. Jodee was completely disconnected from her reflection for now she stared into the eyes of another.

This other sucked Jodee in. Jodee could feel the contempt from just the gaze. What is that saying? "The eyes are the window to the soul." Only, whose soul was it? As if in a telepathic answer, Jodee understood that it was her soul. At least, it was part of it. That part belonged to a different Jodee in a different place. Jodee conjured the name for this other self. It was her Other-land Self. And this other Jodee hated her. Tears dripped down Jodee's face, but she could see none sliding down the face looking back at her. She pulled herself away with a different kind of effort than before. It took all she had not to peek back up. Curiosity always holds a certain power over us all, an overwhelming power.

Jodee wanted to go to bed and forget all about her Other-land Self. But when she shut her eyes, all she saw was dancing colors and shapes that kept moving and changing. It was the kaleidoscope vision the guy and girl in the basement told her about. Those visions would not let her sleep but force her to watch their show for as long as they wanted to entertain. It may have been an hour of this show, it may have been ten minutes, before Jodee began to panic. She tried burying her face into her pillow near the point of suffocation. She rubbed at her eyes with the knuckles of her fist.

Jodee decided she needed to rid herself of the LSD, just like she always did with alcohol. She marched back into her bathroom and grabbed her own toothbrush. She made herself a nice padding on the floor for her knees and kneeled over the toilet. Jodee shoved the toothbrush into her throat and began to wiggle it all about. She brushed the invisible teeth that lined her throat. In success, Jodee lurched forward lumps of food dyed reddish-orange with the color of the tequila sunrises. She gave another heave and a stronger wave of vomit came forth. Jodee closed her eyes to see if that had done it. But the images in her vision still danced. She shoved the toothbrush down and wiggled until all that came up was the slightly foamy acid from her stomach.

So Jodee laid on her bed and waited. She tried to enjoy the kaleidoscope but knew she was fooling herself. She began to shake and cry, waiting for this drug to wear off. She wished for the easy sleep that came with just the right amount of alcohol. Jodee began to time this trip. When the sun shone through her window, Jodee began to cry and shake. It was around six in the morning, and still sleep would not come, the visions would not stop. She wondered if she would feel this way forever, if she had entered a different dimension where she was no longer allowed to oversee the overpowering colors that awaited her at every turn. The green of the grass would leer at her, butterflies would leave rainbow roads in their wake. Jodee began to shake all over.

At four the next afternoon, Jodee found her peace. The visions danced away to find a new audience. She slept. When her body woke her next, it did so with a smile. She had fallen asleep to beautiful darkness. Jodee found the Nikon camera beside her. She clicked through all of her photos from the night/morning and cringed with a giggle. Her face was washed to a dull pale, and not the clean sheen of a vampire. Her eyes were near all black, filled with her pupil. But she could still laugh. And she was still laughing at her ridiculous self the night before on her way into the bathroom to assess the damage. She forgot what had found her on the other side of the mirror. But when she looked at her reflection, Jodee's eyes stuck on themselves. They turned angry. Jodee stopped laughing.

She never laughed when the Other-land Self caught her in the mirror. Tonight, as she tried to fall asleep in bed, Jodee tried to fight off flashbacks to when she and the Other-land first met. But the battle was one she could never win. So Jodee curled into a ball and clutched Scar, trembling as the never-fading memory took over.

CHAPTER 5

The wife beater tank top was a recurring outfit choice for Colby. He wore it underneath a flannel shirt that was unbuttoned enough to see the faded yellow stains that eventually appear on any white shirt. His unkempt hair hung over his scared eyes. But was he just plain scared, or scared to be found out?

Jenson nudged Purdy out of his unwavering stare. *Please let this be the fuckin' guy.* "What?" Purdy asked.

"You ready?"

"Yup, let's head in. I wanna get this fucker, Brian, I really do."

"And if he is our guy, we will."

Morgan Purdy led the way to the interrogation room. Colby was already sitting at the cold, metal table. He was un-cuffed. While Colby was a suspect, he hadn't been arrested. There was no evidence whatsoever. Brian took a seat while Morgan stood in the dimly lit corner.

"Colby, do you mind just stating your full name for us?" Brian asked after he turned on the recorder.

"Uh, yeah, Colby Garrett Jones."

"Thank you. And you are aware that this conversation is being recorded?"

Colby shook his head up and down.

"I need you to say yes or no," Purdy commanded.

"Yes."

"And you understand your rights? They've, they've been read to you?"

"Yes."

"And at any time you can stop the interview and request a lawyer."

"Got it."

"And these are your initials here, on this paper that lists your rights, next to each of these items?"

"Yes."

"Okay. Now Colby, tell us about your relationship with the deceased, Amanda Halkwicks."

Colby let one perfect tear drop down his face. He wiped his greasy hair from his forehead. "She is, uh was, my girlfriend."

"Did you two live together?"

"N-no. I have a separate place."

"But you do have a key to her apartment, correct?"

"What? I mean yeah, I have a key. She's got one to mine too though. Does that matter?"

Brian ignored the question; he would readdress the issue after the openers. "Did you two ever have any problems? Fights, things like that."

"I mean, couples fight, yeah man. We had little arguments. Nothing big though."

Purdy spoke up from his corner, "On the night Amanda was murdered, we have witnesses placing you two together, however briefly, at the bar Ringo's, Colby. They said she ran out crying. What happened?"

"Nothing, another stupid argument, man!"

"About what," Morgan growled.

"I dunno, she gets jealous. It was somethin' like that. I mean, about another girl. Look, me and Amanda wasn't exclusive or nothin'. I can't be on trial for cheating on her."

"You're not, Colby," Brian said. "Right now, you're not on trial for anything. We are just trying to get some facts together."

"Well good. 'Cuz you've got nothin' on me," he said this defensively.

Purdy continued, moving into the light, "How did you find yourself at Amanda's place at the end of the night?"

"Amanda and I, we fight. But then we... you know... we fuck, and everything is fine. So, a while later I made my way over..."

"At what time?"

"I don't know. It could have been around three-forty-five or four."

"It makes a difference, at what time?" Purdy demanded.

"Jesus, man, I don't know! Let's call it four!"

"Well you called around 4:15 in the morning. What took you so long to call it in?" Brian asked.

"Shock, I reckon. Look, my girl was mutilated. She had a damn rod sticking out of her eye! And the blood. God, it made me so sick. I just sat there with her. I don't know."

"You see, Colby, you were the last one to talk to the victim before she went home. And you were also the one to call it in." Morgan looked the trembling boy over.

"That doesn't mean nothin'!"

"There was also no sign of a break in. Either Amanda let someone into the house, or someone who had a key made their own way in."

Colby was visibly sweating now. Morgan imagined how hard it must be to keep his eyes open through all the sweat and grease pouring into the corners. "I didn't do shit! Maybe she had someone else over!"

"There was only one wine glass recovered from the scene. We found the bottle open downstairs and her glass upstairs in the bathroom. Don't you think she would have had a glass *with* any company she might have had over?"

"I don't know! The bitch always drank wine before going out. She might have done that. Maybe you guys didn't look hard 'nuff for the other one."

Purdy rolled his eyes, but they about popped out of his head when his partner exploded out of nowhere. "TELL THE FUCKING TRUTH, KID!"

Colby looked like he shat his pants. His eyes were now filled with tears ready to drop from the rim.

"Colby, we have a bit more evidence that points to you," Jenson went on, now eerily calm after his eruption.

"W-what. What do you have on me?" The veins in Colby's neck popped out.

"Hair."

"Hair?"

Morgan thought, *Hair?*

"Yes. *Your* hair Colby. We found some in Amanda's fist. There was obviously some kind of struggle right before you finished her off."

Colby was at a loss for words, and Morgan cast a long sideways glance at his partner. He had no idea what the fuck Brian was talking about. He also didn't know where this sudden rage came from. Usually Brian was the "good cop," but the roles were now reversed. Purdy slowly retreated to his corner. He was appalled by his partner's behavior and wondered if he forgot they were all being recorded.

"Look, Colby. A few things can happen here. You can confess. And, if you confess here, well, the court looks kindly on those who we say cooperate. A case like this, it can be a hell of a lot of prison time."

"Fucking terrible."

"Well, how does it sound in comparison with the Death Penalty?

"The, Death Penalty? A-are you serious?" Colby was white as untouched snow.

"In the state of Georgia, murder in the first degree earns you a spot on death row. Now, we can take you to court, you can plead not guilty, but with the evidence we have... the jury will have no choice but to convict. Or, you can cooperate with us. Sign your confession now. Maybe the charge gets dropped to manslaughter."

Colby was shaking out tears like a sprinkler now. Purdy moved toward his partner and whispered, "What the fuck are you doing?" In response, Brian only lifted a dismissing hand to his partner. Two of the questions that was supposed to be a part of the interview was being left out, *have you been coerced in any way to confess? Has anyone promised you anything in return for a confession?*

"F-fine. I'll fucking sign. I did it. I killed Amanda. Whatever."

"What the fuck was that in there?" Morgan asked.

"You said you wanted to get him," Brian said.

"Yeah, and you said, 'if he was the right guy.' We don't have evidence on him! We don't have shit!'"

"Look. I had this feeling. I know it was him. Besides, if he didn't do it, he would have chosen to go to a jury trial. He confessed, Morgan, we got it out of him."

"*You* got it out of him. That, and some shit that is probably now weighing down his pants. Do you not realize that what you pulled is completely unethical? Come on, man."

Brian chuckled, but turned serious, "Morgan, we have had so many guys getting away. So many murders have gone unsolved. So yeah, I did what I had to do to get one. It was different, but it fucking worked! We can't have all these people dying without justice. We needed to fucking convict someone for God's sake. And this someone gave his own confession! Just leave it alone, Purdy."

The look in Brian's eyes made Purdy do just that, for a minute. But his mind couldn't stop turning.

Morgan declined Brian's offer for a round of drinks that night after Colby's interview. It was still early, but all he wanted was to be home, a rare desire for Purdy. Not to mention he didn't much feel like sitting across from Brian and getting drunk, not with the way he was feeling toward his partner at the moment. It would absolutely go to blows. So, it was better to go home. Ellen greeted him with surprise on her plain face as he entered the house. She was standing over the stove, cooking what looked like chicken, though it lacked seasoning of any sort. He walked over to her and gave her a peck on her cheek.

"You're home early," she noticed.

"Not early."

"Well, earlier. Didn't have the night shift I mean, on-call. Or the twenty-four hour ones you pull on your own merit. Should I expect a flashlight in bed tonight, along with the rustling of case papers?"

She didn't say any of this with aggression, but with a small smile. She loved her husband, a great deal. He almost loved her, which was all Ellen could ask for to keep her happy. When Morgan had the affair with Miranda, he didn't even try to hide it. It wasn't long lasting or passionate, but more something that came of boredom and ended. The end came about because Miranda and Morgan were two that could never agree on anything. She constantly put down Morgan. It started with little jabs about his soft gut, and then turned into malicious attempts at degrading his worth as a person. Morgan was surprised she never strapped on a dick and forced him to take it.

During the affair, Ellen never said a word or confronted either party. She just wanted her husband to be happy. Marriage was hard, and she knew that. The wild flame of love she felt just being in his presence was enough to keep her satisfied. Though sarcastic, Morgan was a good man. He gently removed the Patricia Cornwell book from his wife's hands. Purdy looked her in the eye, and he told Ellen everything that she had already known.

Tonight he set the table while she finished up broccoli to go with the chicken. Often times he would come home to a nice piece of chicken saran-wrapped in the fridge, with heating instructions followed by a little heart. Morgan took his seat at the table and Ellen served him. He waited until she was seated to cut into his meat. He shoved in forkful after forkful without taking a breath, only breaking to guzzle iceless water. Purdy felt his wife's eyes on him and looked up, strips of chicken hanging from between his lips.

"You okay, honey?" she asked with concern.

He could have lied. Normally, he would have lied to keep things confidential. But he was at a loss with all of the cases that were piling up at the office. So he spilled. Ellen was a vault anyway, mostly because she spent most of her days in isolation reading. He started with Martin Brixx and ended with Colby's interview. Ellen said nothing, so he continued and explained all of the different modes of operation and all of the suspects he thought he had. Morgan reminded her again of the increase in the crime rate in Atlanta. And still, Ellen kept silent. But Morgan felt better. He took in a breath that could swallow some flies in the nearby gravitational pull and finished his meal.

In bed that night, there was the rustling of files, but no flashlight yet. Ellen was also awake, reading. "Have you wondered if it could all be the same guy?" she asked without looking up from her book.

It had been a little over two hours since their one-sided dinner conversation, so the sound of her soft voice took Morgan by surprise. "Huh?"

"Well, you always say every criminal has their one mode of operation. But why couldn't this guy have more? What if he's just... *smarter*?"

Morgan thought about it. "But, none of the victims share any discernable attributes. Serial killers have some kind of pattern in at least one way or another. They're not even connected, aside from living in Georgia. If I'm including every unsolved case in the city over the last few years, the ages of the victims range from eighteen to seventy-three."

"But why can't someone be different from the norm? Maybe this guy just doesn't care about a pattern. Maybe he kills just to kill."

As she said this, Morgan realized just how small his ever-constricting box of thought was. *Say this is the same guy. At least for the majority of the crimes. It is possible... A brilliant serial killer? Aren't they all sort of brilliant in a twisted way? Or someone who's sick and just feels the urge to kill? A schizophrenic?* Morgan tentatively removed the category of "sick people" for the time being to focus his efforts. He didn't think someone who was mentally ill would be concerned with an ever-changing MO. But why not? Why couldn't it be the same guy?

Purdy gently removed the book from his wife's hand and shut off the light by their bed. He kissed her starting from the base of her neck and met her open, expectant mouth. "Thank you," he whispered.

Lanny let himself into his Brookhaven apartment. He was exhausted, but happy from another successful day on the job with Warren. He reached into his shirt pocket and pulled out a flap of skin that was cut in the shape of a jigsaw puzzle piece, in honor of the *Saw* movie franchise. He sat on his favorite sag in the couch and played with the skin. He stretched it and rolled it and finally popped it into his mouth. He let his tongue share in the fun. It flipped the skin over and over, exploring the shape and texture. Lanny pulled it out and decided he ought to put it in a picture frame.

He stood and walked to his bedroom. There was a picture of Jodee and Lanny, before the accident, on his desk. He popped the springs on the frame and slid the picture out. He did not burn, crumple, or wrinkle it. Lanny simply dropped the picture into the mesh wire wastebasket. He placed the skin inside the frame and pressed the back on again. Then, Lanny sat back in his creaky desk chair to admire Warren's handiwork. He wondered where the man learned such skill and precision with a knife. The skin looked like the one piece that goes missing to every jigsaw puzzle. Lanny thought that should now be the solution for every frustrated puzzler. Missing a piece? Cut it from your own skin! Or cardboard. Whatever works.

He pulled open the long, thin drawer that used to be designated for keyboards, before laptops took over. Inside were neat lines, organized by date, comprised of knives and nails, teeth, and one thumb in a plastic bag. He felt himself smile as he traced his finger over each memento. If Lanny ever became a suspect for any reason, this would all have to go before the police obtained a warrant. He planned on burning the entire desk. But for now, he continued to elude the police at Warren's side. In the uppermost corner of the keyboard drawer laid a faux-leather bound journal. It was thick. He carefully picked it up. The thing would never get a chance to collect dust; Lanny wrote in it almost daily.

It was his diary, but more than that. It was his portfolio for death, his death, other people's death, and collective death. There were no bounds or limits. Here he was able to let go and say the things that found solace deep inside of him. Lanny would write his thoughts and feelings, then try and translate them into poetry. Most of the time, the poems made no sense. But, how often do poems reach everyone's comprehension anyway? He only wished he started it sooner... back around the time of the accident.

Lanny flipped past the first pages, looking to his past for signs of change. He landed on a poem he wrote long before he even began looking for his special killer. "Answers in a Circle." He murmured the words to himself, below the decibel of a whisper:

The Unknown deters my courage.
I want to know what is next,
but I am not yet brave enough,
to venture.

I walk along to the cyclical tune
of the world, the universe,
but my shoulders give
further to gravity as
my unanswered journey progresses.

And how would I react if
I discovered life and death
to be
one in the same.
More circles, with no true beginning
or end.

I want to break the circle, or
even find a corner to work.

Life harmonizes.
Could it possibly with
Death?

And if these answers are
what I seek?

If this is all in my head?
If everyone is my creative hallucination?
If I am the God?

Then, I'm alone. And

CHAPTER 5

in the loneliness, more
human than ever.

Warren heard the mumblings of Lanny but could only make out words like "death", "hallucination", and "god" There was no foul stench in Lanny's closet. In fact, Warren welcomed the clean smell of bleach. It was like any other bland closet: a few pairs of shoes on the floor, shirts hung neatly in a row, jeans and pants folded with a crisp crease on one shelf. But on the other shelf sat a Ouija board. The planchette lay on top.

Warren remembered reading somewhere that you were never supposed to leave the planchette on a Ouija board, but didn't care much about the reason why. He thought such things were foolish and quickly turned his attention back on his target. He spied on Lanny through the crack in the barely-open door. His heart hammered in his chest and he wanted to giggle. He felt just like a kid participating in a game of hide-and-seek. When situations were more intense, Warren was completely composed. But, for some reason when it was all a game and getting caught was to be part of the game, all of the normal physiological responses occurred. His palms were sweaty, and he clamped them over his smiling mouth.

Lanny leaned back in his chair and Warren used that squeak to cover the creak of the door hinge as he slid it open enough so that he could slither through. He did so without a sound. From his deep sweatpants pocket, Warren pulled out a thick rope, the kind used to make nooses. He stretched the rope over Lanny's head, and brought it down around his chest, capturing both of the man's arms in the process. As Lanny started to protest, Warren had almost finished his perfected constrictor knot. There was no point in struggling, yet Lanny did anyway.

"Warren, what are you doing?" There was no anger in Lanny's voice, only bizarrely calm fear.

Warren sat up on Lanny's desk and rolled Lanny and the chair back further away from it. He pulled the journal from underneath his butt and gave it a brief glance, before respectfully closing it. He asked, "Tell me Lanny? Which of these was your favorite?" He gestured at the rows of knives. He smirked as he watched confusion come over Lanny's face.

"Uh, um. Well that one," Lanny couldn't move his arm but pointed his finger to the far left, "the first one. That girl, Amanda."

Warren's eyes landed on the steak knife. He remembered that all right, with a little resentment. Lanny caught him off guard that night, outsmarted him, embarrassed him in a sense. Warren picked it up and twirled it around in his hand, acting as if Lanny wasn't there anymore, which was all the more unsettling for the guy in the chair.

"W-warren?" He asked shakily. Warren didn't immediately look up. He sighed, gave his reflected self in the knife's blade a wink, and set his sights back on Lanny.

"Lanny, Lanny, Lanny. Do you know what time it is? I am used to working alone. But we have had some good times, haven't we?"

"Y-yeah, some real good ones, Warren. Really, really good. But, what did I do wrong?"

"Nothing yet, but I want to keep it that way. It's time for you to join this little collection of yours."

"What did I do? I'm sorry, Warren. Mr. Worth. Please. I have been following your teachings, doing everything you say, just don't take this away from me!"

Warren realized that Lanny was not concerned about his life being taken away as much as he was the opportunity to continuing working together. He felt a little warm inside and wanted to both gag and giggle at the same time.

Lanny wished he could pull his safety pin from his pocket to deliver a nice prick to his own thumb. He watched as Warren brought the tip of Amanda's knife to his lips and stood up. Lanny could feel himself trembling. Warren circled behind him and said, "How about a little haircut first?" Without waiting for a response, he began sawing at clumps of Lanny's hair. Lanny watched as the wisps fell all around him. He felt a tear stagger its way from his lid and slowly march down to the corner of his lip. That's all he would allow, one tear. He quickly licked up its saltiness before Warren could see the weak response. If he was going to go out, it would be as the new man he'd become under Warren's tutelage.

"I think that looks nice. It's a great 'post-death' look. Wanna see?" Warren waved the knife in front of Lanny, tilting it to give him a distorted view of his new haircut. It was choppy, but it had always been a straw-like mess anyway. Warren walked back around in front of Lanny. "Player's choice. Do you want a horizontal slit? Or a nice jab in the side of your neck. Personally,

I like the effect of the quick stab. In and out of the artery with a nice blood spatter. But, spilling it is always nice too. Thoughts?"

"Warren, p-p-please…"

"I guess you're more of a passive guy, so a passive spill will do. Ready?" Warren brought the knife to Lanny's throat. He touched the blade to his skin and watched as Lanny's eyes began to bug out of his skull. Warren couldn't take it anymore. He burst out laughing and let the knife drop to the ground. When he caught his breath, he looked back up at Lanny and the completely befuddled look on the fella's face made him double over in laughter again.

Lanny didn't know what to do. Nervous, he began a forced laugh alongside Warren's, waiting for the moment when the powerful man would retrieve the knife and draw it across his neck.

"Oh, fella, I got you! You should have seen your face, it was hilarious!" Warren stooped and picked up the knife. He began to saw through his constrictor knot, still sniggering all the while.

"Wait, so that was, a joke?" Lanny shook out his arms and stared incredulously at Warren.

"Yeah, and a damn good one! I've always wanted to pull it on someone, but most people would be way too serious and hold a grudge. Then, I'd become a suspect in their eyes to any murders in the area. Then, well, I'd probably be caught and go to prison or be sent to death row. Then I couldn't have fun anymore!" *Then I'll have been bested, a shameful, stupid idiot.* "Not you, though. Finally! I got to do it. God, your face had me in stitches. Well, I'll be off, then. Have a fine night, fella!"

And just like that Warren strode out of the apartment. When Lanny heard the door slam, he smiled and felt warm inside.

Morgan Purdy stared down at the body of the man who still had a needle sticking out of his arm. His shoes were without their laces. He would have called it an overdose and went to console the skinny child shaking in the corner with Jenson. But there was a perfect puzzle-piece shape of flesh missing from the underside of his chin. It could have blended in with the other scabs across this man's face and neck, if it wasn't so precise and deliberate. Purdy sighed at how pathetic this copying of a movie was; there's no creativity in it (not that he condoned *any* sort of murder of course) and straightened up. "The kid didn't see anything?" He asked the room.

"He won't talk, to anyone. Looks like he's been holed up in that closet over there," the responding officer pointed to a wooden door. The child had indeed been locked in that closet, but it was before Warren and Lanny came through. Lanny heard whimpers from inside and assumed it to be a dog at first. They were the two to let the kid out… of course it was only after they killed his father. The scenario was one similar to ding-dong-ditch. A turn of the lock (with gloved hands) and an all-out sprint before the child could stick his skinny neck and dirty head into the light.

Purdy broached Ellen's idea with Jenson a few days ago. Jenson had merely scoffed and said they needed to "take serious approaches." The pressure from the media and the public was mounting, and they were feeling it. Jenson had been taking a lot of his frustration out on his partner, who was breaking down the fine strategy-box they'd created over their partnership.

Now they had this guy, Jorge Hernandez, with a beautifully cut piece missing from his otherwise hideous face. That puzzle piece represented another puzzle piece to Purdy. If he were to assume that this all was one killer who had no general mode of operation, then the guy must be smart. However, if he needed to resort to what could be viewed as copyright infringement after a movie then he wasn't as smart as believed himself to be.

"Purdy, the fuck you smilin' about?" Morgan snapped to and found his partner looking at him.

"Nothing. Get anything?"

Brian gave a choked chuckle, "Yeah, get this. Another missing person, another victim. She-"

"Martin Brixx? That kid knows where she is?"

"No, man. Let that one go. I mean, you know, for now. The kid's mom. She's apparently in the fridge in the garage."

Morgan wasn't sure how he was supposed to let go of a missing person's case but said, "Well, let's check it out."

Jenson stood from the child and motioned to one of the blues to take his spot with the kid. He and Purdy walked into the pack-rat garage that would disgust even a hoarder. Crushed soda cans littered one side and full jugs of milk gone bad on the other. Morgan kicked half-full boxes of cereal out of his way and heard a disgruntled squeak. He wrinkled his nose and wished he had a surgeon's mask. The freezer was camouflaged by all of the trash: pornographic magazines strewn about it and books that had probably never been cracked piled in front. Brian swept aside the magazines with his arm, allowing himself a quick glance at a big-breasted brunette spread-eagled on one of the covers before doing so. Brian glanced at Morgan, the way he always did before a potentially big reveal. He lifted the lid that the addict hadn't bothered to lock with both hands.

Thankfully, the freezer was still in commission, so Purdy didn't feel the need to shield his nose from any aromas. He could see just a hand with a finger bent backward against a stack of cheap burger patties. Eggo® waffle-boxes, ice cream lids, and frozen chicken nuggets that had fallen from their box covered the rest of the body. Jenson started pulling the food debris from the freezer, tossing them over his shoulder and adding to the mess behind him. He uncovered her feet first. One was wearing a slipper and the other bare, but both with jagged toenails that could have been used as weapons in a pinch. He continued clearing the mess and revealed hips that were twisted a different way than the top half of her body. They pulled the freezer-burned popsicles off of her face. Yet, the decrepit woman would not let them all go. Two had frozen to her face, one orange and one purple. They stuck there as if they had been super glued.

Her hair was matted down on one side and her body was stiff, and Purdy knocked on it without thinking. The knock was like any thud you'd get from knocking on a solid block of ice. The time of death would be pretty much impossible to determine. There were track marks covering both arms. But her cold lips were caught in a slight smile. There were no signs of foul play, from the initial view anyway.

"*This* one, this one looks like a real overdose. She looks like she's been dead a while now." Purdy left the garage by the same path he'd made for himself earlier. This woman had nothing to do with his guy. Or girl. The dead guy in the other room probably panicked and stuffed his lady out here when her body forgot to breathe. He couldn't have risked jail time and losing his precious heroin. Oh, and his child of course. But now, that guy was dead. The kid would end up in some foster home. *Maybe he'll turn out crazy too. Maybe he'll turn out brilliant. Maybe he'll turn out as a mixture of the two.* His thoughts sent him back to his perp.

Miranda pushed past him through the doorway into the garage while he was on his way out. "Ladies first, for once," she whispered in his ear. Miranda didn't even bother kicking things out of the way. She stepped and crunched right over everything, pausing to take photos all the way. Brian scooted out of her way without mentioning that some of the mess he had added himself and knocked over the Leaning Pile of Books. He rolled his eyes and scooted along Purdy's path and back into the kitchen.

"What're ya thinkin'?" Jenson asked.

Purdy eyed him cautiously, nervous to bring it up again.

"Go on, tell me. I know there's somethin' fryin' in that cracked egg brain of yours."

Purdy said, "I really think this is the same guy. Or girl. As the one who killed the seventy-three year old, and the girl Amanda, and all of the others. I do, Brian, I really do. Just please, consider it and go with me on this."

"Jesus. Come on."

"Where are we going?"

"To strengthen the cop stereotype that much more. I need some coffee for this conversation."

Morgan grinned in spite of himself and followed his partner out to the car. They rode in silence on the way to QuikTrip. Morgan didn't dare open his mouth before Brian was ready to open his mind, which couldn't be done without a caffeine boost. Purdy only wished that they weren't still on duty. He figured a nice alcohol boost would help Brian open his mind a little bit more. Then he started thinking about weed...

"Ok, so you think that all of these deaths, everyone that's gone missing over the last few months, were victims of the same guy?"

"Not necessarily a guy. And more than just the last few months, Brian, the last few years. Think about it. Sure they're scattered here and there, sometimes there's an influx of death, like the past couple months. That only adds to the brilliance."

"Brilliance?" Jenson raised his eyebrows, shocked.

Morgan avoided eye contact before sputtering, "You know. We haven't been able to crack it. I'd like to think we are good at our jobs, as well as everyone else who's worked on unsolvable cases, or those cases where the evidence is one great big arrow at a suspect who can still pass a polygraph claiming innocence."

"Purdy, evidence doesn't lie."

"For God's sake, just open your mind a bit! You are just negating everything I say without a second thought. I know evidence doesn't lie. But evidence can be manipulated to mask the true crime origin." Morgan let out a big puff of air and let it fill the silence. Brian kept his mouth shut, for which Morgan was grateful because it meant he was thinking before speaking. Brian drained his coffee and Morgan hoped every drop was being used to fully engage.

The silence stretched and it was a tense one, while still not uncomfortable. It was just, necessary. Purdy stared at the steering wheel of the Crown Vic and let his eyes slide to a distorted sideways view of his partner. Jenson was rubbing his face and shaking his head. When Brian put his hand down, Purdy swore he could see a phantom of a smile on the man's weatherworn face. He felt his own lips flicker at the corners.

"Well, we haven't worked it out thus far. We may as well try a different approach," Brian finally said. Morgan broke into a grin while Brian laughed as he internally questioned his sanity.

CHAPTER 6

Kaitlyn Rice smiled when she got the email. Jodee just sent it out to the team: the list of who would be traveling to Georgia to play Georgia State University. For once, her name made that list. She was so excited for the chance to play in her first collegiate game. Traveling didn't necessarily mean she'd get any playing time, but it gave her a better chance than would staying in the dorms for the weekend.

Kaitlyn glanced over at her roommate Miley to see her reaction. Miley's was the second name Kaitlyn scoured the list for, and she was secretly glad she didn't see it. Miley's face didn't change, but she did let out a low whistle.

"You good?" Kaitlyn asked, attempting small talk with her roomie.

Miley gave her a dirty look and stuck her headphones in her ears. Kaitlyn rolled her eyes and jumped out of bed to see what the other freshmen were up to. She walked two doors down and pushed the door open without knocking. Chrissy and Lauren were already throwing practice gear into their bags.

Chrissy noticed Kaitlyn first. "Hey, congrats!" she said.

"Yeah, it's about time you get on that bus with us!" Lauren grinned at her. Kaitlyn tried to hide her excitement.

"Seriously." She strode over to Chrissy's bed and plopped down. "But who am I gonna sit with on the bus? You two always sit together."

"Ah, who cares. Maybe you'll get lucky and snag two seats all to yourself. That's what the seniors get. I guess the losers do too," Lauren winked. Kaitlyn threw the stuffed bear from Chrissy's bed at her.

"Hey! Don't bring Fudger into this please," she got up from her cross-legged position and retrieved her bear. "Hey, Kait, we were just about to go over to Jodee's office and grab our uniforms for the weekend. Wanna come?"

Kaitlyn nodded and the three left the room. Lauren made sure to lock the door.

Jodee sat in her office and rubbed at her eyes. They'd been so tired lately; they seemed like they were pulling away from her head. She heard a quick knock at the door followed by the entry of three of her freshmen: Kaitlyn, Chrissy, and Lauren. The girls were allowed to enter in such a way. Jodee wanted everyone on the team to feel comfortable with her. Besides, they'd know when *not* to come in by merely glancing through the window to see what Jodee was up to or whom she was with. It was a very open door policy.

"Hey, Jodee!" Chrissy called cheerfully as she led her pack inside. Kaitlyn Rice was the newest addition to the players traveling. She made quick eye contact with Jodee and grinned slowly, at first trying to contain it. But true joy has its way of breaking through and it couldn't be stopped. Jodee smiled back but didn't say anything, and neither did Kaitlyn. There wasn't any need to make a big deal of it in front of the other girls. She wanted Kaitlyn to feel normal picking up her #36 uniform that was freshly washed.

CHAPTER 6

Jodee listened to the clinking of the hangers as they each picked up a uniform and offered a smile and wave as they exited. She caught a mention of Miley's name followed by a few stifled giggles and ignored it. There'd always be drama on the team, no matter how much team building they did. Cliques came with the territory when you dealt with girls. She sighed and powered down her computer, ready to call it a day. All she wanted to do was go home and curl up with Scar on the couch. She stood slowly from the chair that creaked from relief and turned off the office lights. She needn't bother with locking the door; none of the coaches in the athletic building did. And, in order to get access to the athletic building, you needed a code per entrance.

She hopped in her car and started to back out of her spot, looking in her rear view mirror as she did to check for any obstacles. As she did, Jodee felt the pull. Her eyes glazed over as she stared into the small, rectangular mirror. Her foot was not yet on the gas but raised from the break and the car was in reverse. She was so much in a trance that she did not notice Kaitlyn and the girls walking behind the car to get to the dining hall. The bump felt like the car merely hit a curb, but it was enough for Jodee to pull out of her daze and see clearly in the mirror that Chrissy and Lauren were standing there, looking down with mouths wide open. In horror, Jodee put her car into park and leaped out.

"Holy shit, is that Kait? Oh my God, are you okay?"

Kaitlyn Rice was starting to stand up and dusting asphalt from her knees where fresh scrapes would later sting upon contact with water. There were tears in her eyes, but she wiped them away hoping nobody would notice.

"Yeah, I'm good! Just a couple scraped knees!" Kaitlyn proclaimed, and bounced on her toes to check for further damage. It was more so the shock that hurt her than anything else. And she was okay.

"Are you sure? We can get you in to see the trainer. He can take a further look at you; I think he's still there. God Kait, I'm so sorry." And she was. She could have easily hit Kaitlyn in a worse way and taken her first opportunity, or any, to play in a collegiate game away.

"Hey, I'm fine, I swear. No sweat." Kaitlyn started laughing, as she often did when there was a silence to be filled.

"You're crazy, Kait," Chrissy joined her in laughing and Lauren followed suit. Jodee could see that Kaitlyn really was okay and felt much better. She decided to make a joke to lighten whatever tension was leftover.

"Just make sure those get covered up well. If a referee sees blood in the game, you're out."

The girls laughed and Kaitlyn replied, "I will. Just try not to kill anyone on the way home, Coach."

"Can't promise anything," Jodee winked and got back into her car. She was still a little shaky and waited until the girls were all the way to the dining hall before backing out of her spot again. This time she turned to look over her shoulder instead of using the mirror and made it home without further incident.

Jodee went about her normal routine: let out Scar, ignored texts from Matt, made herself a sandwich, and settled in on the couch. It was just like any other night, save almost injuring one of her own players. When it came time for bed, Jodee splashed water on her face, then dabbed at her squinting eyes with a towel. She felt like a newborn puppy with still-blurred vision. When her vision cleared, her reflection stared back, waiting for her. She tried to ignore it, but it held a certain fascination over her that beat out the terror that brought a quickened patter of her heart. She couldn't help it; sometimes she simply couldn't pull away. Jodee's eyes locked with themselves in the mirror and the disconnect came and was replaced by only a connection with the other face across from her. She stared at her Other-land self. All of her concentration seemed intent on keeping the two faces separate. But, the longer she stared, the harder it became. As usual, the most-centered features of her reflected face morphed into someone hardly recognizable. Those eyes were not her own, but those of someone who was pissed off, someone who maybe wanted to hurt her. Soon, those judgmental eyes were all Jodee could see. They burned through Jodee and seemed to jump out from the rest of the face. Jodee's skin broke out in goose bumps. She wanted to pull away, but the eyes held her still. She felt a tear slide down her cheek. She could hear Scar barking some-where distant, but even that wasn't enough to pull her out of the trance.

As the reflected image drew closer, Jodee felt herself lean toward the mirror. She tried to stop it, but her hips kept hinging anyway. Scar was in the bathroom now, yanking at Jodee's pants and trying to move her even the slightest bit. But the knees, though they trembled, would not budge. The tears began to flow.

At seeing this, Scar bit into her owner, something that she had never done before. She drew blood, but her master didn't so much as scold her or swat her away. She was gone.

The facial features in the mirror began to morph into their true form. It was Jodee, but it was not Jodee. The eyes were still full of hate, but a glimmer of a smile traced on the lips of the darkened face. It grew closer still, hair falling across the face and Jodee felt her own doing the same. Her forehead touched the cool, hard surface of the mirror. A silly thought about the smudge it would leave flitted across her mind. She wished it would have stayed longer, distracted her, so she could secretly escape the force that pressed her to the mirror. Now steady, painful sobs came from Jodee's throat. It was the only sound she could make. She could not scream, she could not speak, and she sure as hell couldn't stop what was happening to her. All she could do was stare into the eyes of her fate and let it take her away.

The mirror began to soften. A scaly hand tested the air before grabbing Jodee by a chunk of her hair. It was almost massaging at first, like she was in second grade again getting her hair brushed and braided by a giggling friend during story time. Jodee let herself relax into the touch. Serenity came. It braided her hair with one hand then followed with light, scratchy strokes that made her skull tingle with pleasure. Then came the yank. It was hard, and more painful than it would have been had it not been preluded by the calm massage. Jodee felt as if her scalp would rip free of her skull. She saw blackness, was in blackness, and then a hard push came from behind and she tumbled forward, further into the dark.

Slowly, light pushed through her eyelids. She opened her eyes and rubbed them, confused as to when she had closed them in the first place. Perhaps it had been when she allowed herself to sink into the massage of a stranger's hand. She didn't remember seeing anyone reflected behind her. Maybe it was because she was too transfixed by her own image. Surely that was it. It couldn't have been anything else. Her Other-land self was a figment of her LSD imaginative memory. She stood up on shaky knees and tried to compose herself. She looked around. Jodee was definitely in a bathroom, but it was not her own. This one gleamed with metallic surfaces. She even saw her face distorted in the curve of the toilet bowl. The shower was occupied only by a bar of soap, which was near identical to the one that sat by the sink. There was nothing else, no shampoo or conditioner, no razor, not even any toilet paper. She opened the cabinets and found bottles of Windex with paper towels. In the drawer there was only a toothbrush accompanied by toothpaste. That was it. She looked up into the vanity mirror that was under soft lights. She looked in and felt the connection, saw her other self. But it lasted only a moment. Now she was alone in the mirror.

She searched her eyes to form the connection, something she rarely did on purpose, but could not. She was alone. Jodee took another look around the bathroom. She was alone at last, but felt she was in more danger now than ever.

While Jodee was tumbling into the abyss somewhere far away, yet still so close, Warren Worth was on his way to his friend's house. The door was locked, as always, but Warren had a key and Noel knew he was coming. He let himself into the apartment, spied Noel sitting on the couch, felt his manhood rise in anticipation, then tore her tank top in half and began kissing his way down between her full breasts.

"Warren…" she gently grabbed his face between her hands and pushed him back. "We need to talk." Noel pinched a piece of her close-cropped black hair behind her ear. When they first met Noel's hair went nearly to her waist and needed to be tied in a thick bun while working. With her amber eyes she indicated that he sit-down. He reluctantly did. "I've been doing a lot of thinking about the future." In truth, she was sick and tired of being someone's plaything. That sort of thing is all right when you're in college and don't know what you are going to do in life, but now she was in her late thirties and an established neurosurgeon. What they were doing felt nothing short of childish and frankly demeaning.

"Really?" His dark eyes glimmered. "So have I."

"You have?" She sat up with the ripped sides of her shirt hanging to the sides like a grungy vest over her nude bra.

He spent hours researching and then rehearsing so that it would sound casual and natural out of his mouth. He inhaled sharply and said, "Oh yes. The two of us, we are beacons of both physical and mental perfection. There are three requirements for natural selection. Individuals in a population have to have varied traits. They differ in the ability to survive, and to reproduce. They pass on traits to their offspring.

"I don't like the idea of having a child. But, neither of us is immortal. The only chance this world has is if some of our gene pool sticks around. I don't want all of our work to be for nothing. Just imagine what the two of us could create. We could train it."

Noel was taken aback. This was unexpected. "So, you want a future too, a family."

"Oh God no," he chuckled. "I want to create something, yes, but not a family. Marriage and all of that is such a thing of the past. Love is a social construct. Society changes every year, one day marriage will be as foreign to civilization as, um, other things that we don't do now that they used to do back in the day." He wanted to punch himself for the stupidity he was exuding.

If it's a social construct, then tell me how I'm in love with you. "Oh," was all she said out loud.

"You could freeze your eggs," he suggested, "then when we are both ready to do this thing it won't matter that you're menopausal and no longer child-bearing."

The thought was depressing. Noel shrugged. "I don't know."

"What's not to know?" He pressed. He needed her to have a baby. She was brilliant and necessary for half of its production.

"That's just not how I pictured my life."

"Don't you remember when we first met?"

Noel rolled her slightly upturned eyes.

"What'd you tell me?"

"I know what I said."

129

"You said you weren't looking for a relationship, you were busy with what was it? Trying to find a cure for schizophrenia and Old timer's?"

"Alzheimer's."

"Huh? Whatever. The point is that you haven't done that yet. What's a relationship good for other than distracting you? I don't want to be your possession. When this whole thing started, I thought we were both on the same page."

Noel felt an angry heat spread through her body. She took three deep breaths as instructed by her therapist. "That was years ago. Things change, as do my wants and desires. And, by the way, I've saved hundreds of lives. Maybe I haven't accomplished all my goals, but I'm sure I've done more for people than you do slinging beers from behind the bar." She was not a cocky woman and hated that he brought this need out in her, the need to prove she was good enough.

Warren figured he probably saved thousands of lives by eliminating his select crop. Of course, she didn't know his true career. He was not insulted by her belittling his bartending job. It was a fun gig and the Atlanta tips left him working three to four days a week and with more than enough money to get by. "Noel," there were no pet names between them, "I am not taking away from all that you've done. All I'm saying is that you'll never be ready for a relationship if you still have goals to realize. It'll just set you back. I'm only thinking of you." He cocked a grin at her.

She wrinkled her nose, stood, and swatted him away when he tried to grab her onto his lap. If there were to be no possessing between the two of them then he needed to stop grabbing her ass as if he had a right to it whenever he pleased. "I'm getting water," she said curtly.

"I'll take a glass." He watched her bottom switch back and forth as she walked away. He was feeling impatient. Warren came over for a quick round, not to be engulfed in drama.

In the kitchen Noel shrugged off her ruined tank top with mild irritation and grabbed a tee shirt sitting still warm in the dryer. She filled two glasses of water and went back to the couch, handing one to Warren saying, "Try not to ruin this one."

He raised his eyebrows and took a sip of water wondering when this mature, sexy, brilliant, woman turned so moody. He figured it must be her time of the month... unless she hit menopause early. If that were the case this would have to be the end of their tryst. He hoped not for he loved listening to her talk and watching the way her mouth moved and cradled long exotic words.

Noel stared straight ahead unable to mask her frustration. She was not a young girl anymore. She couldn't fall into the trap of hoping he'd change his mind and continuing under his terms believing that he would fall in love with her too. No, she would have to move on. Not yet, but soon. This was, after all, only her first time bringing the topic up for discussion. It was a new thought, something he would need to mull over in his own time.

She stood again, grabbing his hand and bringing him to the bedroom. She had some aggression that needed to be worked through.

Warren left his glass on the coffee table and followed, checking this off his mental list and then added a note that he would need to test his protégée. That could wait of course.

"So, how do we go about finding this person. Our victims don't seem to have much in common," Jenson said.

"The one thing that each crime scene has had in common is a lack of evidence, or evidence that could have easily been planted. If this guy, or girl, screws up just once… I don't know. Maybe this is just a fool's errand. Ellen put it in my head. But honestly there is *no* way to go about it," Purdy's head was spinning with frustration.

"Easy there, guy. You talked me into it this far. Let's look at some of our victims. Martin Brixx, Rebecca Caster, and Amanda Halkwicks. Two of which are young females, college-aged, well Amanda just graduated. Each of those three were in a bar just before the incident. Brixx was walking home alone."

"Right. And Rebecca, she was a freshman. But hers we don't know happened at a bar for sure. She got poisoned," even with the doubt, Purdy could feel his wheels turning faster, "but, it was such an intense cocktail and that could have easily been dosed to her inside of a bar. Honestly, that one was completely overdone. I thought our guy was confident, but that just makes him look unsure. Anyway, the time frame fits, before she started getting 'sick' she was out with her sorority sisters based on their accounts. They said she ditched them for a boy. And then of course Amanda Halkwicks, the one who was last seen by her boyfriend Colby and other bar onlookers, running out in a rage."

CHAPTER 6

"So, into the mind of a killer with demented views, well, I guess they all have demented views, we have your average party girls and party boy here. No question about that, and very common. I still think Colby had something to do with Amanda's murder, though."

Purdy shook his head, "No, man. I really don't think so. But looking at these specific victims, they all went off on their own."

Jenson cocked a thick eyebrow in surprise, "Are you saying they deserved it?"

"Of course not. It's just, you see bad things happen on the news all of these terrible things happening to people and you would think it would stop people from reckless behavior."

"Not everybody watches the news. Aside from that, those that do can't fathom such a thing happening to them. You know you've got that same disease. You hear about some crook kidnapping an officer's daughter or killing his family and you still don't believe that sort of thing would ever happen to you, right?"

"That's true. I get that. I'm trying to be in the mindset of someone that doesn't think that way, though."

"You're right. So it's gotta be someone who was raised relatively well in a stable and safe environment. I've certainly given my sons the talk about surroundings. People are crazy out there, whether they want to mug, rape, or kill you. It's not just girls that need to be cautious. We all do. Sometimes I still feel like you don't have to worry about boys like you do a little girl. At least as long as a guy like Jeffery Dahmer isn't on the loose," Jenson chuckled.

"But our victims are more than just females that's the thing. I was doing some research onto other unsolved cases and unexpected deaths around Georgia. There was this guy in Savannah who was killed by a Water Moccasin. Only thing is that he was killed in a bedroom. It wasn't like it happened while he was out on the water. The other guys he was with swear all the doors were shut and locked when they got home, no sign of any snakes unless this guy, Sean Smith, got a knock on the door and said 'Oh, come on in,' to the snake. It doesn't add up. I don't know, I might be reaching. I kind of want to get another opinion on this. You know, a female one."

"You're going to bring Ellen further into this? Man, you need to be careful."

"I wasn't talking about Ellen. I was talking about—"

"Miranda? You sonofabitch. Miranda fuckin' Knox? What are you tryin' to do here really, you dog?"

"Come on, man. She's kind of brilliant. You know her eye is somehow different than anyone else's, on scene and otherwise. She is sure to see something others won't with this."

Jenson only shrugged in response so Morgan dialed Miranda and put it on speakerphone.

"What do you want?" She asked, skipping the formal "hello, how are you?"

"Miranda, I am with Brian. Are you busy right now? We need your help with something." Morgan swallowed his pride with that last sentence and awaited her reply. It came after a bit of a pause.

"Yeah, that's fine, I guess. I'll meet you at Matrix."

CHAPTER 6

"A bar?" Jenson asked incredulously.

"If I have to speak with you two, I am gonna need a drink," Miranda said without a joking lilt in her voice. "I'll see you in fifteen."

And fifteen minutes later Jenson and Purdy walked in to Matrix. Miranda was already sitting at the bar with a Jameson on the rocks in one hand. She was not speaking to anyone, although several other bar patrons looked like they wanted to approach her to converse. It may have been her gray pantsuit and no nonsense tight red bun that held them at bay. She turned her blue eyes to the men as soon as they walked in the door, as if she could sense their arrival. They walked over to her and flagged down the bartender.

"What can I get for you fellas?" Warren asked, noticing the slightly hidden badges clipped to their belts."

"We'll take a pitcher of Bud heavy please," Purdy answered. He surveyed the room as the barkeep filled their pitcher, looking for a private booth. There was one messy, but vacated, and he nudged Knox and Jenson in that direction. "I'll meet you guys over there. Miranda, tidy it up if you don't mind."

She chose to ignore his request and stood with her arms tightly across her chest, then leaned over and asked the bartender for another cold glass to go along with the pitcher. Jenson went with a pile of napkins and cleaned the table himself.

"That'll be twelve dollars," Warren said with the grin that got him tips from men and women alike. Purdy laid down a ten and a five and walked away with the pitcher in one hand and two pint glasses in the other. He joined his partner and Miranda at the table.

"So, what is this all about?" Miranda asked.

"You remember Martin Brixx?" Purdy asked as he tilted his glass and poured a beer first for Jenson and then for himself.

"Oh, Christ. Not this again Morgan. That case is a dead end and you know it."

"But you know the case," Jenson prodded.

"Yeah, I know the case. That guy was a mess. He was probably on the teat too long and couldn't handle living on his own. Always walking into trouble, and eventually found himself walking to nowhere. Disappeared. Gone. Probably stuffed by a sadistic taxidermist somewhere that we will never find. Down a river. Who fucking knows?"

"Exactly. And then we have Rebecca Caster. She was poisoned in Athens, Georgia, with well, what wasn't she poisoned with. Somebody probably gave her it claiming it was cocaine, and she administered it as such. At least that is how it matches up based on the autopsy showing how the drugs were ingested and considering toxicology found Xanax, cocaine, and whatever else."

"And…?" Miranda looked bored as she took another sip.

Those are just two of many unsolved cases we have had in the past year or so. And those two, they have a lot in common," Purdy said.

"They happened in completely different cities," Miranda countered.

"But look at what is the same," Jenson countered.

CHAPTER 6

Miranda looked thoughtful for a moment.

"Think about how you were raised. Would you have ever taken drugs that came from an unknown source on your first experience with them? Would you walk home alone, drunk, on your phone after having not one but *two* experiences with a flasher and then being robbed at knifepoint?" Purdy pressed.

"No. I mean, there were a few nights where I walked home alone in college, but I always had the pepper spray out. Dad gave that to me as soon as I turned thirteen. I see what you're saying there. I never did drugs," Miranda narrowed her eyes at Purdy, "but you're right. Most kids do them in a familiar setting with friends, especially the first time. So, what, are you trying to blame the families? I don't think that'd work. I don't even know why you are still digging around in cul-de-sac cases. My opinion on them? Tough break for that Rebecca girl you mentioned in Athens, though like I think I've pointed out that's not your jurisdiction. She was probably insecure and wanted to be a part of something. Brixx? Shit. Trouble followed that boy wherever he went. He thought he was invincible."

"Okay, I get it, you think we're chasing our tails and not going to get anywhere with this. That's fine. We're just pointing out that both of those two were a little reckless."

"So what, you're into victim blaming now? That and expanding your gut I see," she nodded at his stomach. "Besides, you can't forget about Amanda. She didn't do anything, as you say, 'reckless,' and still ended up with a damn curling iron through her eye. Then there's Hernandez, which you've completely failed to talk about. Why? Is it because he's not a white victim like the rest of them so it doesn't mesh well with your serial killer theory? That's so typical. Ignore the pieces that don't fit, pretend they don't exist, so that you can create some profile that's really an illusion of your imagination."

Jenson let out a low whistle and Purdy bristled, trying to ignore the comment about his midsection. "That was a lot of heat, girl, I can literally feel your blood boiling for you. Told you this was a bad idea," Jenson shrugged at Purdy.

Miranda surveyed both the men in front of her as Purdy drained his glass and filled it again halfway from the pitcher. She shook her head, but a smirk crept onto her face. Purdy knew that smirk; it always came about when she pretended not to want to do something. He clinked his glass against hers for encouragement. "These cases do have something in common, something more that you may have seen after requesting the investigative summary for the one out of Athens. No real evidence was left behind at any of them. There were no latent prints, no fibers or hairs, no way to trace this suspect. So there's a connection. I'll need to look further into this to determine more." She finished her beer and took what was left in the pitcher. "I suppose there's nothing to lose. How's the heat for you now, Brian?"

Lanny met up with Warren in downtown Atlanta. He had put in extra effort at work and taken off a little early. They never really noticed when he came or left, just whether the work was done. And that Asian man's lungs were ready for display. Today he dressed casual and nondescript, remembering what Warren taught him. The goal was never to stand out, and though the weather was turning colder it still would not do to throw on an all-black ensemble complete with leather gloves. Instead he wore faded jeans and a long-sleeved light gray shirt. It might have once said it was from Old Navy, but the logo had long since faded. He skirted into the Matrix and took a seat on his stool. Warren covered the lunch shift today and would be off by four. The lunch shift was a surprising money-pool, a lot of businessmen coming down and spending their lunch breaks tipping back pints or Old-Fashions for an hour before heading back to work.

Almost right at the moment he sat down, there was a ginger ale and lemon juice placed on a coaster in front of Lanny. Warren nodded to him from the other side of the rather empty bar and went about his work. It was 3:30 pm. A man came in and ordered a Miller Lite and the keg blew. Warren replaced the keg effortlessly as his muscles rippled beneath a fitted collared shirt. Warren let the line clear and filled the man a pint in exchange for $3.50. The man threw a five down and waved his hand at Warren, indicating to keep the change. Lanny sipped at his drink. He wanted to make it last until four to avoid filling his bladder. Warren refilled the ice bucket at 3:45 and sighed, glancing at the clock. He cut extra fruit even though there was plenty to last the night and time stretched to 3:50. Warren wiped and re-wiped the bar to the point that it almost sparkled, which would surely dazzle more customers that night. At 3:55 his relief came on duty and clocked in, saving both Lanny and Warren five more minutes of boredom.

However, it was not boring to Lanny. Every time he saw Warren work his stomach flipped like a dog doing a trick. Lanny's gut jerked and jangled around Warren, not in a sexual way but in an admiring sense. It didn't have to be killing, though that is what Lanny preferred to watch. Any kind of work Warren did seem so smooth, precise, and worth watching. Just the way he sliced the lemons and limes was clean enough to impress any surgeon.

With his side-work done, Warren came out from behind the bar, tipped a salute to his coworker, glanced again at the table in the corner, and strutted outside. Lanny sucked down his drink and left a couple crumpled bills on the bar. Although Warren never charged Lanny for his nonalcoholic drink, other bartenders did, and Lanny didn't want to create a scene being chased out of the bar by one of the Matrix employees. Warren was posted up against a light-post checking his cell phone. As Lanny walked up patting his pockets, Warren asked, "Who's it gonna be, fella?"

"What?" Lanny asked, confused. "Give me a moment, I think I left my wallet in the bar." He jogged back down to Matrix while Warren conjured up an unpleasant memory of his seventh grade teacher. He went to her when he realized he left his Walkman in the locker room and returned to find it missing. Instead of helping him track down the thief, she scolded *him* and said that he should be more mindful of his belongings. That bitch.

Lanny returned with his wallet in hand. Luckily, nobody swiped it in the two minutes he left it on the barstool. Warren looked him square in the eyes, his dark blue eyes locking in on Lanny's green ones.

"Uh." Lanny trailed off. He felt put on the spot and entirely too nervous.

CHAPTER 6

"You're picking the fella today, got it? Or the girl. Go on, survey the area and make your choice."

Lanny scanned the busy streets that were starting to pick up with rush hour. On the sidewalk across the street he saw a woman wheeling a baby in a carriage with a cell phone pressed to her ear. By the way she held up her hand to traffic whilst crossing the street when the light had barely changed made Lanny think she was from New York. He spotted a group of young girls sitting outside of the Starbucks, sipping on identical frappuccinos. There was a homeless man on the corner playing a crude guitar. The bucket of money where he kept his life's savings was placed below a sign that simply read, "Thank you and God bless." He may not have believed in God, but a quarter of those who passed by would see that and throw him a buck or two just to prove they were good Christians.

"Him. That guy playing the guitar," Lanny pointed at the man across the street. Warren looked at him like he wanted to raise his arm and whollup him a good one. Lanny realized his rookie mistake and put his arm down. He was literally pointing out whom he was about to kill for anyone who wanted to see. "My bad," he said with his arms tightly at his sides, "but that is him."

Warren shook his head back and forth so fast Lanny thought the bones in his neck would break, sending it spinning around like an owl. "No. Fucking. Way. Fella." Color rose in Warren's cheeks out of anger and Lanny shrunk back.

"But, why not?"

"Well, my question for you is *why?* What is the reasoning behind taking that man's life as opposed to anyone else on this street?"

"Because, I don't know, he's got his money just sitting out for anyone to take. He clearly messed up somewhere along the way, being homeless and all. He's out there living a dangerous life. That makes him a good target in my book."

"Well, throw out your fucking book and pick up mine, Lanny. That man is not stupid. He is working for a living. I have a few rules for this thing I do and one of them is to never touch the homeless. They aren't *intentionally* homeless. The mere fact that they are out there surviving without a damn home and at the hands of the city is pretty amazing to me. That's evolution out there.

"Any and every obstacle is being thrown at them and they are surviving. Plus, he's over there working for his money. He's not just begging for it. He's got that guitar out. Sure, it sounds like shit, but he's *trying*. Killing the homeless is something society does, not me. They are pretty extraordinary and to be *left alone*. Do you hear me, fella?"

Lanny nodded, his face flushed like the teacher had just scolded him in front of the entire class.

"Now, I know who I would have picked. Want to take another shot at it?"

Lanny thought about his options and remembered the way the woman with the baby had put her hand up to traffic. He now recalled the way a car had skidded to a stop, as if it had been ready to test the speed of the light changing from yellow to red.

She put up that hand as if that would always be enough when in reality that car could have easily taken her, and her baby, out. She'd even let go of the baby carriage for that second, still keeping the other hand on her phone. How many times a day did she do that? What odds was she testing? "How about the lady with the baby?" Lanny asked a bit shyly.

Warren nodded and smirked. "That's good, Lanny, I noticed her too. Not only is she risking her own life by not waiting on the light to fully change, but that of her baby as well. I think that kid would be much better growing up with an adopted parent than that woman."

Lanny scratched his head, thinking of his own warped childhood. But his gut had risen in his stomach as if he were going down the big hill on the roller coaster. He found a good target.

"So. Now we have to decide *how* she's going to die," Warren promoted. Lanny's mine flickered to his Smith and Wesson. It was sitting in his truck, still unused.

"Can we shoot her, please?" He looked to Warren with a lowered head.

"With what gun?"

"My revolver? Remember? The one I had that night you killed the girl from the bar? The night we met?"

Jesus if he doesn't sound like a girl about to get angry with her boyfriend for not remembering their first date, Warren thought.

"Lanny, no. I know that gun is registered. And even though bullet striations don't provide the best evidence, they're still there! And the best evidence for our purposes is *no* evidence.

Besides, I very rarely turn to firearms; you should know this by now. It is about creativity. I can now admit the way you chose to off that oaf Pat Creary was unique, effective. Try again. What is the way in which natural selection should have already offed that woman?"

"With a car!" Lanny exclaimed. Warren nodded and gave Lanny a pat on the back.

"Let's begin our stalk," he said as they watched the woman walk into Starbucks. They crossed the street when there was no traffic. It wasn't long before the woman came back out with a coffee in the hand that had been holding her cell phone. The men followed her to the next crosswalk, standing toward the back of the throng of people. The woman was in front and saw a break in traffic. She went, pushing the stroller along. The rest of the people stayed back. Just as she was about to reach the other sidewalk, the hand started to turn into a walking man, and the light was yellow. Warren was swept along with the group of people that began to cross the street. It all happened in that moment: the first steps of the group beginning to cross, the last for the woman ahead of them all in that brief time where the light held at orange. A large truck that had too much speed and would make it across the line in time to beat the red light approached. When the trucker noticed the woman, he slammed on his breaks. But it was too late. He missed the stroller by a mere inch but took the woman and her coffee with him.

By the time the truck stopped, the light had been red for a second or so. The woman laid in a crumpled mess. The coffee cup was still in her hand, but the actual contents had emptied onto the street. Her neck was cocked to one side at an unnatural angle, and splintered bones jutted out. The look on her face was one of anger, like she'd screamed "What the fuck?" as the trucker hit her.

"Now what?" Lanny asked Warren as he peered at the clearly dead woman.

"Huh? Now nothing. New target. Sometimes natural selection works just fine on its own. Come along Lanny." Warren smiled and led his mentee away from the scene.

CHAPTER 7

Jodee stumbled out of the bathroom into a room that had a table, stove, and a simple full-sized bed that was positioned under curtain-less windows. She wondered if she had traveled back in time before there was electricity, but quickly dismissed the thought as the glaring apartment lights shone down on her. The sun beat through the large window with anger. She was missing the blackout curtains in her own home that protected her from such light. Sweat was already beginning to web around her neck hairs.

Jodee tottered over to the table and picked up the remote, searching for the television. That's always the thing to do when in doubt; turn to the comfort of the TV. The power button was easy enough to locate. That symbol with a line going into the broken circle would never change. She pushed down on it and her vision began to flicker. Jodee hit the button again and everything cleared with an audible snap. She took in a breath and turned whatever the remote was for on again.

The flickering lasted a moment. They were almost like strobe lights and she took a moment to be thankful she didn't receive concussions throughout her soccer career like Kaitlyn Rice. Before they were fully formed in front of her, she heard them.

"And the temperatures tonight are going to drop to around a cool seventy-five degrees Fahrenheit. Back to you, Skyla."

Just as the weatherman was finishing his spiel, he arrived in front of Jodee with a smile so bright she had to squint. He only came in like a camera flash because he disappeared as soon as a deeply tanned blonde woman with narrow slits for eyes appeared.

"Thanks, Cobra. Boy, I'm sure missing those 120-degree summer days right about now. Tonight's top story is about a man who stayed still for too long while visiting one of our fine plots up north. Stay tuned," Skyla winked at Jodee and a CNN logo came whooshing around Jodee's head. She ducked in fright and jammed a sweaty thumb on the power button. She stood, shaking, and swept her arm through the air where Skyla and Cobra had just been standing.

Where the fuck am I? Sweat dripped from all surfaces of her skin. She wiped at her neck absentmindedly. What she really needed was a glass of ice-cold water, and to turn on the damn air conditioning. *Cool at seventy-five degrees?* She walked into the kitchen-esque area and found a glass in the cupboard. She turned on the waterspout and greedily watched it fill the cup. She took a chug and was dismayed to find it almost hot. Jodee was at least hoping for room temperature. She turned to the icebox and opened it. Inside, there was only meat, no bag of ice. But some ice chips had frosted across the top and bottom of the box, so she scraped that into her cup. They began melting almost on impact, but at least made the water slightly cooler.

Jodee searched the walls for a thermometer and found one that was higher tech than what she was used to. A warning label was above it and read "*Warning. Do not place thermostat below*

CHAPTER 7

68° Fahrenheit. Results could be fatal." Jodee scrunched her eyebrows at that. She usually popped the thermostat down to 67 or 68 when going to bed and left it at 73 during the day.

She looked outside and saw workmen in coveralls cleaning up giant, raggedy, plastic tube-like things off of the sidewalk. She walked back to the bathroom and stared at her eyes in the mirror, so hard that they began to cross and give her a headache. She looked around the bare apartment again and that is when the tears came. Her heart ached for Scar.

Jo slipped easily through the mirror, grinning as she went. She had finally done it. Her consciousness was stronger than Jodee's, so she had the upper hand. A dog met her with bared teeth, barking spittle at her. She grinned at it and tried to give it a pat on the head. The thing snapped at her, so she gave it a good smack across the face. Let it learn who was in charge here sooner rather than later.

Jo wanted to get to Lanny right away, but she knew she had obligations to this football team that Jodee ran unless she wanted to raise any suspicion. But at least they were about to travel to Atlanta, and she knew that was where Lanny would be. She knew from listening to Jodee through reflecting surfaces that the team would be leaving the next day on a bus. She smirked at the ancient concept of a bus, or even a car, and hoped that she wasn't the one expected to drive it.

She shivered in the cool air and looked down at her beautiful, shiny skin. Though no goose bumps were breaking out, she could feel the cold shutting her down. She needed to find some long sleeved clothes and turn up the thermostat ASAP.

Warren decided to call it a day with Mother Nature doing her own work, so he sent Lanny home with the assignment to find their next target. As he watched the man who was about fifteen years his junior turn and look both ways before crossing the street, he felt an overwhelming sense of pride. Here was a boy who he watched transform into a man with Warren's careful guidance in just a matter of months. It was someone he shaped, a brain he molded into his own beautiful mutation with lessons he would carry for life. Warren decided right there that he was ready for a child and thought of ways he could convince Noel to hop off of her pill sooner. He briefly considered giving her placebos but didn't know how long it would take for them to wear off. She was being testy lately after all. No, Warren would have to convince this woman of higher knowledge that it was time to bring a gift to the earth, another being that could be molded and serve as Warren's heir to greater understanding and a wealth of knowledge.

Warren sent Noel a text message that he was on his way and would pick up beer. She responded with a brief 'O.K.' and within half an hour he was unlocking her front door. She let him take her to the bed and laid there for twelve minutes, feeling disgusted with herself and even more like she was being used.

Warren noticed her lack of involvement but didn't let that distract him in the moment. He finished and rolled off of her, needing a moment to catch his breath before again broaching the subject of their child.

As Noel was using the bathroom to force any bit of urine out and avoid a UTI, Lanny was pondering his assignment. He was having difficulty concentrating since work kept butting into his brain. He had made a mistake that he only just came to realize and was hoping that nobody would catch it. Normally Lanny was the one to discover such a mistake and report it. The lungs he last worked with had a faulty provenance. Even though the lungs weren't to be used as evidence in some kind of investigation, all records were still held to the same standard of arrangement in the chronology of ownership and custody. He had forgotten to mark the location they had been just before he sent them off for display. It didn't seem like such a big deal, but he knew it was. Fortunately there was a low probability that anyone else would notice and he sure wasn't going to tattle on himself. But the lungs still persisted to capture his attention and that's when he decided on the next target.

"So. . . what do you think?" Warren asked when Noel failed to give a response. He didn't wait for her to get to the third beer and cursed himself for his own terrible impatience.

She sighed and gazed at him with her amber eyes boring their way into what might be his soul. "I don't know, Warren. Why now? I don't think I am ready for this."

"But I am! And there is nobody else better suited to be the mother of my child than you are. I want to start the process of raising a superior human being before my own brain turns to mush."

"Warren, you're barely fifty. And what is all of this talk about a superior human being?"

"Yes, I know. But I want to have at least eighteen years of training. Who knows what could happen in that time? Yes, I know I myself am an evolved human, but accidents happen every day. I do not want to take the risk of waiting too long and then it being too late. Impatience may be one of my fallbacks, but in some ways, it acts as strength. You know it is better to get a head start on things. 'Never leave that till tomorrow which you can do today.' Ben Franklin. Come on, Noel." He returned her gaze and pushed back harder with the invisible current, hoping she would crack.

The more she listened to him speak the more insane she thought him. "Training? A child? It's called raising, Warren. And what's all this about 'superior beings' and you being 'evolved'? Evolved compared to what? You sound insane, fumbling out whatever quote you memorized for the day like that." The more she thought about it, the more Noel realized she did not love this man. Listening to him talk like this made her cringe. She thought she was in love, but now this would be easy to cut off. He was desperate and she shivered thinking what a man like this would actually do with a baby. Still, she tried to place a comforting hand on Warren, but he shook it off. He rubbed his temples in frustration and for a moment Noel worried that he would tear through the thin skin.

He thought he would rather be called insane than stupid. "Don't talk to me like that," he said. Then he thought for a moment. "Your eggs!" He exclaimed.

"What about them?"

"You set them aside, right? When we last spoke of child-birth?"

"Yes…" Noel trailed off, regretting that she spoke honestly.

"Give them to me! I can find a surrogate! The baby can be mine; you don't have to have any part in its life. All I need are your genes."

"Are you fucking mental, Warren?"

"Noel, you know good and well the kind of man I am. I am superior to the rest of my kind, and you to yours on the side of females. I know what I am doing. The time, it's now. I feel if I wait any longer it would be too late. Please, Noel."

"What is this to you? Who fucking talks like that? Hell no you can't have my eggs. You are not superior. You do not have life figured out. I don't know where you get this sense of entitlement as if you're Albert fucking Einstein when you're actually quite the opposite. Honestly, you're undeniably attractive, but I'm not sure what I ever saw in you. This is over. All of it."

Warren looked at Noel in disbelief. A red rage began to blind him. He clenched and unclenched his fists, the knuckles turned white. He snapped his eyes to hers and locked in hard. The Albert Einstein comment, that was it, she called him stupid. "You've really fucked me. You stupid cunt."

The words came out in such a vile spit that they hit Noel like a slap across the face. She could say nothing in response. Warren rose from the bed and stalked out of the room, slamming the door shut on his way out.

Jo could hardly contain her excitement, for it was the morning that she would depart for Atlanta, Georgia. She planned on reuniting with her brother that evening. Unfortunately, she would not be traveling alone but with an entire team of girls, as well as a couple assistant coaches and a trainer.

Earlier in the morning she had tried to figure out how to work the oldest model of a car she had ever seen. But she hadn't been able to turn it on, let alone drive the thing. So, she'd picked up the ringing telephone she had found in Jodee's place and answered it. A man that the phone identified as Matt had been on the other line and sounded pleased that Jo had answered. She'd told him she was feeling ill, which wasn't untrue considering the drastically different environmental conditions, and he had picked her up and dropped her off at the field house. Throughout the drive, he kept taking his eyes off the road to stare at Jo, compliment her hair, comment on the "glow" she had about her, until Jo nearly hissed at him. Instead she slammed one hand down on the dashboard as if Matt had almost hit something when he wasn't paying attention. He was silenced for the rest of the ride, until he tried to give her a kiss goodbye. Jo faked a cough, "I'm sick," she said and slid out of the car.

Now Jo sat bundled in a Patagonia sweater waiting for all of the girls to file onto the bus. A blonde girl walked up to Jo and said, "Wow! In the past three and a half years I have never seen you stray from anything but the black 'do. I like it!" Jo squinted down at her own white-blonde hair, confused. But she knew the comment ended in a complimentary way.

"Thank you," she said.

Another, younger girl walked past and noticed Jo's ensemble. "How are you not dying? It's gotta be like, seventy-five degrees out!" Kaitlyn Rice exclaimed.

CHAPTER 7

"Yeah, Coach, we never get weather this hot at this time of year. Embrace it! Me, I'm hoping to catch a little bit of a tan," another girl said.

Jo bristled at their comments, annoyed, but tried to keep it in check. "I'm feeling chilly," she said.

"Hope you aren't getting sick!" The second girl said. "It'd suck to go on this bus ride with a cold."

Jo noticed that these girls were the last that needed to get on the bus and felt herself getting more annoyed at them for prolonging their departure. She knew that Jodee, as their coach, had some authority over them.

"O.K. no need to worry about me; just get on the bus, we've got to get a move on!" The girls shut up at once and boarded the bus, and Jo sighed in relief. She spent the duration of the bus ride ignoring everyone, no small feat considering the girls felt the need to fill the silence with singing, chatter, and movies. She groaned inwardly each time they had to stop for food, though that disdain didn't stop her from devouring a burger and ordering two others. She completed the meals with French fries and ice cream, enjoying the envious stares from all the college-aged girls who could not eat like that the day before a game. She had to admit that for all of this time's fallbacks, they knew what they were doing when it came to food.

As soon as they arrived in Atlanta, she found her way to her hotel room. Luckily, it was all to herself. She lay on her bed and was awoken by a hard knock on the door.

"Jodee!" a voice she recognized as belonging to one of the assistant coaches rang out. "We've got a practice to run, let's go!"

What the fuck? Is every minute planned with these people? Don't they rest? I have to find my brother, I've no time for this! "I've been, uh, throwing up. I can't get out of bed. You run it. Please leave me be."

"Are you sure? Can I come in?"

"No! I'm worried I may be very contagious. Definitely have a fever. Just, keep out."

"Okay," the voice muffled through the door, still unsure. "Get some rest. We need you well for the game tomorrow."

Jo heard the retreating footsteps and breathed in a sigh of relief. She slithered over to the window and watched as the bus once again filled up and drove away without her. She needed to figure out where Lanny lived and how to get to him. The chime of the phone, which she'd heard girls on the bus refer to as a "cell phone," grabbed her attention. There were words on the screen from Tony Anderson, the assistant coach, telling her to feel better. She ignored the message and began fiddling with the device, trying to find the list of contacts. Once she succeeded, she scrolled to the Ls but could not find a Lanny. She scrolled down to the Ps and found his name, Lanny Pape. Just seeing his name was enough to bring tears to her dry eyes. Without thinking she clicked on the call button immediately.

Lanny was disappointed with how the day turned out. He had been excited to watch Warren kill again and felt only confusion when Warren had been satisfied with the day's work. He hadn't done anything! A trucker had, and by accident. There was no way Lanny would lick the spoon of such a sloppy amateur. His stomach started turning as he was deep in thought, though he could not figure out why. A moment later, his cell phone began to ring its standard chime. When he saw the name of the caller, he nearly dropped the phone.

Many a time had Lanny sent texts and calls to his sister, but they had all been in vain. He never thought the day would come that she would reach out to him again. He answered and choked out a simple, "Hello?"

Hearing her brother's voice again made the tears flow without the option to even turn them off. "Lanny? Oh my, I can't believe it. Is it really you?" She cried into the phone.

"It's me, Jodee, I just can't believe it's you!" He sobbed with her, unable to process the moment but fully surrendering to it.

CHAPTER 8

Whenever Warren needed to channel his rage, he always turned to the same thing to calm him down... the gym. He counted on his workouts to release the endorphins and clear his mind. Warren felt like Noel had handed him a death sentence when she refused to have a child with him, or merely give him her eggs. They never fought in the past, never had a disagreement of any kind. This was the first and would most likely be the last. Of course, if she issued an apology, he was apt to change his mind.

Warren wasn't a journaling man. He internalized everything. Noel didn't accept him for who he truly was. She mocked him, belittled him, made him feel *stupid*. As he pounded on the treadmill after lifting weights, his mind spun for an answer. He almost considered going to therapy, but actually laughed out loud at the idea. When his mind finally delivered a feasible option, he hit the STOP button and stood on the sides of the treadmill until it stopped running. He breathed hard, both hating and loving himself for finally realizing that he *did* have someone he could turn to about this, and it was Lanny.

His sweat turned cold by the time he reached Lanny's place in Brookhaven. He gave the door his usual rap and it opened a second later. Lanny's face fell when he saw who was on the other side.

"What, expecting someone else?" Warren asked. As far as he knew, Lanny had no other friends.

"Yeah, actually. But come in! Of course please come in!"

Warren noticed a bit of a shake to Lanny's hands. "Is this a setup, fella?" He asked, cocking an eyebrow in suspicion.

Lanny looked taken aback, "What? No, of course not. I wouldn't betray you like that, Mr. Worth. You gave me a purpose again, remember?"

"Then what's got you in a tizzy? You can understand that I don't fully trust this situation. In fact, why don't you hand over that little gun you keep, just to keep me at ease."

Without a word, Lanny grabbed the revolver from underneath the sag on his favorite couch. He changed its hidden position almost weekly. He handed it to Warren to appease him and waited as Warren checked to see if it was loaded so that he could spill his excitement.

"My sister is coming!" His voice nearly squeaked in a pubescent way.

Warren looked up in confusion. "Beg your pardon?"

"Jodee! She called! And she's coming to see me!"

"Your sister? I thought you two didn't speak, that she abandoned you."

"None of that matters now. I've been waiting for this day for a long time."

"And you just don't care? After all she did to you?"

Lanny, for the first time, sent the look of utter disbelief in Warren's direction and said, "Of course I don't. I love her, and I can't really blame her. We had a tough life. I think it was her way of blocking everything out and forgetting. But maybe now she's ready to push through that barrier that has been blinding her for all these years."

"Forget what, Lanny?"

"My first spoon-lick of course! Not including licking the brownie batter bowl she always gave me."

Warren remembered the wistful look Lanny had gotten on his face the night they first met at Amanda's place. He had stuck the knife in his mouth, and it sent him into a trance, one that Warren had been nervous to lift him from. He leaned forward, interested. Before, he hadn't cared about Lanny's past. Before, Lanny had been nothing to him but a student. But he had wanted to confide in Lanny, and still did. He was starting to view Lanny as a younger brother of sorts, and Warren wanted to know the life Lanny led before he become such.

"Please, Lanny, do elaborate."

Jodee decided to go outside and find anyone who could explain to her where she was. She went up to one of the workmen she saw and gasped at his appearance. She tried to mask it as a yawn so that she wouldn't appear rude. His eyes were slits and almost glowed yellow in color. His skin looked like he was covered in water or oil, yet she could see nothing dripping. His teeth all ended in points, like he could tear through any kind of flesh within seconds. She started to take a couple of steps back, suddenly scared.

"Ma'am, are you okay?" The soothing baritone of his voice caught her by surprise.

"Uh…" she couldn't conjure up any words.

"You don't look so well. Maybe you need to go see a doctor, or lay out some? Visit a sauna? You look about all dried up, I'm sorry to say."

He was kind, even though she was too nervous to look him straight in the face. Her body broke out in goose bumps despite the sweat that spread along its surface. "W-where am I?" She finally mustered.

He raised his thick eyebrows in concern. "You're in America. . ." he was confused by the question.

"No, but where in America? Am I in Greenville?" She noticed that the word had no meaning to him. "South Carolina?" She tried.

"I've never heard of those things," he said, "but you should really go see a doctor. We are in America."

"But where am I? What part of America?" She shrieked and it echoed on the streets.

"The south," he responded.

"Can you go on? South what?"

"The southern plot of America? Town 12 to be exact."

"South America?" She asked incredulously. "But I live in North America. And what is 'Town 12?' I've never heard of that."

The workman looked her up and down. "Well, that makes sense. You probably live in Town one hundred something if you're from up north. But I've never heard anyone refer to it as South America as if it's its own separate continent. It's the *southern* America. We are just a bit lower than you folks up there in the northern parts of America. You can talk to some

162

other folks around here who may know a bit more about the old cities and towns and countries and consonants or whatever from years and years and years ago, but I'm not gonna be able to give you those answers because I never went to school to learn all that bullshit."

She could see that he was starting to lose patience with her geographical questions, and that brought her to the next question. "And what is that? All of that you're cleaning up?"

The workman started to look a bit agitated, "Look lady. You're here, just like the rest of us. I don't know how to simplify it for you. As for all this? You act like you've never seen shed skin before."

"Like. . . snakeskin?" She felt terror creep over her as she looked at the size of the vacant skins and thought about the snakes that must have filled them prior.

"Excuse me? That is just rude, lady. We don't call or poke fun of mutants like you. Callin' us snakes. Come on now. We may have snakelike traits, but that doesn't make us snakes!"

"Mutants like me? Seriously? What the fuck?"

"I can see that sweat pourin' down your face. You obviously are one of those unevolved that run scared up north because you're not equipped to handle the world as it changes. But let me tell you, there's not many of you left and Mother Nature will eventually wipe you out, hate to give it to you so straight but I don't take kindly to insults. Now get on your way, go to the Tip if you have to. Find you some nice 65-70 degree weather if you can," he chuckled and turned his back on her.

She began to walk away in a daze. The sun glared down on her in an unforgivable way as if with a vendetta. Jodee's head initially began to lighten, like it would fill with air and abandon her "unequipped" body. All at once, it seemed to fill with lead and then introduced her to the ground.

When she opened her eyes, the bright light greeted her. She thought it could possibly be the tunnel of light to Heaven of which everyone spoke. But it burned her eyes, blinding her, and she sat up in the middle of cracked concrete that singed her bare legs. She was not going to Heaven. Her past finally caught up to her and brought her to this Hell.

The thoughts from Jodee's mind almost seem to pour out of Lanny's mouth and into Warren's ears at the same exact moment. The combination of their two memories seeking that day together connected them across dimensions in that time, though they would never know it. They could only feel the increased sharpness of their brain recalling something that was once so distant for one, and a constant dream for the other.

Jodee Pape listened to her parents fighting. She gazed at her little brother whom she'd finally soothed to sleep with soft music from her Boom box. But she still had to listen and could no longer take it. She gazed down at her fingernails, at her cuticles that were torn apart. She pulled on her stringy blonde hair, yanking until clumps broke free into her hands. She'd separated them from their roots, what they had always known, and nothing changed. The hair was still dead, but it was also still there. Each time one of her parents' voices slammed its way past her closed door, she pulled again. She would not be able to take this much longer.

A few hours later, Lanny Pape sat there, licking his knife like the spoon of batter. Jodee turned to him swiftly.

"Lanny, I love you. You will always have me," she swallowed and looked at their parents. "Are you done licking the spoon?" Lanny stuck the knife in his mouth to the handle, defying any gag reflex, and pulled it out clean. He nodded while refusing his tears the privilege of sliding down his baby-soft cheek.

"Take it away, Jodee."

Jodee gently pulled the steak knife from his grasp. It was the same knife that had been set on the oval oak table through multiple family dinners. She placed the clean knife back into her mother's blood, drowning it in its thickness. She then put it back in the side of her father's neck and left it there. Jodee shook off her mother's cleaning glove and left it in the stickiness between their two bodies. The blood from both ran together and joined beautifully between them, connecting them after death.

"Now cry, Lanny. Let me take you to your room, and we can cry together." Lanny granted a fat tear permission to fall down his flushed cheek. "Lanny, what happened?" She asked.

"Dad. . . and Mom… they killed themselves, they left us." He looked at his big sister with widened eyes, pupils enlarged. They almost popped out of his head like a pug's. "Jodee?"

"Yeah, Lanny?"   .

"What's going to happen now?" He stared, mesmerized by her red-stained hands, worried only for her future and not his own.

"Now, Lanny? Now, hopeful- well, someone *will* adopt us both, together. If not, well, when I am eighteen, I will adopt you myself. And, and everything will be fine. I promise. I'll always be here for you."

As she spoke, red and blue lights began to dance on her face in a brilliant ballet. She pulled her little brother close and gave him a tight squeeze. The police were in the house moments later, and then in the room with the children of the deceased.

"Disgusting," one of the officers mumbled, "that they'd leave their kids like this. It is absolutely selfish."

Warren held on to each word that Lanny said. As Lanny spoke, a ghost of a smile played on his lips. The memory that was being replayed was one of Lanny's fondest and last with his big sister. It was clear that he favored it because he saw what Jodee did as heroic act for the benefit of Lanny. When Lanny finished, a heavy silence hung over the room. Warren was for once unsure what to say next and Lanny was not quite ready to leave the cloud of memory where his sister's words echoed forever, 'Lanny, I love you. You will always have me.'

"So, she's coming here?" Warren broke the silence with his handy knife used for cutting the tension. "When's the last you saw her, fella?" He asked softly.

Lanny reluctantly focused back on the present. "I guess it was the time she brought me to Olive Garden. When she left me even further behind to go play soccer."

CHAPTER 8

Before Warren could respond, there was a quick knock at the door. Lanny turned to Warren with the same look a girl might give her mother before going on her first date. Lanny rose from the couch and walked to the door. He felt as if he were moving underwater, and his gut was pulling him backwards. Without checking the peephole he opened the door.

On the other side, Jo stood, with tears already brimming her eyelids. The doorway was only opened enough to show a third of her brother's body, but it was there. He was there, and alive. She lifted him into the air and gave him a whirl around.

Lanny's arms stayed tight to their sides while enclosed in Jo's grip. She squeezed him hard, to the point that it felt like she was crushing his lungs. He was…confused. He'd been expecting her of course, but not this excited a version. To be so wanted just threw him off guard. Nobody ever really wanted him.

Jo set her brother back on the ground and stepped back to survey him. It was her brother all right, albeit a much scrawnier version. But it was in a body that was not savagely destroyed. It was just as pathetically unevolved as the last one, but Jo didn't hold that against him. She grabbed his face in her hands and again felt the urge to squeeze out her excitement.

While Jo held Lanny's face so close, he noticed how different she looked. She had abandoned the jet-black hair that she began dying as a teenager; instead white-blond hair spilled from her scalp and almost seemed to glow. Her pupils were narrow and looked like a deflating balloon while the rest of the eyes were filled with army green. He wondered if she had taken to wearing special contacts. Her skin looked moist, but smooth. She was different, but she was his sister. "Jodee, I cannot believe you're here!" He exclaimed.

"Lanny, I've missed you so much. The world isn't the same without you!" She embraced him again and then, as an afterthought, added, "Also, please call me Jo."

Lanny pulled his sister into the home and shut the door behind her. Jo looked around the room, pleased. This place was much lighter than Jodee's had been. The windows were left naked to allow the sun entrance into the home. Her pivoting tour halted when her eyes landed on Warren Worth.

Warren couldn't move from his perch on the leather chair. He had never seen someone so beautiful, nor so captivating. He wanted to speak but felt even he was not strong enough to pry his jaw from the floor.

"Who is this?" Jo asked Lanny though keeping a distrustful gaze on Warren.

"Jodee- Jo. This is Warren Worth. He's taken me under his wing, like an older brother," Lanny said with a wide grin. He couldn't believe how lucky he was, sharing a room with the two people he loved most in the world *at the same time!* He wanted to be pinched, but instead he slid his hand into his pocket and pricked his thumb on the safety pin. Lanny pulled his hand from his pants and eyed the ruby red bubble that was forming from the puncture. It was real.

"Much older, by the looks of it." Jo noticed the faint lines and crow's feet on Warren's handsome face.

Warren finally found his voice, and footing, and stood to greet his soul mate. "Jo, I'm Warren. I've heard so much about you." He offered her a strong hand and left out that the majority of what he'd heard about her had just been said moments prior to her arrival.

Jo stared vacantly at the hand Warren offered, unsure what to do. She did not like him, which she could tell right away. So she ignored his reach and took a seat on Lanny's sofa. She initially sat down in the middle but realized there wasn't enough space for her brother; so she scooted over and pulled him down to join her.

Lanny was oblivious to Jo's disinclination to Warren, but Warren could see and feel it clear as anything. It was almost like she was sending waves of hate toward him. But that would not act as deterrence. For Warren, it was only a new challenge. Noel and her treason to their unborn baby had, for the moment, left his mind.

"So, how did you get here?" Lanny asked.

"A cab," Jo smiled at her younger brother. "I'm sorry it took me so long." For Jo and Lanny, this meant completely different things. But one thing remained in common, and that was how devastatingly long it had taken. Warren sensed all of this transpiring through the room and let himself out, allowing the two to reconnect.

CHAPTER 9

Purdy and Jenson sat in the office next to a pile of folders, each containing active cases in which they reached dead ends, quite a few now cold. They pulled page after page to see if they could find any link between the suspects. The MOs were all over the place: one girl who was drugged, one stabbed in the neck (and in the eye with her own hair tool), a druggie who could have overdosed himself but held a missing flap of skin in the perfect shape of a jigsaw piece, etcetera.

"I don't know, man." Jenson looked at his partner. "Do you still believe these are somehow connected? This is a bit outlandish."

"I'm not sure. But I don't want to give this up. I really think if we can catch the guy for one murder, we have him for all. If it is the one guy, and he has killed this many people, he's got to be one proud son of a bitch. I bet we find pictures of all his victims tucked away in a box under his bed in place of a stack of Playboys.

"Miranda should be here soon. We can see what she makes of all this." Purdy put his head back down, straining to find any kind of link. On cue, the red head and her heels marched into the room. She pulled up her own chair and sat with the men at Purdy's desk, which was previously cleared save for all of the case files. She grabbed each without a word and began to flip through them.

Morgan and Brian looked at each other and shrugged, then leaned back to wait on what her conclusion could be. As she scanned each page, her eyebrows drew together in fierce concentration. She would randomly smirk here and there, and the men had no idea on how to interpret that. Purdy realized she wasn't going to talk, or share the folders, until she read them all cover to cover, so he nudged Brian and said, "We're gonna go grab some food."

Miranda's eyes only flicked left to right as she continued reading. "Want anything?" Purdy asked. Her lack of response was answer enough and the two men ambled away, letting her try to make something of the mess.

When the two returned, wiping sandwich crumbs from their chests that landed on their slightly protruding stomachs, Purdy's more so than Jenson's, Miranda had produced her own little folder that she covered with notes. She noticed them and gave them a look of irritation. "Well, sit down," she commanded.

The men did as they were told without a complaint. Miranda gave them a few seconds to adjust to a comfortable position and find their focus before releasing her spiel. She loved doing her spiel. In every case, it was her time to shine and show what she knew. Nobody was better at putting puzzles together than she.

"Okay," she began when both men gave her solid eye contact, "assuming it is one murderer, a serial killer, he or she is an impressive one. Among the many other things, he made one body disappear, drugged another supposedly in public and unsuspected, and has the skilled hand of a surgeon. The last is in reference to that jigsaw cut when I met you guys at the scene of

Hernandez. As for the girl, Amanda, the curling iron shoved into her eye isn't what killed her, obviously, it was the knife that perfectly punctured her carotid artery.

"The work was done by someone who knew what he or she was doing on all accounts. Getting rid of a body undetected, someone like us can do no problem. All the crime scenes were organized, aside from the ones that appeared deliberately disorganized, like that of Hernandez. Little to no evidence of our unsub was left behind."

"So this person is obviously educated in some way," Morgan said.

"Extremely. The fact that he or she almost always takes the murder weapon is another thing to consider. We never recovered the knife that jabbed Amanda's neck. Another interesting note is that one of her pillowcases was missing, an odd thing to take indeed. Also I would like to point out that the majority of the murders have taken place in Atlanta, followed by towns on the outskirts like Athens, Georgia. I have a guy looking into unsolved murders in other parts of the state; he's going through all the clippings he can find and will have a list of towns for us within the next couple of days."

"So what kind of person are we focusing on here, Miranda?" Jenson asked.

"Based on what I see, it is an educated person in the Atlanta area. However, this person is insecure. Smart, but not the smartest and embarrassed by that fact. He's complicated, wants to believe he's God but knows he isn't. This person could either surround himself with a lot of lesser educated people *or* people of higher education to feel like he is of the same caliber. Again, that does not mean this person is 'dumb.' He, well or she I guess, clearly takes the time to study what he needs to know in order to do his bidding. Could be a parent or teacher that told him he was stupid his whole life and wouldn't amount to anything, something like that.

"There were deliberate leavings and takings at each crime scene, and the extended knowledge necessary for knowing how and when to administer a drug undetected, where to stab a person, how to get rid of a body, how to make it look like an accident, etcetera. This person likes to play God. And what kinds of people are known for that? The suspect could potentially be a surgeon, or there's the possibility that he is one of us. Someone on the force. I want to look through background checks of all surgeons in the area and leave you guys to search for any flags on men and women who wear the uniform. It's going to be a bit like salespeople doing cold calls at first, but it's the only way to begin.

"I'm leaning toward the perp being a male, but I don't want to solidly say that yet. It's also someone experienced enough, and I reckon that he or she is in their early forties to mid-fifties. However, back to that puzzle piece, that was cheesy and unoriginal. While this guy knew what he was doing when it came to cuts and killing, he missed the mark on that Caster girl. He's clearly unaware when it comes to drugs and lethal amounts. As you recall, a moment ago I said that it is possibly a surgeon. Well, a surgeon would have that sort of drug knowledge. In which case, he might have purposefully overdone it to throw us off any scent," Miranda sat back, satisfied.

Jenson looked up from his pad full of notes. "We can handle all that. And keep our eyes out for any suspicious activity, of course. If we find this guy, two things will happen."

"What's that, Brian?" Purdy asked.

"Well, the good thing, we'll have taken a crazy killer off the streets."

"And the bad?"

"We are going to be severely punished for the Colby kid situation." Jenson sighed and rubbed his forehead. Morgan knew that his partner was thinking of the forceful way in which he had made Colby confess in order to close the case. Purdy was wrapping his head around the point Miranda made, that either this guy didn't know anything when it came to drug administration, or he knew everything and was clever-minded enough to make himself look like an amateur. He felt the beginnings of a headache trying to consider the many possibilities.

"I also pulled some case files from the past ten years, all of the unsolved homicides, as well as DOA's that were inconclusive. Let's head down to the evidence room and pull what was taken from each scene, see if there's anything we can make sense of. Come along, boys." Miranda stood and turned from Jenson's desk. The two men followed without hesitation. They jumped into the Crime Scene Unit van without bothering to buckle for the one-minute drive.

When they got down to the bleak, basement-type evidence storage unit, Miranda leapt out of the van and clicked her way inside. There was a stack of folders under one of her arms. She found her way to a steel table and separated the folders into three stacks. "Look at the Chain-of-Custody sheets inside of each. They should all be up to date, and the items will be in the boxes from 2003 onward." She gestured toward a wall that had shelves holding hundreds of cardboard boxes. They seemed to be never-ending as they crept around a corner and continued on into a back room.

Miranda pulled on a pair of latex gloves and offered the box with size Large gloves to the men. Jenson shook his head, but Purdy grabbed a pair. The three took their stacks and began sliding boxes off of the shelves, pulling the evidence from each, and putting it in neat piles on tables in the spacious center of the room. Jenson jumped when he found a dead rat inside of one from 2007. He slid away from the box while Miranda and Purdy were bent over their own and slid on a pair of gloves. The majority of the boxes held dead beetles and pieces of stretched out webs vacated by the previous eight-legged tenants. When they pulled all of the evidence from each case, they surveyed the contents on the table. There was not much to be pulled from each, a rare thing for murders, which usually came with a plethora of items to be collected.

They began to sift through each pile. There was a wallet with the homicide from 2011 that belonged to Martin Forrester. It had been staged to look like a suicide, he was found hanging in his living room, but later reopened as a possible homicide. The autopsy had confirmed that the man was dead before he was tied up and left to hang. Purdy flipped through the contents of the wallet. He found a Triple A card, a few credit cards, a business card from a bartender, six bucks cash, and one of those cards that you punch a hole in each time you purchase something from the mall pretzel shop. He had been one punch short from getting a free soft pretzel.

"I'll be honest, I don't know what I am looking for," Purdy announced to the others.

Miranda looked up from a pile that was from a 2004 murder. "Connections. And I've found one. I remember working this scene. I don't know why I didn't remember this before." She held up a stained, lilac pillowcase that was inside a sealed plastic bag. "We only collected this pillowcase, the other one was missing, stripped from the pillow. Just like the Halkwicks scene."

"So, looks like our boy's been busy a while now," Jenson said. "Jesus Christ. One guy, all this time." He gave a low whistle.

Lanny had left his sister in his apartment and went grocery shopping for the first time in months. His sister was ravenous and all that graced his cabinet shelves were cans of soup. He picked up everything he could think of, things that they had loved as children. There was a jumbo-sized box of brown sugar cinnamon pop tarts, a twelve-pack of both Coca-Cola and Dr. Pepper, bologna, turkey, and three packs of bacon.

Jo jumped at the sound of the door opening. Her brother walked in and she relaxed, but only slightly. She dreaded the return of the man named Warren and felt ill at the prospect of meeting again. She rose from the pea-green couch and helped

Lanny unload everything into the kitchen. At the sight of the bacon, Jo licked her lips greedily.

"I'll put some in a frying pan right away!" Lanny promised his sister, noticing the way she eyed the meat. He also noticed she was too hungry to wait and slid the bologna toward Jo, along with a can of Coke. "Here," he said, "a snack while you wait for your snack."

Jo laughed at this and pulled a piece of bologna from the package. She sucked it into her mouth in one bite and washed it down with the crisp soda.

As Lanny turned on the stove, he wiped his forehead onto the back of his hand. Beads of sweat broke out all over his face. He checked the thermostat and saw that the room was set to a staggering ninety degrees. "Damn it," he cursed. "Jo, I'm so sorry. My air conditioner must be broken. I'll call my landlord right away."

"Don't," she said, "I, I was so cold. I'm sorry Lanny. I changed it. You can set it a little lower, I'm feeling a bit better now." Lanny raised his pale eyebrows in surprise and bumped the thermostat down to a compromising eighty degrees. He stripped off his shirt and returned to the kitchen in just his undershirt. Jo tittered at his paleness. Some things would be the same, no matter the universe. The bacon began to crackle, and Lanny flipped it onto Jo's plate. Without waiting for them to cool, Jo grabbed a handful of bacon and put it straight into her mouth. Lanny flinched, expecting to hear a squeal of surprise from Jo's skin burning at the touch of the bacon, but she emitted no such thing. There were only groans of satisfaction coming from his sister. She finished the bacon and looked at Lanny expectantly, asking him with her eyes to cook some more. Lanny threw some more strips onto the pan and laughed to himself. Jo sure had worked up an appetite.

"So you were in town with your team for a game?" Lanny asked.

"Huh?" Jo managed between bites.

"You know, with the soccer team."

"Oh, oh right. Yes. But I felt it was more important that I spend time with you."

"Well, when do you have to go back? Is the game tomorrow or Sunday?"

Jo ignored the distracting glow from her cell phone. "Umm, I think it is tomorrow."

The phone continued to buzz and glow to the point of pure irritation for Jo. "Fucking hell," she muttered as she answered the phone. The caller ID read Kaitlyn Rice.

"Hello?" Jo couldn't keep the annoyance from her voice.

"Coach?" Kaitlyn sounded timid.

"What is it?" Jo asked.

"Well, I just heard from Tony that you left. He said you hadn't been feeling well…" the girl trailed off.

"Yes? And?"

Kaitlyn was caught off guard by the impatience in Jo's voice. "Well, are you coming back? Before the game I mean? Tony said he's been trying your phone and you haven't been answering him."

179

Jo looked at her brother standing over the stove and popping bacon when a feeling of nostalgia crept through her. "You know what? Let's call this my official resignation. I think I'm done with coaching."

Kaitlyn was shocked by what she was hearing and at that moment wished she had stayed in the room with the other girls listening in on speakerphone instead of doing it all alone on the stairwell. "You- you're joking. Right?"

"No, no I am not much of a joker, Kaitlyn."

"But, you're the one who recruited in me! You believed in me! You said you had big plans for me! You can't leave me now, Jodee. You can't leave this team. I'm sorry I messed up and came into the season unfit, but I am ready to prove myself to everyone else now. Please, please don't do this."

"Well, sounds like you've got all the stuff. Do let the assistant coach know that he's in charge, will you?" Jo hung up the phone on paralyzed Kaitlyn Rice.

"You're staying?" Lanny inflated with excitement. Jo turned her attention toward her brother.

"Yes, Lan, I will be staying with you."

Lanny threw some more bacon down for his sister then ran off to change the sheets on his bed. He would give her his bedroom and take the couch for himself. As he stripped the sheets, he heard a hearty burp echo into the bedroom. Lanny grinned and felt himself shake with excitement. There was so much going for him. The desk drawer called to him and he went to it. He pulled it open slowly, lengthening the build-up. Lanny took in the sight of all his treasures and ran his fingers over them. Amazingly, he did not nick a finger on any of the sharp objects. He felt the energy they held from each special moment.

Lanny heard his sister's footsteps and closed the drawer much faster than he had opened it. "Jo, you can sleep in here," he said while leaning against the desk.

"Are you sure? I'll be fine on the couch," Jo said thinking of the large window in that room.

"Please, I *want* you to stay in here, Sis."

Jo shrugged and spied a window in the room. The sun was going down but at least it would be able to shine through on its morning schedule. "Fine, that'll be just fine. Thank you. I think I'll retire for a little while; this day has absolutely wiped me out," Jo said, and it was not untrue. Lanny nodded and left the room, closing the door gently behind him. He figured he could meet up with Warren. It just dawned on him that Warren had shown up to his house for some reason or another before Jo had. He felt a mixture of worried excitement- worried that he might be in trouble for something and excited that it might be about their next victim.

He called up his mentor who bid Lanny to come by his apartment. Lanny was shocked with excitement, for he had never been inside Warren's home. He had only seen it from the outside. There was nothing extraordinary about it. It was in a nice complex with nice cars parked all around, but that was it. The place was nice, if not a little dull and repetitious, like a cookie-cutter suburbia before entering the real suburbs with a family. But he knew that the monotony would stop as soon as he opened Warren's door.

Jodee found her way back to the apartment, which she had been forced in to. Like it or not, it seemed to be her home. Just like a cell became the home to its prisoner. She had left the door unlocked merely because she could not figure out how it worked. It was a plain door, albeit very tall, and silver, like you would describe the walk-in cooler of a restaurant. The "handle" barely stuck out from the door, and there was no apparent lock to it. It worked like a button, all she had to do was give it a slight push and the door gave way to her cell. Jodee let herself in and shut the door. She immediately collapsed to the ground in tears but found relief from the slight coolness the floor had to offer.

Just as she was beginning to sniffle from her fetus-position, there came a knock at the door. It boomed around the room, like the sound of a bomb exploding outside of a shelter. Jodee trembled at the thought of who it could be. Maybe it was the true owner of the apartment, but for some reason she did not believe that to be the case. In a weird way, the place forced her to be its owner in a way a scraggly puppy with big eyes on the road would work its magic on a little boy. This was no puppy, yet it still held some kind of effect on her. She could feel the acceptance in the air and worried for a second that the walls would close in to give her a hug.

The booming did not cease, and then a female voice rang through in between knocks. "Jo! Open up! Where have you been, I thought we were going hunting today? I took the rabbit all for myself and that is what you deserve!"

The voice sounded friendly enough, yet Jodee still wished for the door to have just a peephole so that she could see whom she was opening to. She pressed her ear against the cold door, took a moment to appreciate its touch, and then listened for the voice again. Instead came the startling slam of a knock.

"Jo, seriously open up. Are you okay? I haven't been able to get a hold of you."

Jodee never went by Jo in her life, but that was close enough to Jodee. And the voice seemed concerned, and like a friend. She decided to let the woman in and pushed the button that had slid in and poked out on the inside of the apartment now.

The door opened quickly, and the woman stepped inside. She immediately gave Jodee a once over and grinned, showing off fangs for teeth. Her eyes were not as frightening as the workers outside, but her skin gleamed in intricate patterns that, in Jodee's world, would have been something to avoid eye contact with out of respect for the skin disease that it must be. Her skin was a pale pink with deeper tones of the color in splotches lining her arms and neck.

"Oh my Lanza," the woman said, "She actually did it! I can't believe that Medusa pulled it off!"

"I'm sorry?" Jodee asked uncertainly.

"Why on earth she would want to go to such a disgusting, low-level place is beyond me. Well of course I know *why*, but that wouldn't be enough for me. Still, the fact that she did it," the woman paused from her monologue to look at Jodee again, as if still not believing what she was seeing. "This is just… incredible. No wonder I couldn't get through to her telepathically." She finished and stared at Jodee with her eyes that also cast a pretty pale pink sheen.

"Can you please just tell me, who is Medusa? And who are you?"

"Well, of course the real Medusa is a mythical creature with snakes for her hair," she giggled, "and I only use it in jest when describing Jo. I believe it's what your kind would use as an affectionate 'bitch.'

"As for me, my name is Celestria, Jo's best friend, and descended from the Grand Canyon Pink Rattlesnake." She grinned, showing off her sharp, shiny teeth.

"What the fuck is going on," Jodee muttered to herself. She had no idea of anything this Celestria was saying and just wanted to wake up from the nightmare she was evidently in. There was no way this was real life, extremely lifelike, yes, but not *real*.

"I can understand your confusion. I'll sum it up," Celestria began to answer Jodee's muttering even though it was clearly a rhetorical question, "Jo is my best friend. But, she's also you."

"Are you saying I have dissociative identity disorder? Because I've never met you in my life, that I can remember."

Celestria chuckled, "No, no, no. Oh, you poor thing. You haven't met me in your life, but you've met me in hers. Also yours, but a different one than you've been experiencing."

"Is this a riddle? Can you please not belittle me and be serious or leave."

"Oh, calm down please. I'll take it slow. Just sit, okay? Because this is obviously going to take a lot of explanation. Oh, and fetch me a blanket, would you? You've got the temperature set awfully low in here," Celestria shivered.

Jodee obliged and tossed a blanket from the bedroom to the woman. She sat down on the steel chair, and Celestria sat opposite to her.

"Please, begin," Jodee gestured in a let's get on with this motion.

"Well, I want to see how much you know. What year is it for you, exactly?"

"2013."

"Holy, holy Lanza. Okay. Well, you've at least had to have heard of Robert Lanza, correct? I believe he first published around that time."

"Sorry, no. I have no idea who that is."

"Wow. Okay. Well, simply put, he is the Father of Biocentrism."

"Biocentrism," Jodee rolled the word around in her mouth, "I think I have heard of that. It's what celebrities do; they freeze themselves or something. To be honest, I don't know much about it."

"No, my dear, you are thinking of scientology, which is absolutely laughable. Biocentrism is basically the belief, and truth by the way as we now know, that it is consciousness that creates the universe. I think in your time it was believed to be the opposite, and you creatures had beliefs in such things as gods and wizards."

Jodee tried not to be offended by this as she was a Christian. "We believe in evolution too," she came back with a hostile edge in her voice.

"Well, snaps for you," Celestria rubbed her thumb against her middle finger in a condescending way. "Anyway, Lanza says that the body receives consciousness. He says that there are multiple universes, well really infinite, and they all exist simultaneously. So really, there's infinite yous as well."

Jodee felt like she was back in Philosophy 101. She remembered how difficult it was to change her way of thinking to adapt to the course, and it was something she had not kept up with over the years. She could already feel her brain twisting in preparation to flip upside down. "I'm going to play along with this nonsense, because as soon as it's over I can wake up. What all does this have to do with me being here?"

"It's kind of a long story. I wish Jo had warned me that she was doing it so that I could have avoided coming here."

Jodee couldn't believe how blunt this woman was. "Just talk."

"I really wish you could use your telepathy, it's so much easier to transfer information that way."

"Well sorry I'm not some kind of clairvoyant," Jodee said, annoyed.

"No, apologize for being too ignorant to be aware of how unevolved you are. Anyway, your brother, Lanny, died here-"

"He lived this long?" Jodee asked, shocked.

"This would be a lot easier if you just shut up and listen. Evolution gave you two ears and one mouth, yet you seem to use your mouth twice as much. So, Lanny died in our universe. It was murder, I don't really know the details. I just know that Jo was completely heartbroken by it. All she wanted was to be reunited with her kid brother, and then seek vengeance.

"So, based on biocentrism, you can die in one universe, but only the body really dies. The consciousness cannot be created or destroyed. It simply merges with consciousness in another universe. They converge and grow ever stronger, but it is all the same. So, when you regain consciousness after dying, you enter a world that is similar to what you remember as your own.

"Jo is brilliant. She wanted to find her brother, so she had to find a universe that his consciousness traveled to. There are infinite ones, of course, but some are held closer than others. Think of wavelengths, we use them to describe every type of relationship or comparison these days. She needed to find a universe that was matched perfectly to ours, to which the peaks hit at the exact same rhythm. Perfect compatibility would be a universe in which the peak hits as our trough does. That would be good for peering into the world, but not actually *travelling* to it.

"You see, what Jo did has literally never been done. I thought she was driving herself crazy trying to find a way to do it. Before I saw you, I'd thought she had finally gone off the deep end and chanced killing herself, hoping she'd wake up in a similar enough universe to where Lanny still existed.

"For some reason, your universe is attuned to ours. So, Jo was able to travel to 2013 by switching places with you." Celestria smiled, she felt quite pleased with herself and wondered if she should go back to school to become a history teacher.

"That doesn't make any sense. For one thing, this is obviously the future of my world and not some alternate universe. So, I think what you're talking about is time-travel, but she wouldn't have needed to switch places with me," Jodee said.

"Ah, the frivolous concept of time once again rears its ugly head. No, she did not travel through time. The past, present, and future as they're titled all exist simultaneously and are ongoing. Lanza likes to use a record player as an example. Humans can only experience time linearly, like an arrow. But, when you use a record player, you can stop it at any point in the beginning, middle, or end of the song and the music is still there. Just because we cannot fully experience this as the needle in one part at a time does not mean it isn't true. You could also think of it as a video player that is broken up frame by frame."

"I'm not even going to try to process all of that right now. Next question, *how* could she switch places with me?"

Celestria giggled behind her palm, "I'm going to assume that you have tried lysergic acid diethylamide, and I realize that it is taboo in your society."

"Lysergic acid... LSD?" Jodee asked, incredulous.

"Yes! LSD."

"That's just a hallucinogen," Jodee pointed out.

"Yes... and no. You see, many drugs are used to enhance senses that you didn't even know you have. I think... if I can remember my lessons correctly, your world leaders at the time had them all illegal to better keep you under their thumbs. I think it was also to save you from yourselves becausethey feared many of you would experience overstimulation and have a mass freak-out creating the end of your world.

"We now believe in a moderate, day-to-day intake of small doses in our air supply because we believe in experiencing every part of our consciousness. And oftentimes, the only way to do that is through drug use."

"This is insane," Jodee exclaimed, "there is no way all of this is real. You guys are all about evolution, apparently, but LSD and drugs like it are manmade!"

"That doesn't mean it's not the product of evolution. Initially, when humans were nothing more than mongoloids dragging their knuckles along the ground, the only kind of adaptations they had were purely physical. This is much like the evolution of birds and their beaks. But evolution has become more about the mental game.

"I guess you could say even evolution has evolved, the adaptations used to center on the physical, now it is more about the mental."

"Okay, so you guys can sense more. I'm still not seeing the whole picture," Jodee was growing frustrated.

Celestria, equally as frustrated, continued, "Well, if you were able to use LSD, then you could peer into other universes in the same way that we can peer into yours. And, if you were snooping at the exact moment Jo was, then the connection can be formed. It is quite difficult to do, like I said before, nearly impossible, because most people on LSD avoid looking in reflective surfaces. It isn't as exhausting and terrifying when you have a supplemented amount of LSD put into your system each day, but I'm guessing yours was a lot taken at once, causing a panic within you.

"So, when you looked in the mirror, good ole Jo was looking back. She's told me about you, the things she's seen and heard. She said you're never around your brother, but you talk about him on rare occasions. She said you are doing nothing with your life but slaving away to a career and watching the television. Jo said you have a barely-there relationship with another human, and hardly any friends that come to your house. She doesn't like you at all, really," Celestria looked thoughtful.

"Well, I don't think I like her much either!" Jodee felt the old fury building up inside of her. "How do I get back to my world?"

"Like I've said multiple times, seriously don't you listen, it is nearly impossible. You would have to up your intake of the drug if you wanted to switch fast or live here long enough to where it becomes part of your system. Then, you'd have to catch Jo's eyes looking in the mirror at the same time you are. The mirror can act as a portal, but it's more like a window, between consciousnesses.

"But if Jo wants to be there, and stay there, then I doubt she'll be looking in any reflection long enough for you to make a connection, or at all. And in the off chance that she did, you would have to physically fight her and pull her back to this side as you went to yours and she's a tough Medusa. Basically, you don't have a chance. You're stuck here."

Jodee blinked hopelessly at this realization. The majority of what Celestria had said went in one ear and out the other, but that last bit hit her like a truck. "Get out," she pointed at the door.

Celestria shrugged and walked toward the door, realizing she was far too impatient to ever become a teacher. "You may want to move as far north as you can get," she called over her shoulder.

CHAPTER 10

Lanny thud his clumsy fist against Warren's front door only twice. On his third wind-up the door opened. Warren looked at Lanny's closed fist that was ready to strike again and smirked, amused.

"Thanks for coming," he said and stood back, allowing Lanny to walk inside. Lanny was expecting to see a place that was decorated in either completely black or completely white furnishings and accents. He thought that there would be cold, informal statues watching and judging his every move, and perhaps a weapons room somewhere in the back. Instead, he walked into a warm environment. It resembled something a suburban mother would cook up, followed by the scent of cookies baking in the oven.

Lanny did smell something sweet and wondered bewilderedly if Warren had decided to bake him some cupcakes. The vanilla smell came from the candles that sat on Warren's heavy, antiqued coffee table. Warren's couch looked even more inviting than Lanny's favorite pea-green sag; it was a large, rich brown piece with leather that was perfectly worn in and rustic. Plants covered enough of the room space to the point that Lanny thought he would see a butterfly flutter past. On the mantel of the painted-to-look-aged armoire there were three different photographs. One was of a dashing couple kissing on their wedding day, and for a brief moment Lanny puzzled over whether the man in the photo was Warren and if his mentor had lost a lover at some point. On closer look, he could see it was a man who only resembled Warren, holding a beautiful blonde woman in a romantic embrace, scratched into the frame read 'Dr. and Mrs. Worth.' The other photo showed a young boy between the same couple, the man and woman were a bit older now. The last was of that boy who was now just coming into his manhood. Lanny could see Warren's handsome features despite the awkwardness that plagues every preteen. Warren's arms were clasped around a Newfoundland's neck, partially hidden by the thick fur that lined the beast. His smile in that photograph was one that Lanny had never seen on Warren's face, nobody had in a long while. It was one of pure, simple happiness.

"His name was Duke," Warren said from over Lanny's shoulder. It entered his ear almost in a whisper, with a touch of nostalgia.

"He's a handsome one," Lanny responded correctly and nodded to emphasize the point. He had never pegged Warren for an animal-loving kind of guy.

"And smart," Warren said in a defensive tone that changed to one of a wistful nature, "He didn't need all the commands. He understood the way I spoke, the way I moved. Fella, I swear we communicated telepathically half of the time."

Lanny gave the photograph one more respectful nod and then turned to face Warren straight on.

"Warren, I've been thinking about our next victim. He or she has to have a specific characteristic, but it is one that is easy to find. I think-"

"She really fucked me over big time," Warren interrupted Lanny. He collapsed on the couch and his bare triceps made a fart-noise on the cushion.

The woman that was hit by the truck? Lanny was about to ask Warren who he was talking about, but he continued on his own.

"Lanny, I'm no spring chicken anymore. I know that. One of the most important parts of natural selection is reproduction to ensure the continuation of your own. I had that opportunity, to create another Worth, to create someone who I could train to be an even better version of me, a Warren 2.0 if you will.

"He was going to have both me and her to learn from. You can't do better than her as far as I'm concerned, at least for my needs. Yes, she holds the outer attraction, and believe me when I say the outward appearance of an animal does play a role in natural selection, but she was also brilliant in a way that I guess I can admit I am not. She is a neurosurgeon. Together we would have created the perfect child, an über-human that probably would have solved all the world's problems."

Warren paused again and Lanny wondered if he should say something or ask a question. He waited a moment and Warren continued to purge his anger.

"She wouldn't do it! She denied my seed nourishment, and I cannot bare to wait any longer!" Warren pounded his fist on the coffee table and the lucky bamboo plant atop it shivered.

"Who are we talking about?" Lanny asked quietly.

"Noel, but it doesn't fucking-matter, now does it? I just don't know what to do, Lan," both the men stiffened at the awkwardness of the attempted nickname but ignored it.

"She's a bitch, man," Lanny himself sounded awkward attempting to mimic the "guy-talk" from locker rooms growing up.

"Exactly, and I need one of those to continue on and create my legacy. This was just a big blow to me, you know?" Warren looked at Lanny expectantly. His deep blue eyes were completely unguarded.

"You can find someone better. Someone who is even more like you, more evolved as you might like to put it. Someone who understands the importance of, um, reproducing."

Warren nodded and thought about Jo. "I need a distraction," he said in a voice that was decidedly harder.

Lanny perked up at this, "I have an idea for our next victim!"

Warren tore his mind away from Lanny's sister and leaned forward, "Let's hear it, fella."

"Let's go find ourselves a smoker, a real chain-smoker," he said. "Every day I see a pair of damaged lungs, Chinese men and women that lost their lives because they couldn't put down that cancer stick. They knew the warnings before starting, most people do, yet they begin anyway.

"Why is that? I understand starting before you know the risks, but if you know what cigarettes can do, why would you begin smoking them in the first place? We have this large bin at The Exhibit, and it is filled with smoke cartons. Many of them are more than halfway full, so we feel like we are getting through to these people. Sure, the beginning fourth of the bin was filled with cartons the staff bought to get the ball rolling, because people are like sheep. They're more likely to start or stop something if everyone else is doing the same thing."

Warren grinned a rare smile that reached his eyes. He felt extremely proud of Lanny in that moment. His mentee came up with a fantastic idea for a target and backed it with facts that followed Warren's line of thinking and beliefs. Warren leaned forward and pulled Lanny into a hug, something he rarely, if ever, did.

Lanny had been enveloped twice in one day and had to hold back the amount of emotion he felt. He gave himself an imaginary pat on the back as Warren gave him a real one.

Warren pulled back and stood up, then straightened out his slightly wrinkled black shirt. It clung to his lean, muscular figure, but not in a way that was too "showy."

"Well, let's get a move on," Warren snapped his fingers and Lanny stood with a smile of his own.

"Where to, Boss?"

"Downtown. Like you said though, not someone who began smoking and got addicted before everyone became aware of the major possible side effects. Anyone up to age, hmm, let's say thirty-four? Honestly, though, I prefer younger. Smoking's not the worst thing. Just like walking home alone drunk isn't the worst thing. But it certainly isn't the best for you and that's all I need."

"Thirty-four and younger, got it. But wait, what about weed smokers?"

"What about them?"

"Should we include them in the pool? That's pretty bad for lungs too, isn't it?"

"Uh… I'm not…uh… let's just do regular smokers for now."

Lanny gave a small salute and followed Warren out the door. "But, what do you want to use to do it?"

"What part of the body does smoking usually target and kill?" Warren asked his student.

"The lungs."

"Right, so we are going to cut off his or her air supply!" Warren stood aside and let Lanny out the door, then locked the two locks behind them. "We'll take my car," he said, and the headlights of the matte black BMW blinked in greeting as it unlocked its doors.

"Purdy, come and look at this," Jenson called his partner over to his workspace. "I started with all of the doctors and surgeons in the Atlanta area, just checking their histories and background checks. I threw out the ones with non-violent crimes, you know speeding tickets and burglary type of stuff, and narrowed it down to these few."

Morgan looked at the list in front of him. Brian had printed the background checks of the three possibilities as well as blown up pictures of each. There were two men and one woman. The men looked like they could easily pass for a doctor or a senile old man. The woman, though, was devastatingly gorgeous.

"Noel Leach," Morgan murmured.

"Yeah, she's quite somethin'. Guess what she got locked up for."

"What?"

"She beat the hell out of her boyfriend when she was in college. Apparently, she found him using cocaine. She claimed her best friend died from it and that he knew it. He had to be hospitalized. She really hates drug use."

"Interesting," Morgan looked thoughtful, "what about the other two?"

"This guy, Dr. Shultz, he sexually assaulted his assistant. He was a psychiatrist, no longer practicing." The only thing that stood out about Shultz was his blinding white teeth. Other than that, his face looked like sweating clay.

Jenson tapped at the last photo, of an old man with white caterpillar eyebrows. "And this is Dr. Leonard Cross. He poisoned one of his own patients. Allegedly there may have been others he killed with medicine throughout his career, but there was only the proof of this one."

"He's not still locked up?"

"He was released about two years ago after serving fifteen years. Had a damn good lawyer, pleaded guilty due to negligence. Made it seem like the doc had no idea what he was doing, that he wasn't doing anything on purpose and killed the guy by accident."

"That's not surprising, rich old white guy getting off easy," Purdy huffed out his anger at the biased justice system.

"So, what do you think?" Jenson asked.

"That one girl, Rebecca Caster, was killed with a cocktail of drugs. That sounds like something our friend Cross would do. As well as Hernandez, the apparent overdose. I don't want to cross off Dr. Leach just yet, but I think we can knock off Dr. Shultz.

None of our victims were sexually assaulted or raped in any way. Even the girl we found in lingerie wasn't found to have been the victim of sexual assault."

"So, we should call them in, I guess. See if they'll come talk to us. Let's start with Dr. Cross."

Purdy let his eyes linger on their other suspect for a moment and nodded. "Bring him in."

Dr. Cross came in that same day, apparently excited to help in any way that he could. "I've been seeing all these headlines in the newspaper, boy oh boy, just terrible what has been going on these days!"

Purdy and Jenson glanced at each other. "That's right. Do you know about how long this has been going on?" Jenson asked innocently.

"I reckon a few months now, right?" Dr. Cross beamed, showing off his overlapping teeth and yellow smile.

"Well, it really seems to have been going on for just inside of a year now. Say, doc, when were you released?"

"Now, son, don't get all suspicious on me. I was released *two* whole years ago, and I've been a boy scout! Haven't done one thing, and the only time I did a thing was by accident!"

"Nobody's accusing you right now, Dr. Cross, we are just trying to look at this case from every angle. I know it was a little while back, but do you happen to know where you were on May tenth of this year?"

"Don't sell me a dog here, officer. May 10th? Do you know what day of the week that was?" Purdy was straining to understand the man through his thick southern accent.

"It was a Saturday, Dr. Cross," Jenson helped.

"A Saturday let me see let me see. Boys, don't get nervous, I'm going to go into my jacket pocket and pull out my planner."

Purdy chuckled and watched as the old man pulled a dated planner from inside his coat. It's binding was leathery and looked as worn as its owner. He watched as Leonard Cross licked his gnarled fingers and flipped through the pages. Cross finally landed on the desired page and jabbed it with his index finger.

"Yessir, right here. I was visiting my sister in Helen on that weekend."

"The entire weekend?" Purdy pressed.

"The whole thing. I was with her and the kids. Watched them go tubin'. But I didn't join in on that, water and inflatable tubes doesn't sound like much fun to me anymore."

"Would you mind if we gave your sister a call, to verify this alibi?" Jenson asked.

"You can call her up right now if you'd like." The old man turned to Purdy, who was taking down notes on a pad. "Hand that over, son, and I'll give yuh all her info. Address, telephone, husband's name, date of birth, whatever you need." He reached for the pad and pulled it out of Purdy's light grip, then proceeded to write down all of the information as promised.

"Well, uh," Purdy stuttered. He didn't see any reason to keep this man, who came in voluntarily and without a lawyer, then gave an alibi, any longer. "Jenson, you have anything else?"

"No, I'd say you're good to go Dr. Cross. Thank you for all of your cooperation."

"And thank you, gentlemen. I sure hope you find this sucker." Dr. Cross picked up his hat and tipped it to the officers, then left the office.

As soon as the door shut behind Dr. Cross, Purdy turned to Jenson, "He is awfully likeable and trustworthy for a retired serial killer."

"Sure is," Jenson scratched at his goatee.

Lanny followed Warren's brisk pace as they walked through downtown Atlanta. There was a plethora of young smokers to choose from, and one young woman trying to inconspicuously smoke a joint, and for a brief moment Warren wished he could light the entire block of bars on fire. But, for every smoker stationed outside despite the impending cold there were three or four non-smokers on the inside, just enjoying a beer. Warren had to keep that in mind, to only take from those who take from themselves. He turned into a bar at random and Lanny jogged after him.

"Warren Worth! How ya doin' man?" A small guy with facial hair lining his jaw greeted Warren.

"Hey, Sam. I'm good, how about you fella? Haven't seen you in Matrix in a while." Warren gave the guy an amiable smile.

"We fired three bartenders at once, someone's got to pick up the slack!" He smiled in a way that didn't quite hide his annoyance. "Want a Budweiser?"

"Please." Sam turned to fill the pint and set it in front of Warren with just a bit of the head sloshing onto the bar.

Lanny stepped out from behind Warren's shadow and managed, "Can I please have a ginger ale and lemon juice?"

Sam turned his attention on the wisp of a man next to Warren. "I'm sorry?"

"A ginger ale and lemon juice, please?"

"Throw some gin in there," Warren commanded.

Sam surveyed Lanny and said, "I am going to need some ID, then."

"He's good," Warren said. His dark eyes flashed and warned Sam not to cause any problems. Lanny was well beyond the legal drinking age; Sam was just being a dick.

"Sure, coming right up."

Sam threw together the cocktail with little flourish and set it carefully in front of Lanny.

"Thank you," Lanny said, feeling like a kid who had to get his older sister to beat up his bully.

Warren put some cash on the bar, enough to leave a 50% tip, and led the way over to the window seats so that they could comfortably stalk their prey.

"How do you know that guy?" Lanny asked with a wrinkle in his nose.

"Bartenders know bartenders," Warren said distractedly. He had his eye on one guy in particular. He looked to be about twenty, chain-smoking a pack of Marlboro's without pausing to take in a breath of air. Lanny noticed Warren's sharp gaze and fixed his own on the guy outside. He was skinny, wearing a beanie that was covered in some sort of animal's hair, with his own greasy hair coiling out of the bottom. Warren could spy two cigarettes left in the pack, which meant their greasy friend would soon have to leave the bar and buy new ones.

Warren drained his beer, meaning to leave the bar before their victim. He eyed Lanny's still-full drink. "Finish up," he said.

Lanny took his first sip and contorted his face. "I can't, Warren, I'm sorry. I don't drink, this tastes disgusting."

Warren sighed and took the drink from Lanny's hand, finishing it himself. Lanny felt disappointed in himself for failing his mentor on such a minor level. Neither said anything, they just stood up and left the bar.

The pair crossed the street as dark fell. The darkness and hordes of people worked as their mask. Almost perfectly on schedule, the greaser stood up and dropped his empty pack on the concrete that Sam would later have to sweep. He gave a few handshakes out to his cohorts and left the bar.

"Ready?" Warren asked Lanny.

Lanny nodded in reply and slid his hand into his pants pocket to deliver a prick to his thumb. But then he noticed the excited and confident boyish look on Warren's face and pulled his hand out, blood free. "Let's do it," he said with a smile that reached beyond his eyes.

They mirrored the steps of the prey from the other side of the street a few blocks down to where it was less busy. They waited patiently as the man went inside a convenience store and came out with another pack. He slapped it against his hand and pulled a fresh cigarette out immediately. He lit it and took a great inhale as if he was asthmatic and finally located his inhaler. The puff of smoke he let out dissipated into the air above him and he began his walk again.

Instead of heading back to the main bar area, as Warren would have guessed, the guy continued on his path to the sketchier parts of town. Warren kept his face forward, but spoke sideways to Lanny, "Have you ever gone to catch a dog while in your car before?"

"Huh? Lanny asked, confused.

"Like, seen a stray then gone to try and rescue it?" Warren asked.

"Uh, no, can't say I have. I was never an animal person."

"Well, it's best to drive ahead of them. That way you're in their path and don't have to chase them as much. You just intercept. See what I'm getting at here, fella?"

"But we left the car way back that way. Why, he could turn at any corner in the time it would take us to get the car and we'd lose him!"

Warren gave Lanny an exasperated look and began to run.

"Warren, what are you doing?" Lanny whisper-yelled after him. Warren didn't respond, only kept at his run. Lanny had no choice but to run after him. They only went a few blocks with Warren surreptitiously peeking over his shoulder to keep tabs on their prey, and Lanny was already wheezing. Warren crossed the street with Lanny in his wake. They were far enough ahead and under minimal enough lighting that their grease-ball wouldn't have seen them unless he had super-vision. Warren pulled Lanny into an alley. Both of their eyes had begun to adjust to the dark, so they could make out the outlines of each other's faces in the dank side street.

They peeked around the corner like boys in the game of hide and seek and saw the bobbing flicker of orange light coming from the end of the cigarette. Warren was so excited that he had to stifle a giggle. Something about the cool air and outdoors had given him an extra spring in his step. He peeked around the corner again. "Ready?" He asked Lanny. Lanny, who was unaware of the actual plan, took a step back.

"N-not really," he answered. Lanny's wavering reply went unnoticed by Warren.

Lanny never saw Warren in a true predator-prey moment, where he actually had to capture his prey like a cat would a mouse. It all happened in a flash; Warren leaped out onto the sidewalk and snatched the guy back into the alley with him. Lanny wondered about the kind of agility workouts Warren did to keep such quick motion at his age. He was as spry as a jackrabbit!

The man was startled, but not enough so to the point that he lost his cigarette. He'd been ambushed mid-drag, and the thing still hung from his mouth like an oddly shaped tumor. He was still breathing it in and puffing it out as Warren held him in a headlock, although the puffs came out smaller and smaller. He began to struggle, fiending for a breath of fresh air for probably the first time in his life. The guy scratched at Warren's forearm, delivering a good-sized nick, however it only urged Warren to squeeze harder. Instead of returning eye contact with the bulging ones of the victim, Lanny admired the flex of Warren's bicep as he gently guided his catch to the ground.

Warren switched positions as swiftly as an MMA fighter and placed himself on top of the smoker, now with his large hand around the man's neck. He leaned forward to put all of his weight behind his forearm and held his position even minutes after the guy had stopped struggling. Warren like to be sure about everything. Leaving a job without fully knowing whether it was completed or not was something for *stupid* people to do.

Once satisfied, Warren sat up and examined the scratch on his arm. It wasn't anything too deep, nothing a bit of alcohol and a cotton swab couldn't disinfect. He held up the corpse's right hand, the one he had successfully used to scratch at Warren. Warren's vision had improved much with the night, but not enough so that he could clearly see the guy's fingernails. As always, it was better to be safe than sorry.

"Lanny," Warren said from his dominant position, "Do you have a toothpick or something skinny and sharp?"

Without a word, Lanny felt for the safety pin that was always in his right pocket. He pulled it out, unclasped it to clean the point, and handed it to Warren. Warren set to work cleaning the undersides of the deceased's fingernails with such dexterity that he could have applied for a salon job. Each time he swiped the pin under a fingernail, he wiped whatever remnants collected on the inside of his own pant pocket. Once satisfied, he looked at Lanny and smiled, then jabbed the safety pin into the wrist of the man, who was conveniently already cut up in that area.

"Got a little blood for you right here, fella." With one drop of ruby red hanging onto the pin, Warren handed it back to Lanny who immediately placed it on his tongue. "That was fun. I feel much better." Warren rose to his feet and sauntered away. They would take the long way back to the car, so as to enjoy the brisk night.

CHAPTER 11

Jodee was on her back staring at the fan-less ceiling. She hadn't left the apartment since Celestria's visit and felt nauseous at the thought of eating the second half of meat in the fridge. Jodee didn't know what sort of meat it was but when she initially ate some it just felt *wrong* in her mouth. She just drank water and hoped it would be enough to fool her belly into thinking food was mixed in there. She could already feel the large muscles throughout her body depleting. Three days had passed, and she was still unsure what to do. Go back out there into a land she was foreign to and find food, lay in bed until she rots and dies, or hang herself to get it over with quickly. Each scenario would most likely lead to the same outcome. And if it were true that there were infinite universes, and that her consciousness would just transfer to the next? Well that would be fine. Maybe the next one would suit her a little better.

She did wonder though, if it would work the same way considering her consciousness was switched across space and time. Jodee opted to stay in the minor comfort that the apartment had begun to offer her. She was getting really good at sleeping through most of the day and night.

Scar occupied the majority of thoughts while she was awake. She wondered how her baby was getting on without her, if there was anyone taking care of her, and her own heart ached to be back with her love. Jodee actually found herself wishing that she could just give Matt a call and have him check in on her dog. Though she didn't know it that was exactly what he had done as soon as he heard Jodee had gone AWOL.

A thud on the door interrupted Jodee's mindless wonderings. She assumed Celestria was back and rolled her eyes, letting them fall shut at the end of their cycle. But the knocker was incessant. She pulled herself out of bed clad only in a sports bra and some ratty running shorts she had found. The logo that appeared on them was one she did not recognize.

Jodee took her time getting to the door, as there was nobody in this world she worried about pissing-off. *Maybe it's that overly defensive street cleaner from my first day. Maybe he'll rape me and eat me. Or just eat me. Just as long as I die.* She smiled as she pushed the doorknob to the other side and let whomever it was inside.

There were two people waiting for her on the other side and they were… familiar. It was a man and a woman. The latter rushed her way into the apartment and embraced Jodee in a tight hug. "This is incredible," the woman murmured in her ears. When the woman finally released Jodee, the man stepped forward. He had a bag in his hands.

Nothing Jodee had ever seen was as beautiful as that bag with the signature golden arches on the side. The bag designs had changed, but the arches never would. The smell of fast food lingered around Jodee's nose and her stomach ached for it. She was more focused on the bag's contents than the two strangers in front of her. Jodee finally broke her gaze from the meal dangling in front of her and met the man's eyes.

"Who are you?" She asked.

He had narrow slits for pupils, but also crow's feet that Jodee remembered calling "twinks" when she was a child. Aside from his eyes, he looked like any older man from her own world. The woman had a tight bun and was a bit more frightening, as her lack of a nose made Jodee think of Voldemort from Harry Potter. Instead there were two skinny lines holed out. Her teeth were all sharp, something Jodee had seen before, but they still curved into a warm smile.

"Jo," the woman breathed.

Jodee pointed a finger at herself. "Me? No, it's actually Jodee."

"Jodee! Of course, of course! That is what we named you but is what you refused to be called since you were, I don't know," the woman looked at her partner as if to get his help on guessing the age, "six I think."

Jodee felt cold for the first time since arriving in this universe. Her skin broke out in goose bumps and she trembled. The food was no longer fighting for her attention. "Are you—" she tried to choke the words out of a dry mouth, "are you my parents?"

The woman beamed her sharp smile and pulled Jodee in for another hug. Tears pricked at the corners of her eyes. The man stepped forward and embraced both of the women, still with the bag of McDonald's in hand.

Guilt hung and wrung itself in Jodee's midsection and she pulled away from the group hug. "Please, come in," she said and gestured at the sparsely decorated apartment. They all found themselves seated around the stainless steel table. "I, uh, I don't know what to say," Jodee admitted. She felt awkward. Here were the people she'd killed, but now very much alive. It was awkward enough when she thought of it alone in her thoughts at night, that she was once capable of murder.

"We are sure you're very confused. But, by the looks of it, very hungry as well. Please, eat first and then we will fill you in as best we can."

Jodee's father pushed the bag toward her and she opened it hesitantly. When the smell of a Big Mac hit her nostrils, all hesitation was lost. She devoured it within two minutes. A small fry accompanied the burger and she poured them into her mouth with such lust. She licked the remaining salt from her lips and wished for more.

"There will be more," her father said, as if reading her mind.

"So Jo- I mean Jodee. We have spoken to Celestria, so we know how much she's filled you in on our world. It's quite magnificent, isn't it?" She asked without expecting a response.

Jodee jumped in and said, "Do you even remember your last world?"

Her mother ignored it and continued while her father watched her face carefully. "You and your brother, at least in this universe, were very close. Jo was absolutely devastated when he was killed. Since then, this was about a year and a half ago I would say; she's shut herself off from the rest of the world.

She quit her job and devoted all her time and energy to finding a way into your universe, so that she could be reunited with her brother.

"We didn't think it was possible," she paused and looked at her husband who nodded, "we just thought, well, that Jo was losing touch with reality. We've only seen her twice in the past year and a half and both times she had this look in her eye, it was absolute madness! We were frightened and tried to get her help, but she sent us away.

"It's been hard. Losing both our son and daughter," different kinds of tears found their way down her face and she broke into loud sobs. Jodee's father placed a hand on her shoulder and picked up where she left off.

"It has been hard. Losing both of our children. That's not the way it's supposed to go. It's supposed to be you guys burying us! But, after Celestria reached out to us, we got excited. We knew we had to come see you. We want to help you. And, to answer the question your mother chose to ignore, we do, and we don't, remember the last world. We see it sometimes, in dreams. I think we are peeking into the lives of our other selves while we dream. So, yes, we see it in bits and pieces, although we are not sure what could be real or not."

"So, you think you see events and things you went through in your past life?" Jodee asked with more than just a tremble coating her voice.

"Yes," he answered simply.

"So… do you remember… well do you see anything with me?" Jodee released tears from her eyes like she was turning on a faucet that had been off for far too long. Her cries were loud and childlike; they seemed like they would never stop.

Jodee's mother placed a hand on Jodee's greasy one. "Darling," she said, "we know that you may have done something bad to us, horrible even, but we don't know exactly what. You are our daughter," she said with force, "And we love you despite anything you may have done. We are together again, and that is all that matters."

Jodee looked at her parents through blurred eyes. They were both so old, to an age they didn't even come close to in her world. *I didn't give them a chance. I hated them for hating each other. But now, now they look so happy.*

"I killed you guys. You fought constantly. I thought I did it for Lanny's sake, but maybe it was for my own. Maybe I was the one who went crazy." She looked at both of them in the eyes and remembered their empty stares from that night. "I killed my parents. Who in God's name does that? What kind of psychopathic—"

"Who's God?" Her father looked more confused by this than Jodee's confession.

"Remember, snakelet, with the time of Christians and all of that."

"Ah, yes."

Jodee looked back and forth between them and said, "I'm sorry. I'm so sorry. Words will never be enough, but I am. I've tried to forget that little girl and be independent, be helpful, be as good a person as I can."

"Shhh. You can't kill what can't be created nor destroyed. We really are happy," Her mother smiled, and the slits of her eyes became straight lines for a moment.

This realization only caused her to cry harder, and both of her parents stood so they could hold their baby again. A warm embrace when one is crying almost always makes the person cry harder, because sometimes that is exactly what they need.

After a few minutes of hard crying, Jodee slowed it down to wipe the snot that had started to run from her nose and into her mouth. "N-now what?"

Jodee's parents looked at each other and then smiled at Jodee. "We would like you to move in with us. As long as you don't kill us again," her father winked. "But we spoke and thought that we should all move up north together."

Jodee's heart flattened against her chest. "But, won't it be too cold for you guys?"

"Honey, we can put on as many layers of clothing that we need to. But you can only take so much off!" Jodee's mother laughed. "So, what do you think? Make the best of this place with your folks?"

Jodee nodded and felt her eyes well with tears again. She wondered if this was going to become a common thing for her. Scar entered her mind again, and she knew that she needed to stay alive if she were to ever see her again. Or maybe there was another piece of Scar's consciousness just waiting for Jodee to find her in this universe. Again, she fell into the arms of her mother and father.

Morgan Purdy was lying in bed with his wife. She was, as always, reading one of her Patricia Cornwell novels. He nuzzled the top of her head with his scratchy chin. He was so grateful to her for guiding him in a new direction with the case. They may not have gotten anywhere with Dr. Cross, but they still had Dr. Leach to question. He was hoping that the interview, would she come in, might bust the whole thing open.

His mind was always on his caseload, even when he wished he could forget it for an hour. Morgan was starting to that night in bed with his wife, with possible sex on the horizon, when the phone rang. He answered it immediately.

"Investigator Purdy," he said and then felt old school for not checking his caller ID first.

"Morgan, it's Miranda."

"Miranda? What is it?" He tried to sound annoyed for the sake of his wife, who had shifted slightly away from him. Ellen kept her eyes on the book, but Morgan could tell she wasn't actually reading, just hanging on every word he said.

"We have a DOA, potentially another victim of the same killer. You don't need to come down here, another of the guys from your office did. Max Porter. Once again, nothing left at the scene. We ran a background as well. Turns out he's been arrested more than once for possession."

"Possession of what?"

"Cocaine."

"Really?" Purdy scratched his chin thoughtfully.

"Didn't you and Jenson narrow down the list to those couple of doctors? And what's her name. she beat up her boyfriend for just that."

"Holy shit! I'll have to call Brian right away, see if he ever got a hold of her. Fuck! Thanks for the call. Find anything else interesting? Any signs of a struggle?"

"No sign of struggle, clean fingernails, but he was strangled. Maybe the doctor… what's her name again?"

"Noel Leach."

"Right. Maybe Dr. Leach lured him into the alley with a proposal of a blow job or something."

"Have you collected any samples from his mouth and genitals?"

"We swabbed the area; the guys are bringing it back to the lab now to see if we can find anything other than his own DNA."

"Awesome, thank you again for calling. Please keep me updated."

Miranda clicked off on the other line and Morgan ended the call on his own. "Wow," he murmured.

"What was that about?" Ellen tried not to sound jealous.

"It's about the fact that you're a genius. We may be cracking down on our killer soon." He gave her a long kiss on the mouth, to which she reciprocated.

Jo was sitting on the couch, waiting for her brother in the wee hours of the morning. She was getting frustrated, wondering where he was and hoping it wasn't with his friend Warren. A soft knock came on the door. Jo thought at first that it might be

Lanny finally returning but realized he probably would have his own key.

Jo opened the door without looking out the peephole. She didn't know what a peephole was as she could usually see who was outside just by reading their thoughts. She swung it open in an annoyance that only grew when she saw who was on the other side.

"You, you're one of the girls on the football team, right?"

"Uh, yeah Coach, it's me, Kaitlyn."

"Ugh," Jo's facial expression changed from one of confusion to disgust. "What do you *want*? Didn't we already cover all of this on the phone? Shouldn't you be back in, where is it, Greenville by now?"

"No... not yet. We still have a game Sunday."

"Do the other coaches know you're here?"

"Does it matter?"

Jo smirked at the young girl's sass. She was bullheaded, as was Jo. "How did you find me?"

"Can I come in?" Kaitlyn asked, almost begged.

"Fine." Jo stepped out of the way and let the small girl into the room. She really was a little thing, albeit packed full of muscle.

"Can I sit?"

"Yeah, yeah. Have a seat."

Kaitlyn plopped down in the leather recliner, so Jo found herself sitting in Lanny's favorite sag.

"I'll ask again. How did you find me?"

"It's really not that hard. Searched around your Facebook page and found you have a brother. He actually has his phone number listed there. So, I looked him up on White Pages. Again, it's not that hard to find someone these days."

"Well, what do you want," Jo asked, trying not to be impressed. She didn't have that kind of technology to where she could track just anyone down without help from a police officer (and you had to have a good reason for that). That kind of information was not available to the public in her world.

"I want an explanation. The whole reason I came to Furman was because of you! You appreciated my style of play and you came after me. You offered me that scholarship. I'm not being cocky, I'm just, I don't know. I don't understand why you're doing this now. Especially at the beginning of the season!"

"Look, kid, I don't know what to tell you. If I'm the only reason you're playing, well, do you really think that is good enough? Maybe you should quit."

Kaitlyn looked taken aback. She wasn't expecting a response like that, not by someone who commended her for being so tenacious on the field and known for not giving up on a play. "W-well, I- I don't know. No, I'm not going to quit, but please can you just come back? Does this have anything to do with your recent change in, um, appearance?"

"Look, you're starting to get annoying. No, you passed that. But I see a little of me in you, that's why I haven't ripped your head off yet. You need to just hop back in whatever cab you came here in and get back to your team." Jo could see by the look on the girl's face that the team thing struck a nerve. "Yeah, you don't want the girls to turn on you too, do you? You want them to have been abandoned by me, and then you too?"

A determined face quickly masked whatever emotional response Jo had pulled from Kaitlyn. "I'm not leaving here without you."

Jo rolled her eyes. "Then you're going to be here a long time."

"Fine." Kaitlyn crossed her legs in the chair and settled into it. "I can wait." She noticed a cloudy look in Jo's eyes and found herself transfixed, but to Jo it only appeared as if the girl was keeping her eyes locked and focused on the goal.

Jo didn't know how far the girl was going to take it. But between her presence and the absence of Lanny, it was beginning to be a bit too much. She felt an angry heat spread through her body.

"Seriously. I'm not coming. You need to get the fuck out of here."

Kaitlyn flinched, but still did not move.

"Fine," Jo said, "I'll come with you. Let's go." She stood and walked to the door, ready to open it and lock the pest outside.

Kaitlyn raised her eyebrows. "You really think I'm that stupid? You're just going to lock me out!"

Jo didn't know if Kaitlyn was reading her mind (or maybe reading her mind subconsciously) or just annoyingly intuitive. Either way, it was enough to make her blood boil. "GET THE FUCK OUT!" she screamed.

CHAPTER 11

Kaitlyn's face turned red. "I'm not leaving here without you. For real." A light sweat had broken out on her face. She was nervous, but still determined.

Jo's eyes were blinded by rage for a moment. And in that moment, she crossed the room to where Kaitlyn sat. Kaitlyn recoiled as if worried Jo might throw a punch, but she threw something worse instead.

In one quick motion, a jerk of the neck, Jo shot forward and clamped her teeth down on Kaitlyn's arm. She may not have had much in the way of fangs, but they held a venom much more powerful than any other person she knew, or snake for that matter. Kaitlyn struggled to get her wrist out of Jo's mouth, but Jo locked in tight like a dog. She shook her head a little and bit harder, trying to release as much venom as she could.

"What the hell are you doing?" Kaitlyn shrieked. She'd been bitten before, in jest, but this was different. The inside of her arm began to tingle and prickle, much like the way her whole body had felt when the doctors had injected her with something prior to a CAT scan. It was uncomfortable, unbearable, and unstoppable.

The light sheen of sweat on Kaitlyn became excessive. She began to gag, and Jo finally got out of the way as the girl spewed vomit. Blood poured from the wound. Jo sat back on the couch to watch the rest of the show. Kaitlyn looked at Jo with eyes widened in disbelief. She tried to get up and run to the door but fell to the ground immediately. More vomit forced its way out of her mouth. She looked at Jo to help, but only got a shrug in return. She tried pulling herself across the ground, believing that just getting a crack of fresh air would solve everything. As she struggled, Kaitlyn checked behind her to make sure she wasn't being pursued by whatever beast Jo was. But the bitch just stood there, and Kaitlyn swore she saw a glimmer of satisfaction on her face. She rolled her eyes back front and gritted her teeth through the searing pain that was spreading through all of the veins in her body. She felt like she was inwardly on fire and knew that stop, drop, and roll wouldn't do the trick here. "AAHHHHHHH!" She finally released a scream in pain when her mouth was momentarily clear of vomit. She let out a few wails before another wave came through. The throw-up splashed into her face and landed in front of her. The smell alone caused another round to come forth.

Kaitlyn tried again to sit up. Her whole body shook with effort and the burning feeling beneath her skin made her want to curl into a ball and weep for her mother. She got to her knees and lifted her hand toward the door, which was still a good three feet out of her grasp. Kaitlyn shuffled forward on her knees but was off-balance and fell into her own pile of puke. She cried out again. Her face was white with effort, but once more she tried to stand. She put one leg out in front of her in lunge position and pushed forward, propelling herself to the door. With excessive momentum she lacked accuracy and instead of grasping the knob in her hand, she hit her tooth on it, sending it flying from her gums. Now her mouth was an unhealthy mix of leftover vomit and blood. It all sloshed together and dribbled down her chin. She lifted her hand to the door, but it was too short to reach from her position on the ground. Kaitlyn cried out again, refusing to give up and ready for another go at regaining her legs. She began to stand, to really stand on both legs, but in that same moment, and despite all her efforts, she began to convulse. Kaitlyn fell straight onto her back and with it came a sickening thud between her skull and the ground. It was not enough to bring her to unconsciousness, which she would have welcomed. Her eyes rolled to the back of her head and Jo wondered what all Kaitlyn could see back there and clapped her hands at the entertainment.

Kaitlyn finally fainted after all of the convulsing, and when she came to, she did not even attempt to walk. The fire in her veins only increased. On top of that, she could not feel anything in her right arm at all, couldn't even waggle a pinky finger. She lay on the floor, terrified at the sound of her own heart beating so fast that she thought it might explode. "Fuck you," she said between gales of childlike crying. Her terror only increased when she gasped for air and failed to bring enough oxygen into her body. Her panic level rose each time she tried to fill her lungs and failed. She fell unconscious again, and this time it was one from which she would not return.

The show was over, so Jo stood and stretched her limbs. She peered down at herself and noticed a slight swell in her belly from all of the food she had been consuming. She then walked over to Kaitlyn's body and thought about dragging it into Lanny's bedroom, not quite sure what to do with it. Murder was a crime, obviously, and she didn't want to get Lanny into trouble. That being said, she didn't want to get herself into trouble either. So, for the moment, she heaved little Kaitlyn Rice into Lanny's bathtub and left it there, figuring she and Lanny could turn it into a little brother sister project, if he ever got home.

Jo felt nauseous and irritable, so she lay down on the bathroom floor next to the bathtub. She didn't want to believe what could be happening was happening, after all she was a full-grown woman, but there's always that possibility. She looked down again at the swell of her stomach that was more than just food waiting to be digested and groaned. She'd gained weight, all right, and in more areas than the one. Jo had been overeating prior to the switch with Jodee, stress eating, and she'd been greedy with food in this universe as well. She didn't want to admit that she was getting a bit chubby, but it was true enough. Jo stripped off her clothing and heaped it on top of Kaitlyn's body. Her vision was clouding over, and she wished desperately for some oil.

Jo fumbled with the cabinets under the sink and groped for anything that might help loosen her skin. She found a bottle of conditioner and figured it was better than nothing. She began to cry out in frustration and cursed herself for letting it get to this point. Jo wiped her face against the cold floor and cried, then tore open the bottle of conditioner. She slathered it all over her face to try and make her shedding as painless and easy as possible. The tile floor wasn't doing enough; she needed something rough. In a fit of great effort, Jo flung the top half of her body up to snatch the towel that hung from the door. She rubbed her face against it to no avail, but kept at it, rubbing to the point that would usually lead to rawness in an unevolved.

CHAPTER 11

She was on her knees with her head bowed to the ground where she laid the towel, rubbing her forehead vigorously. Finally, the skin on her forehead began to peel away. She used this breaking point to continue the peel. The hard part was over. She continued the rub down to her chin and her face was done. In an inchworm style, Jo continued to scrape her body against the towel. It only took about an hour for her to completely squirm out of her outermost skin. One thing she could be grateful for was that in her evolution, the shedding process lasted an hour compared to her ancestors who endured it for a week.

Jo did not yet shake her feet from the skin and looked down at herself, admiring the clean shed the way one would admire a great big peel of the skin after a dreadful sunburn. There was something awfully satisfying about it. She put her head down on the towel that was now folded to act as a pillow and let herself nap.

CHAPTER 12

Lanny stayed the night at Warren's. The two men were celebrating and just enjoying each other's company on such a wonderful night, up until the wee hours of the morning. Lanny looked at his mentor and smiled, "I, I am just sho' grateful fo' you, Mister Warrrrr Worth!" He clapped Warren on the shoulder.

Warren, who was only tipsy, smiled at his comrade. "And I for you Lanny. We make a great team, that is for sure." Warren continued drinking his Budweiser as Lanny drained his third drink. Warren figured that the gin was too powerful a taste for a new drinker, so he had traded out the gin in the ginbuck for vodka. The results were obviously favorable. Lanny could barely taste the vodka, mostly just his regular ginger ale and lemon juice. For the first time in his life, the man was not only drunk, but also plastered.

And because of this, Warren decided to open up to him, but only a little. There was a good chance he wouldn't remember, but Warren needed to start small. "Lanny, do you want to know a secret?"

"You have a secret, Mr. Worth? Other than, ya know, killin' folks for a livin'?" Lanny giggled. The bit of sarcasm that came out of Lanny's mouth pleasantly surprised Warren.

He chuckled. "Yes Lanny, I have a secret. Remember that time we went to Clarenceville?"

"Oh, yesh. Pat Creary and the vomit and the Grey Goose bottle. Sounds like a good title for a book." His laugh was saliva-coated.

"Well, do you remember the house we camped out inside? And the bartender?"

Lanny tried to dig through the archives of his memory, not an easy task considering his state. "Hmmmm. House for sure. So creepy. I swear I saw a ghost in there. And-"

Warren was interested in this. "Wait, really?"

"Yeah, but that's not surprising in a creepy 'ole place. You see things. The mind, it plays tricks on fools. And the bartender, kinda. Older guy. Gimpy."

"Not gimpy, Lanny, he. . . never mind. Well, that house used to be Scotty's."

"How d'ya know that?"

"Because Scotty is my uncle."

Lanny's jaw dropped in a comic fashion. He did a double-take even though it was something crazy he had heard and not seen. "No way."

Warren laughed again. "Way."

"What the-?"

"He used to have a son. But the kid died in that house. One of his friends was over, they were about twelve at the time, and he had found his dad's gun. Brought it over for a little show-and-tell.

"And you know kids, they aren't the brightest, not developed yet. Anyway, he accidentally shot Johnny DeLello. Scotty

228

couldn't stay in that house, but he didn't want to leave his bar. So, he moved, and nobody else ever took over the place."

Lanny was hanging on every word, unblinking.

"Scotty calls me every now and then. When there's some kind of trouble, in a small town like that it really sticks out, he lets me know. He doesn't give me any names; he doesn't need to. He knows what I do. He just likes for me to clean up the streets in the way the police force down there can't."

"Wow," Lanny was in awe. "So that's why you are the way you are?"

"Excuse me?" Warren was confused.

"Wait, I gotta queshtion. How come you like to make me feel so stupid sometimes? I'm smart, I know I'm smart, why don't you see that? I'm not much but that I am. I was magna cum laude," he burped.

Warren ignored the question. "What did you mean by 'the way I am'?"

"Well, serial killersh. They get like that 'cause they go through bad stuff, right?" Lanny forgot about his own question. For this, Warren was grateful to the booze. What could he say? That he made people feel stupid because that's what teachers did to him his whole life? Told him he wouldn't amount to anything? Absolutely not, for some things he would take to the grave.

"Oh, I didn't go through anything bad, Lanny. I hardly consider myself a serial killer. No, I didn't really know Johnny. We'd only met maybe one time in our lives. It was no real loss to me, but I felt for my uncle. That hit him hard. So, he supports me in everything I do. Always has."

"That is crazy! Crazy cool!" Lanny might have begun to mull over what he just learned, maybe tried to record it to memory, or maybe he was just too tired to say anything else that could be part of such a deep conversation.

"Hey, Lanny?"

"Yeah, brudda?"

"Tell me about your sister. She seems… amazing." Warren thought of Jo and the way that her skin shone, the way that her eyes were more alert and observant than anyone he ever met. Her blonde hair almost shimmered to the point of being white. He was absolutely enamored.

"Jodee. I mean, Jo. She is my sissssta. And you are my brothaa," Lanny giggled at himself and his eyes fluttered. Warren knew that his friend was about to pass out and was in for a nasty hangover. But then he said, "Now I have a question for you…" he could barely keep his eyes open though.

"And what might that be?" Warren asked, figuring it was back to the other question and annoyed that Lanny of all people could make him feel uneasy.

"Did you do that guy, uhhhhhhhhhh. . ." Lanny's 'uh' was so long Warren found himself thinking about Peter Griffin stubbing his toe after getting a golden ticket in the show *Family Guy*. It started off funny, but then got annoying, and funny again. Just as Warren was about to cut off the baritone pitch exuding from Lanny's throat, Lanny remembered. "Brixx! Martin Brixx! Was tha' you? I know they said he went mishin' and all…"

"Yes, that one was all me, fella." Warren smiled softly, that was a fond memory of his.

"Where is he?"

"Into the air, my friend." Warren laughed when he saw Lanny's look of befuddlement. "I took him from a parking deck. He was wasted and only had eyes for his cell phone. He was walking home alone in the wee hours of the morning too, and through that damn parking deck. Anyway, I brought him into some woods surrounding Clarenceville. It must have been five or six in the morning; not a soul in that town was awake. I set him on fire. Watched him burn for a good while. Anything that didn't burn, teeth and what not, I grinded up and fed to the wind. That was a hard day's work, but man it was enjoyable. I basically made him disappear into thin air, gone without a trace. I felt bad about the mother though. It destroyed her. Normally I don't have to see the effect of my damage, but she came into my bar, absolutely haggard after a day with the police. I recognized her from the newspapers. I did take care of her first round, though. You know—"

Lanny fell asleep. Warren smiled and took the empty glass from Lanny's hand. He found a blanket in the closet and put it over Lanny, who was now murmuring indistinguishable words.

"Good night, fella," Warren said with a smile and gave Lanny a tender kiss on the top of his head. Lanny fell asleep instantly after that.

Purdy greeted his partner with a little dance the following morning. "Ready to get this bitch?"

Jenson chuckled. "Let's give her a call." Jenson dialed the number listed for the hospital and listened to the phone ring. He was directed to a desk nurse, who told him to wait while she paged Dr. Leach.

"She might be in the middle of a surgery, or just finishing up. Please hold on for one second," Jenson turned the phone onto speaker so that he and Morgan could listen to the annoying boop together. After about seven minutes, a woman picked up.

"This is Doctor Leach," she said in a curt voice.

"Doctor Leach, this is Morgan Purdy and Brian Jenson with the Atlanta PD."

"What can I do for you?"

"We are investigating an ongoing crime spree in Georgia, and we wanted to bring you in to ask you a few questions."

"Why? Is one of the victims a previous patient of mine?"

Morgan looked at Brian and shrugged with a furrowed brow, both unsure how to proceed. "No, Ms. Leach-"

"*Doctor* Leach," she cut him off.

"Right, Doctor Leach, not that we are aware. We just wanted to ask you a few questions."

"With all due respect, gentleman, I am not going to take the time out of my day to visit with you. I have back-to-back surgeries and lives to save. Unless you are going to arrest me for any reason, I think this conversation is over."

The phone clicked off on the other end and left the two men in silence on their own end. "Terrific," Purdy grumbled.

As anticipated, Lanny woke up with a murderous headache. He opened his eyes carefully and squinted against the sunlight that shone in through the windows onto all of Warren's many plants. Through his half-vision, he could see a tall glass of water with no ice and a few Advil sitting next to the lucky bamboo plant. He pushed himself up, and the movement sent a whoosh of queasiness through him. He clapped his hand over his mouth and dashed to the bathroom, opting to save the medicine for *after* he rid his body of last night's contents.

Warren sat in the armchair, slowly reading a book, unnoticed, and smirked like a father watching his son experience his first hangover. In a way, that's exactly what it was. He heard the hurling in the distance and shook his head, merely turning to the next page in his book. Lanny flushed the toilet and returned to the room, still squinting and holding his head.

"How are you feeling, fella?" Warren asked with a grin.

Lanny jumped at the sound of Warren's deep voice and sat back down. "I didn't see you there," he mumbled, "and I feel like hell."

Warren leaned forward and nudged the water closer to Lanny. "Well, drink up," he said, "and then we can take you home."

Lanny guzzled half of the water then threw back the three Advil and finished the glass. Without being asked, Warren picked up the glass and refilled it, just as he did for all of his customers. In silence, Lanny finished it again.

"Ugh. I forgot. Jo is at my house. She's probably been worried sick!"

"You look like the sick one to me," Warren chuckled.

Lanny laughed a little as well. "Either way, I've gotta get home to her. Would you mind taking me?"

Warren was already planning on that, as he was excited at the prospect of seeing Jo again. "Of course. I have a bottle of water in the fridge you can drink on the way over." Warren retrieved the bottle and followed Lanny out of the apartment. He locked the door behind him and unlocked his car door. Lanny made his way over to the flashing lights and got comfortable in the passenger seat while he waited for Warren to join. He slumped low in the seat and drank from the water bottle in an absurd manner. He didn't want to continue tilting his head back, because it made him that much more nauseous, so he held the bottle and squeezed it from the bottom up, like he was eating a push pop. Air kept filling his mouth and Lanny realized how unsuccessful this was.

Warren slid into the car and put the air conditioning on despite the impending cold weather. He knew that cold air in the face felt great when hung over. "Just settle back, we'll be to your place in no time."

Lanny did just that. He leaned his head against the window and squinted against the intrusive sunlight streaming into the car. Mercifully, the traffic wasn't too terrible, and they made it back to his apartment in less than thirty minutes. Lanny stumbled out of Warren's luxury car and made his way to his own apartment with Warren at his heels. He tried the knob first, to see if he would have to tangle with the keys, and the door was unlocked.

Lanny never left his door unlocked, but maybe Jo had stepped out for a walk. He let himself in and heard groans coming from the bathroom. Whatever nastiness he felt from the night before completely vanished and was replaced by worry.

The door unlocked and the sounds coming from the bathroom were two things he did not like at all when put together. He stepped inside and felt something sharp. He looked down and saw a tooth resting in the carpet. He crept over to his television center and pulled open one of the drawers below the television. Nestled in a small towel was his two and a quarter inch barreled Smith and Wesson revolver. He sniffed the air and noticed the piles of vomit scattered around the room like unearthed landmines. Warren watched all of this with great curiosity as he followed Lanny toward the bathroom.

"Jo?" Lanny called with trepidation. The response was only another series of groans, not unlike the ones Lanny himself was making this morning. "Jo, is that you?" He nudged open the bathroom door and didn't know what to address first. Lanny immediately turned his head away and darted from the bathroom to his kitchen sink to vomit again.

Jo was laying on the ground of the bathroom, looking quite sick and quite naked. Behind her lay a sheath of what looked like a giant sunburn peel, and in the tub was a dead girl. "Well, good morning Jo!" Warren said under his breath with a smile. He grabbed a blanket off of Lanny's bed and covered the naked woman with it. As always, Warren was a gentleman first. He then stroked her hair gently to wake her up. "Jo?" He called. "Wake up, Jo."

Jo did. She blinked her eyes open and was grateful for the clarity with which they could see. But any feelings of gratitude disappeared as soon as she focused in on Warren's face. "What the fuck are you doing here? Get out of my fucking face! And what have you done with my brother?"

"I'm right here, Jo. What happened last night?" Lanny answered from just outside the door, still too queasy to look inside. "I mean, what's on the ground with you, and who's that in the tub? Did you kill someone?"

"I'm not answering any questions until this creep is out of my face!" Jo demanded. She was not in the mood for strangers or judgment, and only owed answers to her brother.

Warren backed away from the room and leaned in to whisper to Lanny. "Don't worry, I'm not going anywhere. I'll just be out in my car. Call me when you need a hand with, well, all of this." Lanny nodded and turned back toward the bathroom as Warren let himself out. Lanny still had the revolver in his hand, tense and ready from the shock. Warren eased it from his grip and slid it into the back of his jeans, then nudged Lanny further into the bedroom.

"Jo, you're going to have to come out here. I can't take the smell of whatever you've got going on in there."

Jo pushed herself up with some effort and swaddled herself in the thick blanket Warren had put on her. She was thankful for the heat it offered. Jo shuffled out of the bathroom and sat herself down on Lanny's bed. Lanny still could not sit down, he stood in front of the bed and at an angle to the bathroom that he could just see the end of Jo's shed-skin.

"Jo, what is that?"

Jo glanced at her old skin and shrugged. "I've gained a lot of weight. That shit hasn't happened since my last growth spurt," she chuckled.

"Why is it happening at all? I don't know what that is!"

"Lan, please sit down," Jo implored. Lanny obliged wordlessly. "That's my old skin. When I grow, I go through ecdysis, like a snake."

"So, you have a skin disease?"

"No, no, no. I'd say it's the opposite of a disease. It's an evolutionary trait really. Where I'm from, a good many of us go through ecdysis."

Lanny began to feel light-headed. His smattering of freckles stood out even more in contrast to his skin as it paled. "What do you mean, 'where you're from?' We came from the same womb, Jo. Right? Or have you never been my sister?" Tears sprang to Lanny's eyes as his heartbeat quickened. His breaths came in unsatisfying rasps.

Jo sighed and sat next to him. She placed a reassuring hand on his shaking shoulder. "Of course I'm your sister. I'm just the better version of her."

"What the heck?"

"Lanny, I'm from the year 3038."

Lanny slid his hand into his pocket and found his safety pin. He delivered himself a prick and stuck his thumb in his mouth. as he listened to Jo's tale. It was unbelievable and incredible, but it didn't take much to convince him that it was true.

"So, what, she just pissed you off?"

"Let's just say that it wasn't a good time to be trying me," Jo explained. "But look, now that all of that is out of the way, we've got to get the body out of your apartment before it stinks up the place."

"Alright. What should we do with it?" Lanny began to stand up.

"Actually, wait a second," Jo said, and Lanny paused. "There's one more thing we need to address." Lanny sat back down. "What is the deal with you and Warren?"

"What do you mean?" Lanny asked.

"Like, what is your relationship. Are you, together, or what?"

"What? No, Jo. He's my buddy. He's been looking out for me. Teaching me. Helping me grow."

"How? Look, Lanny, I don't like him. I will be straight up with you on that."

"But, why? You haven't even met him, except for a moment at a time! He looks out for me, Jo!"

"Well, I'm here now. So you don't need someone else looking out for you. Especially someone like him. I don't get good vibes from him at all, Lan. I don't trust him."

"So, because you're here now, he's got to go? What happens if you abandon me again?"

"We've already been through this! *I* never abandoned you, not in the lifetime that we lived together anyway. If anything, you left me when you died. But Lanny, if he stays in your life. . . I won't."

Lanny fell into a silence. He finally asked, "What do you want me to do?"

"He needs to go."

"I'm not going to kill him, Jo. I love that man."

"We don't have to kill him necessarily, but I want him out of your life."

Lanny didn't like the sound of where any of this was going. But this was his sister. He loved her more than anyone, no matter the universe or lifetime. He couldn't lose her, not again. And it was clear that his fantasy of Jo and Warren falling in love, marrying, and Warren becoming his brother for real wasn't going to happen. Jo wasn't giving him any other options.

"Does he have any soft spots?"

Lanny swallowed the lump that formed in his throat. He felt tears prick his eyes, so he shoved the safety pin into his thumb and stuck it in his mouth while he thought. The salty and bitter flavor eased him. "Yeah. I mean no. Well, maybe. It's aging. He's scared of what it may do to him. When he came over yesterday, before you got here, I mean, he was fuming about this woman—"

"—Who's the lady? And why was he mad?" The ever-impatient Jo interrupted.

"Um, Noel. And because she won't have kids with him. Something like that."

Jo chortled. "You said he helps you, looks out for you. Get him to help you with that," Jo gestured toward the bathroom where the rotting Kaitlyn Rice still hung over the tub. "He's still outside, isn't he? I know he is. So go get him and have him help you with this. You are going to leave it as a little present for this Noel," Jo was coming up with the plan at the same rate her mouth was running. There was no pre-planning involved at all. If she wanted to get things done, she needed to act fast, so she just trusted her mouth to lead her in the right direction. "When you get the call, you get the fuck away from Warren with whatever excuse you need. Understand?"

Lanny's gut was turning upside down, but still he nodded without making eye contact with his older sister. "Yes, Jo. Wait, but no. That won't work. What do you expect me to say to him, especially if we ride there together?" Lanny was hoping this would be a fatal enough flaw to call her sister off of the betrayal. Of course, it wasn't much.

"I don't know, say the corpse is making you sick?"

"That won't work."

"And why won't that work?"

"Because-" Lanny couldn't very well expose everything he and Warren did together to his sister, at least not at that moment. "Because I work at Bodies: The Exhibit. I deal with the deceased every single day, and in much more graphic of ways. Sorry, Jo, that just won't work."

Jo felt a heat creep over her skin. Her tongue flicked up and down inside her closed mouth, but she was trying to stay calm. Here was her own brother, technically her own blood, choosing solidarity with the *other* side. And that was enough for Jo to feel like he was against her. "Well, Lanny, we are going to figure something out. He needs to go. Do you understand me?" The last question came out as more of a command. It was the way a mother might finish the lecture she gives her child for talking back.

"Okay."

"Okay? Okay what? Are we in this together?"

"Jo," Lanny sighed, "this is all happening so fast. You don't even know him!" Lanny was sweating profusely, but whether it was from the heat of the apartment or the heat of the conversation he couldn't be sure. His voice was starting to squeak with panic. "Please, Jo!"

"ENOUGH!" It came out in a terrifying combination of a yell and a hiss. Lanny cowered away and lowered his eyes from Jo's increasingly beady ones. She had begun to shake back and forth ever so slightly.

"I'm sorry," he whispered.

Jo tried to calm herself down. She stopped the shaking and took a deep breath. "Lanny, this is about us, and our time to be together. I have strong intuition, and I know that guy is no good. I don't trust him. I don't like him. And frankly, I don't even like how attached you are to this person. He has to go. So, whatever you can do to make that happen, do it. You're a smart guy. Be creative."

Warren pretty much pounded the importance of creativity into Lanny, although Warren seemed to lack in that area. Lanny realized he really was the one with the good ideas. The man who, in the presence of his sister, felt more like a boy glanced at his desk drawer where he kept everything. He couldn't bear the thought of parting with his treasures but knew that he must. He may as well sacrifice everything at once and wipe his hands clean.

Lanny grabbed a drawstring bag from the closet and dropped in a few of the items, but not everything, just enough: the knife from Amanda's house, the framed flap of jigsaw skin, and a few teeth.

"I don't want to know," Jo said, not flinching at the contents of the drawer. "Just bring him in."

Lanny patted his pocket to make sure his wallet was in it and then sent Warren a text. He could hear him bounding up the steps moments after. Lanny noticed a bulge in the front pocket of Warren's black jeans.

"Alright, let's get this show on the road!" Warren's voice boomed merrily through the apartment. He walked into the bedroom where Lanny and Jo were sitting on the bed and grinned at them both. He loved the idea of framing Noel with the murder of the dead girl in Lanny's tub. It was quite inspired, and he just knew that it came from the cunning mind of his female counterpart.

Jo smiled sweetly back at him. "Thank you so much for your help, Warren. And your discretion, I hope! I made a mistake. I'm sure Lanny can fill you in on my condition while you guys take care of our little problem."

"Yeah, that's no problem. Whatcha think, Lanny, want to throw her in the bed of your truck?"

Before Lanny could answer, Jo cut in and said, "Don't you think that's a little obvious? I mean, she's not exactly a deer that'll be thumping up and down and, unless you're driving a hearse, a dead body in the back of your car doesn't look so good.

Don't you think?" She smiled a sickening smile at Warren again, and her eyes flashed from beneath her white-blonde hair.

"Smart woman," Warren pointed at Jo. "I like her, Lanny. She's right. We can load her up in my trunk; I already have some tarp back there. Always do. Because, well, you never know." Warren headed into the bathroom. He reached into his front pocket and pulled out a syringe.

"You do this with a snake?" Warren asked, impressed. He recalled the time he used a snake to kill a man. "Creative. I like it!" He said and sent his winning smile toward Jo. Warren decided the puncture marks already there would be the perfect entry for his needle. Lanny peeked from around the door while Jo stood inside the frame, both watching with disgust as Warren turned the needle this way and that, looking for the last bit of blood flow. He really dug the thing into her and shoved it to the left, then right. Each time he tried a new position, he pulled up on the syringe, only getting a drop of blood. They could all visibly see the needle snaking this way and that from the bulge it created against her skin. There was none of the gentle touch of a seasoned phlebotomist. Finally, Warren hit the sweet spot. Blood spurted from Kaitlyn, for its last time, and filled the tube about half-way before losing pressure. But it was enough. Warren pulled it from the hole and slid the syringe into a plastic tube before pocketing it again.

"Ready, fella?" Warren asked, not expecting an answer. He grabbed Kaitlyn by her arms and indicated for Lanny to grab her by the feet. Warren walked backwards while Lanny walked forwards with the body. "Wait," Warren spoke again, "Jo, my keys are in my front pocket, the left side. Do you mind popping the trunk, and acting as our lookout? It is pure daylight out there right now. We want to get there before she gets home, which seems like plenty of time, but it could quickly get away from us. She usually doesn't get home until about 8, maybe 9 o' clock.

"Once we are a safe distance away, we make an anonymous call and I'll pretend to be a concerned neighbor and describe the stench of the apartment. We can splat a bit of blood outside the front door; the police will use this as enough evidence to enter without a warrant, and voila. The bitch goes to jail. She'll try and use her surgeries or job as an alibi, but they'll easily be able to tell that the time of death was last night."

Jo watched Warren with a mixture of disgust and pleasure, pleasure at getting rid of him. He was so sure of himself that he would never see anything going awry.

Jo leapt up from the bed to where Warren stood with the lower half of Kaitlyn's body. She shoved her hand deep into Warren's front pocket and found the keys. She let it linger for a second just to give him a brief thrill, toy with him a bit, and by his quickened heartbeat she could tell she had done just that.

"Just follow me boys!" She basically skipped her way to the front door and threw it open, and then fumbled with the car keys until she hit the button that lifted the trunk. She gazed around the empty parking lot and called, "Let's move it!"

The men came out, Lanny grunting with effort while Warren did most of the work. They tossed her into the trunk and slammed it shut. "Good luck! And be safe, brother." Jo gave Lanny a kiss on the cheek. She watched him climb into Warren's car then found herself face to face with Mr. Worth. "You know, he really does love you. Take care of my brother," she said and gave him a kiss on the cheek as well with her thin lips.

"I will, ma'am." Warren gave her a wink and climbed into his car. He took off in a display of revving engines and they headed to Noel's.

"Your sister sure is something," Warren said as he drove.

"Mhum."

"You okay, Lan? Still a bit hung over?" Warren looked at Lanny.

"Yeah," Lanny said, and looked out the window, avoiding Warren's gaze at all costs. It was a beautiful day, sunny and crisp outside. They could have been heading to the river for a picnic. But this would be no picnic for Lanny. He wasn't sure he could go through with it. He watched Warren from the corner of his eye and smiled at the chiseled jaw. He loved him—almost in the same way that a son loves his father. It was a rocky start, but they accomplished so much together. And then Jo decided to come out of nowhere and ruin, no, Lanny didn't want to use the word *ruin*, but she did mess with the flow a bit.

It was a short drive. Noel lived in a nice little townhome with a green front door. Warren still had the key and fished it from his pocket. He clicked open the lock and took a good look around outside before swinging the door open. The parking lot for the townhomes was empty, most people were probably at work or happy hour. Lanny certainly was tapped out for sick days. Warren stuck his head in the house and called for Noel. There was no answer. He nodded at Lanny then rejoined him at the car.

They hoisted Kaitlyn's dead body from the trunk and quick-shuffled into the house. They were barely inside the entrance when Warren let his end, the top half, drop. It made a thud that would have definitely resulted in a concussion.

"What should we do with her?" Lanny asked.

"Well, we've gotta do what Noel would most likely have done. Bring her to the bathtub and fill it with ice." He surveyed Lanny's pale complexion. "Are you sure you're okay? I don't want you getting sick in here."

"I'm fine, swear." Lanny forced himself to smile, but it came across as a grimace.

"Okay…" Warren said doubtfully. He grabbed Kaitlyn again by her wrists and dragged her into Noel's pure white bathroom. It looked like she bleached the room every day. There wasn't even a trace of mildew on the pure white shower curtain, and the hand towel hung in a crisp fold by the sink. Warren hoisted the body into the tub and laughed. He knew how much Noel hated a mess.

"Can you bring in some ice?" He called to Lanny. "There is a big popcorn bowl in the bottom cabinet, second from the right of the sink." Warren could hear the cabinet open and then a moment later the sound of ice pouring into it.

"I don't think there's gonna be enough ice to fill the tub. . . even with her inside of it," Lanny said, brow crinkled in thought.

"That's okay. We can just start filling it with cold water. Hand me that towel." He gestured at the one by the sink. Lanny tossed it to him and watched as Warren used it as a buffer between himself and the faucet. He let the water run on its coldest setting. Lanny heaved up the bowl of ice and dumped it around the body, then retreated to the kitchen to fill it again.

After two more refills, Noel was out of ice. But it was enough. Kaitlyn was surrounded by ice that began to chunk together at the surface of the water.

"Well," Warren brushed his hands against each other up and down in the way one might after finishing a tough job. "That's it!"

"What about the blood on the door? That we were going to smear?" Lanny asked, still nervous about how this would all end. It was all he could do to keep his voice from shaking.

"I'll do that on the way out. Wipe down that bowl wherever you touched it and put it in the sink." Lanny did as he was told and then followed Warren to the door. Warren stepped outside, ready to create a red masterpiece before vacating the area. He began to shut the door behind them.

"Wait," Lanny stuck his foot in the door. I think I might have dropped my wallet in there."

"Go on, then. I'll just be out here playing Armstrong." Warren shooed him off to go back into the home using the artist who did all of the crazy portraits as inspiration.

Lanny went back inside and was overcome with guilt. Enough so that he didn't take pause to wonder what Armstrong, either Louis or Neil, had to do with blood spatter. Warren, the most careful and untrusting human Lanny ever met, did not suspect anything in the slightest. He trusted Lanny, and now Lanny was going to betray him. He almost couldn't do it. He thought about Jo and felt a strong wave of fear. Lanny pulled the drawstring bag from inside his pants. It was previously tucked into his briefs against the inside of his leg, the opposite side of his penis. He dumped the items onto the kitchen table in one pile. Lanny proceeded to pull out his wallet and root around for Warren's business card. It wasn't hard to find, as Lanny didn't make a habit of collecting business cards. He crumpled it a bit with his hand and then wiped it on his shirt, in case they could pull fingerprints off of paper. He figured they could and wanted to play it safe. He stuck his hand beneath his shirt and gripped the card through the material with his thumb and forefinger. Lanny brought that into the bathroom with Kaitlyn and left it on the ground and in the corner, so that it might look like it fell out by mistake. He took a shaky breath and went back outside, wanting to undo everything he just did and feeling so wrong about it.

Warren was shooting the syringe at the door when Lanny opened it, and a little got inside. It was fine, and more authentic that way. "You got it?" Warren asked, still not suspecting a thing.

"Right here!" Lanny held it up with a trembling hand.

"Well, I think I'm about done here. Let's get out of here. Tell Jo she can go ahead and make that call. I'll drop you off, but then I've got to get to work." Warren marched to his bimmer with Lanny in his wake.

Jo ran next door and rang the neighbor's bell. The scruffy, professor-looking type man opened up, confused as he was not expecting any guests. Jo could smell the freshly brewed coffee inside his apartment. "Sir, my cellular phone died. Can I please borrow yours, it's an emergency!"

The man took one look at this pretty blonde's concerned face hidden beneath waves of hair. "Of course, sure, here it is. No passcode on it. Would you like to come inside?"

"No, that's okay. I can make the call from out here. But, uh, do you mind if I got a little privacy? It's a family emergency."

"Yes. Just knock on the door when you're finished."

Jo smiled at the man and thanked him, then dialed 911 as soon as he shut the door. She did her best to sound shocked and distressed, "Hello? I'd like to report, well, I'm not quite sure what. I live in Crescent Valley Townhomes and I smell something quite awful from next door. It smells like something has been dead in there for a long while, and it's all I can do to keep from vomiting! Lighting candles has done nothing. And, well, I tried to knock on my neighbor's door, but she didn't answer. I noticed a little bit of something just in front of and a little bit on the door. It looked like blood!"

"Ma'am, what is your name?"

"I'd rather not say; I want this to stay anonymous. But the apartment number is thirty-seven! Please just come! My neighbor, she scares me. And she's always hanging around with this man who's got this wild look in his eyes! Please get here!" Jo hung up the phone and knocked on the door.

"Everything alright?" The man asked.

"I think everything will be. Thank you so much." Jo handed the phone back to the man and retreated down the steps. She waited until he shut his door to let herself back in to Lanny's apartment, and then she sent him the text.

CHAPTER 13

Purdy's phone vibrated next to him as he sat as his desk. He answered and listened. Jenson walked up while Purdy was on it, so he gave him the index finger. "Yes, thank you for calling me. We're on our way." He turned to his partner with a grin stretched across his face that could give the Cheshire cat a run for his money.

"Well?" Brian asked. "What is it?"

"There was an anonymous call. A woman called to report a stench of 'death' and blood from her neighbor's house. Guess who owns the place?"

"No fuckin' way," Jenson formed a smile that matched his partner's. "Well, let's get the fuck over there!" The men jumped up and literally sprinted to Jenson's car. He tore out of the parking lot and zoomed toward Crescent Valley.

"Ready to go?" Warren asked Lanny, consulting his watch. If Jo already made the call, they needed to hit the road. On top of that, Warren had to be at work in thirty minutes. "I'll drop you off but then I've got to get going. We good?"

Lanny nodded, afraid to look Warren in the eye. He didn't say a word the entire way back to his place and sunk in his seat when Warren put on "With a Little Help from My Friends" and sang out loud to it.

"I'll see ya, fella. If not tomorrow, the day after that," Warren tipped Lanny a two-fingered salute and sped off toward

Matrix. Lanny could barely lift his lead-filled arm to offer a pathetic excuse for a wave back to the man he'd betrayed.

Jo was waiting outside the front door, like a woman waiting for her man to come home after war. He could imagine her waving a handkerchief this way and that. "Come on inside!" She yelled. "I want to hear all about it!" Lanny made his way through the apartment door. Each motion or movement he made was difficult, as if every cell in his body was propelling him to do the opposite, as if every cell was trying to pull him backwards, back all the way to the moment he dropped Warren's business card and his treasures in Noel's apartment.

Purdy and Jenson arrived at the townhomes. The door to unit thirty-seven was covered in blood. Purdy gave an impolite, thunderous bang on the door. There was no answer. He tried again, announcing himself along with a warning that they would kick down the door if necessary. But still, there was no response. Purdy nodded to Jenson, who had the thighs of a linebacker. It took him two kicks just next to the doorknob to bust it open. The doorframe splintered off its hinges and they forced their way inside. Each had his hand on his gun holster, but there was no reason to pull it out just yet.

"Is there anyone here?" Jenson was calling to either Noel or a potential victim.

"Brian, look at this." Morgan was standing by the thick, wooden table with his mouth agape. There was a flap of skin in a jigsaw shape, the missing piece from Hernandez, some scattered teeth, and a knife. Although, the knife shone clean, Purdy was willing to bet that the width would match the wound on the deceased Amanda's neck.

"Holy shit." Jenson tightened his grip on his holster, almost expecting Noel to come out of nowhere and surprise them.

"I'll call Miranda. You radio dispatch. Let's check the rest if the place and make for certain that there is nobody here." Morgan made his way further into the townhome. He checked closets, the bedroom, and under the bed. When he was coming up from his knees while looking under the bed, he saw something odd through the cracked bathroom door. He stood up and made his way toward the bathroom, pulling out his gun. "Anyone here?" He asked again, not expecting an answer. He pushed the door open with his toe then jumped inside the bathroom. Morgan covered his mouth in shock at what he saw.

He didn't have to call out to his partner, Brian appeared by his side. "We got the bitch."

It didn't take long for Miranda and the Crime Scene Unit van to arrive. She busied herself taking photographs and collecting all of the evidence. Purdy and Jenson stood to the side, consulting with one another on the unsolved cases and the likelihood that it really was Noel Leach behind it all. *Doctor* Leach that is.

"Hey, did you guys notice this?" Miranda came up to them, holding a small plastic bag between gloved fingers. Inside the bag was a crumpled business card. It read **Matrix** and below that **Warren Worth** *then* **Bartender: Private Parties and Events**. "Boyfriend? What do you think?" She asked.

Morgan glanced at his partner, who spoke for the both of them. "We'll go check him out. Could just be that she wanted him to bartend a party or something," he laughed through his nose, "but I doubt it. Maybe they are the new Bonnie and Clyde. Michelson?" Brian turned to another detective. "You guys going to the hospital to find Noel?"

"Yep. We'll call you with any updates."

Jenson turned to Purdy. "Morgan, let's go."

"Thanks, Miranda." Morgan nodded to his former lover, not feeling as much as the fuel of hatred as he did in the past. "Let's go," he repeated Brian's words back to his partner. He held the bag containing the business card and looked at it closely. He remembered seeing some sort of bartender's business card in the murder from 2011. It was formatted differently, though, and he didn't remember the name that was on the last one. He was already in the passenger seat of Jenson's car, so he sent a quick text over to Miranda asking her to check Forrester's wallet when she got the chance. He settled back into his seat, his mind turning in all sorts of directions, scrambling to put everything together.

Warren shook ice, peach schnapps, cranberry juice, and Crown Royal in his mixing tin. He wanted it to be good and frothy. He then expertly strained the concoction over four shot glasses. "Cheers, ladies." He grinned.

"Oh, come on, take one with us. Please," said the woman with short blonde hair and a big nose.

"I'd love to ma'am, believe me. But I don't want to upset the boss. Now you all drink up." He flashed his winning smile, which widened as she pulled out a twenty-dollar bill for a tip.

"Ma'am," she laughed, "so formal." But she clinked glasses with her friends, and they drained the shots. Warren slid the twenty into his palm and put it into his tip jar. He was wiping up the spillage from the shots when he noticed two gentlemen approach the bar.

"What'll it be for you fellas?" He asked through his smile.

Morgan Purdy pulled out his badge and showed it to the bartender. "We'd like to speak with a Warren Worth please."

Warren froze, but his smile didn't falter. It did, however, feel more forced than usual. "Well, that would be me. What can I do for the two of you?"

"Mr. Worth," Jenson began, "can you tell us where you were tonight?"

"Well, sir, I've been here at work."

"How about before that? What time did your shift start?"

"It started at eight in the evening, sir, but I arrived at about seven-thirty. I always get here a little early because I know the bar will be in disarray from whoever was working before me," he laughed.

"Mr. Worth, do you know a Noel Leach?" Purdy asked, scratching his chin.

Warren scratched his smooth chin, mirroring Morgan Purdy. "Why, yes, she used to be a regular of mine. Cool girl; could really handle her liquor. Why?"

"We found your business card at her residence."

"That's not surprising. I hand out my card to a lot of people. In fact, would you gentlemen care for one?" Warren grabbed two cards from a stack behind the bar and slid them to the detectives. The men both took them and put them in their wallets. "Is she okay? Is she hurt or something?"

Morgan smiled at Warren. "We will give you a call if we have any other questions. Thank you."

"Alrighty, see you fellas!" Warren called out through gritted teeth as he watched the detectives leave. He felt completely hollow, and like he was watching himself from somewhere else; like in a game-film, he was waiting to be reamed out by the coach for the mistakes he made.

"Yoo-hoo, bartender, another round please!" Big-nosed blonde waved a twenty at Warren.

"Coming right up," he said without a smile.

Warren stared at his reflection in the mirror. He stared until his eyes began to cross and the image looking back at him became unrecognizable. "You fucking *stupid* idiot," he literally spat, and specks sprayed the mirror's surface. "How the fuck could you be so stupid?" He asked. His brows curved in and up, he was both hurt and angry. He felt like a dog being reprimanded. Only he was the dog, and the owner as well. "You can't blame Lanny; this is your own doing you disgusting piece of shit! How could you trust someone with the real you! How could you show yourself, and expose yourself, to an outsider?" It was the reverse of the mirrored pep talk guys give themselves in high school prior to asking the popular girl to prom.

He looked down and tapped the nose of the revolver against his head. He saw water droplets lying in the sink, though the faucet was off. Tears. Actual tears were free falling from his face, abandoning him. And he didn't blame those salty buggers either. He would abandon himself too. He looked back into the mirror; his handsome features distorted with every emotion he never took the time to feel. "You are sick! You are the disease! You are one of *them*!" Warren flicked open the chamber and saw a full house. He swung it shut and pointed Lanny's gun at his reflection. "You deserve this, you stupid fuck!" He turned the snub-nosed Smith and Wesson so that the barrel was looking him dead in the right eye. "Fuck you," he said and pulled the trigger.

There was no opportunity to fight. He was there, and then he wasn't, in the length of time it takes a camera to flash.

"Well, suicide in the wake of a murder is essentially admission of guilt," Purdy said, looking beyond the large star-shaped hole and into the mush of brain that was once Warren Worth. "We've still got to bring in the doctor for this. They probably worked together." One of Warren's eyes was still open, and the blue lost its vibrancy. The other eye was jumbled below the wound, the right side of his face messier than a Picasso painting. He peered down at the text he had received from Miranda not even an hour prior.

The bar named on top of the card is Voodoo. The name at the bottom is Warren Worth. Hope you've found something. Let me know.

EPILOGUE

Warren's tracking skills were second to none. His long tongue flickered about, smelling the air and searching for his next victim. He hated the unevolved. He found their presence to be a nuisance and spent a great deal of his time in power business offices fighting to increase the air conditioning tax. Warren believed that the unevolved shouldn't get to create their own safe world inside their homes and should pay more for the ridiculously cold air they craved. He hoped the price increase would chase the unevolved up north, and away from everyone else. But, in the meantime, he tracked down these unevolved anomalies and took care of them himself.

Warren didn't believe it was cannibalism per say. For one thing, he didn't eat the entire body. Well, only some of the time if he was *really* hungry and didn't feel like searching for one of the few bodies of water in which to dump the body. Secondly, he didn't count the unevolved as being in his same species. So it *wasn't* cannibalism. But he still kept his practices to himself.

The sun was out, and the day was full of potential. The unevolved had a certain smell about them, and it was especially strong considering they all lived in the same block of homes on the outskirts of any of the towns. There, all of the townhomes and the couple of stand-alone houses were painted all white. He strutted down the pavement with his hands in his pockets, alternatively whistling and smelling. The aroma that filled the air where Town 12 ended and Town 13 started was the salty smell of sweat. He grinned, showing razor sharp points of teeth. He had naturally pointed teeth already but filed them into spikes, so it made an easier time of tearing through flesh.

The 110-degree weather didn't stop some of the unevolved from milling about and jumping through sprinklers. Yet another thing that those-kind wasted—water. What was the point of spraying it into the air to jump through? Sure Warren liked to dip himself in a bathtub or pool on the special occasion, but only indoors! There wasn't enough water to spare for everyone, yet here were the mongrels using it as a source to cool down while *outside*. The sun would eat it up anyway. It was disgusting and wasteful.

One of them was separated from a social group of frolickers and gossipers. He was just strolling, hands in the pockets of his shorts and head down, scuffing the ground as he walked. He was shirtless and slathered in the "sunscreen" that the unevolved all wore when they made the ever-so-bold step outside of the comfort of their iceboxes of homes. This one man, however, was absolutely covered in the white, semen-like substance. Warren could tell he was headed for the shade on the other side of the townhomes, most likely to lean against the cool, stone wall. This also meant he was about to be out of sight and out of mind from the rest of his freaky little community. Warren smirked and continued his way past the rest of them, basking in the smell of the sweat that dripped from their bodies. He offered a few of them a wave, but kept his lips shut over his teeth. He didn't want to set off any alarms from a squealing little mini-mutant.

Warren rounded the corner of the white-painted stone building and found his target just sitting on the ground tracing designs in the dirt with his finger. "Hey there, fella," Warren said mildly. He allowed his white fang-filled mouth to spread into a smile.

The guy looked up and peeked nervously through his long, messy, straw-like hair. He was nervous because he wasn't used to anyone approaching him. The only person he interacted with was his sister twice a week. "Uh, h-hi," he replied.

Warren looked at the guys face and took a step back with a start. He stared into his hazel-green eyes and his own blue ones darkened. He felt a rage crawl through his veins, from his feet and boiling all the way up to his ears and then his temples, which began to pulse. "You, feeble little fink." Warren didn't know the guy, at least he didn't now, but he recognized him from one of his dreams.

Lanny paled so that his face was the same color of the cream that covered his body. "I-I don't know you, sir," he said to this man who was barely his superior. He shrank further against the wall, wishing he could flatten to it completely.

"You may not now, but you will." Warren didn't give the guy a chance to respond. He leapt forward, teeth first, and tore into the guy's jugular. He teethed a flap of skin and pulled it, peeling the skin from around Lanny's neck like one would peel the skin from an apple. Blood spilled in waterfalls and Warren collected it in his hands then force-fed it to Lanny. "Lick the spoon, you fucking coward." Lanny had no choice, as he couldn't push the blood back out. As he swallowed, Warren further ripped into the neck, tearing apart both the trachea and esophagus so that Lanny couldn't fully swallow it.

Lanny died with a mouthful of blood that dripped down his chin and a neck that was one inch from being disconnected from the rest of his body. The red fell into the sunscreen and created a beautiful pink that was like an ombre from the dark red on his face and throat. His dead eyes stared downward, hopeless and empty.

"The universe is not only queerer than we suppose, but queerer than we can suppose."
-John Haldane *Possible Worlds* (1927)

About the Author

Spoonlicker is Cassidy Barker's debut novel. She is a recent graduate from the University of Georgia with a degree in Criminal Justice.

Cassidy now resides in Atlanta, bar-tends part-time, and is currently at work on a next novel.

71385640R00164

Made in the USA
Columbia, SC
25 August 2019